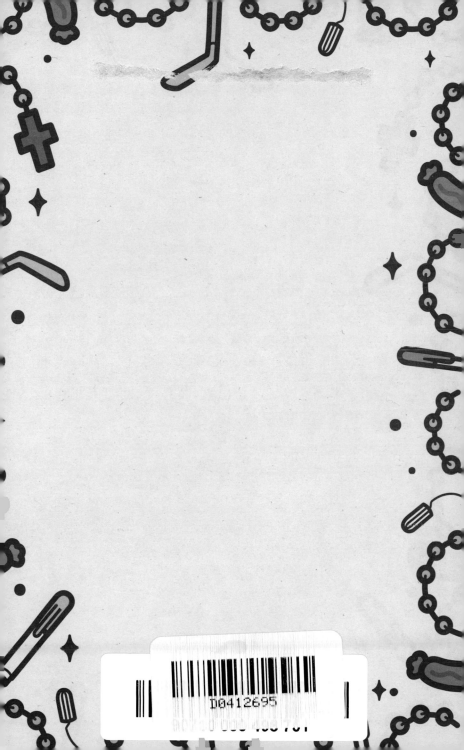

BAD Habits

BY

FLYNN MEANEY

PENGUIN BOOKS

PENGUIN BOOKS

UK | USA | Canada | Ireland | Australia
India | New Zealand | South Africa

Penguin Books is part of the Penguin Random House group of companies
whose addresses can be found at global.penguinrandomhouse.com.

www.penguin.co.uk   www.puffin.co.uk   www.ladybird.co.uk

First published 2021

001

Text copyright © Elizabeth Flynn Meaney, 2021
Illustrations copyright © Ellen Porteus, 2021

The publishers are grateful to Third Side Music o/b/o Meriwar Music, Songs of Ty
Joyce and R&Bling Music and Larry Spier Music o/b/o Stan My Music for permission
to reproduce lyrics/lines from 'My Neck, My Back (Lick It)', written by Khia Chambers,
Edward Meriwether and Michael J. Williams. Published by Larry Spier Music o/b/o
Stan My Music (administered by Atlas Music Publishing). Copyright © Third Side Music
o/b/o Meriwar Music, Songs of Ty Joyce and R&Bling Music, 2001. All rights reserved.
'My vagina is a fish' (page 70) refers to the line 'My mother is a fish' from *As I Lay
Dying* by William Faulkner, published in Great Britain by Vintage Books (1930)
Excerpts from *The Vagina Monologues* are from the 20th-anniversary edition of *The
Vagina Monologues* by Eve Ensler, published in Great Britain by Virago (2018)

Every effort has been made to trace copyright holders and to obtain their
permission for the use of copyright material. The publisher apologizes for any errors
or omissions in the above list and would be grateful if notified of any corrections
that should be incorporated in future reprints or editions of this book.

The moral right of the author and illustrator has been asserted

Set in 10.5/15.5 pt Sabon LT Std
Typeset by Jouve (UK), Milton Keynes
Printed and bound in Great Britain by Clays Ltd, Elcograf S.p.A.

The authorized representative in the EEA is Penguin Random House Ireland,
Morrison Chambers, 32 Nassau Street, Dublin D02 YH68

A CIP catalogue record for this book is available from the British Library

ISBN: 978-0-241-40719-6

All correspondence to:
Penguin Books, Penguin Random House Children's
One Embassy Gardens, 8 Viaduct Gardens, London SW11 7BW

For all the loud feminists with purple hair . . .
and the quiet feminists with killer French braids

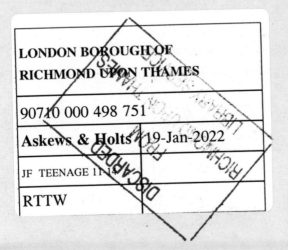

August

1

Don't look down, I told myself. *If you look down, you're friggin' screwed.*

There I was, hanging from a second-floor window of St Ambrose Hall in a denim miniskirt and my motorcycle boots. As my bare legs dangled, my sore biceps suddenly reminded me that I had *not* in fact done ten pull-ups during the school physical-fitness test last year. I had lied. In reality, I had done three, twerked a little in mid-air, then bribed Amy Horner with my Shameless Hussy red lipgloss to write down ten. *Crap.*

'Alex!' Colin Nowakowski stuck his head out of the window. He was fumbling to button his shirt over the silver cross on his chest. 'I don't know if you climbing down is such a good idea!'

Last year, I thought Colin Nowakowski was kind of a little turd. But tonight, when we reached for the same hot dog at the back-to-school barbecue, I saw that a summer growth spurt, plus a cool shorter-on-the-sides haircut, had transformed him from turd to quasi-hot hipster. So I'd put my number in his phone, suggesting we hook up later.

Now, seeing him all anxious and twitchy like a meerkat with irritable bowel syndrome, I regretted it. Here's a pro tip: if you ever sneak into a guy's dorm room to hook up and he's got a Michael Bublé station on his Spotify, just turn and run.

'Psh, it's fine!' I said cheerfully. 'I've snuck out of every boys' dorm on this campus! Once P. J. Keller lowered me from the fourth floor on a bedsheet. This is no sweat!'

In reality, I wasn't as chill as I sounded – either literally or figuratively. *No sweat* had been real bullshit because I was sweating heavily in the hot August night. Those friggin' Minnesota mosquitoes were all over my bare legs, I couldn't get my boots to grip on the dangerously smooth stone wall and my hold on the windowsill was slipping.

Suddenly there was a growl below me.

'Was that a *dog*?' I hissed. 'Is there a *dog* down there?'

Before I could stop myself, I looked down. *Crap.* The distance to the prickle bushes made me dizzy and, much worse, there was a giant yellow-white beast whose demon eyes gleamed in the dark. Razor-sharp teeth flashed in its black, cavernous mouth with each bloodthirsty bark.

'Charlie,' Colin told me. 'Father Callahan's dog. He lives in our dorm. He's a Labradoodle.'

'Charlie the Labradoodle?' I squinted at the monster down below, which now looked to be foaming at the mouth. 'That's not Charlie the Labradoodle! I follow Charlie the Labradoodle on Instagram! Charlie the Labradoodle is adorable! He wears fedoras with ear holes! THAT down

4

there is some genetically modified wolf from a horror movie! Do you hear how he's barking at me?'

'I don't think he likes girls,' Colin babbled anxiously. 'I mean, he lives in a dorm full of guys, where girls aren't even allowed, so I think he's kind of –'

'A MISOGYNIST?' I burst out. 'Your dorm priest has a MISOGYNIST Labradoodle? What, Father Callahan isn't scary enough, with the Rasputin beard and the thunder voice?'

Right on cue, like the approaching rumble of a summer storm, we heard that very thunder voice boom out. Father Callahan, Colin Nowakowski's dorm priest, was coming around the back of the building, calling out in the dark, 'What is it, Charlie boy? What's going on back there?'

'Oh FUDGE!' Colin Nowakowski gasped. 'Father Callahan! Father Callahan's coming!' His face was so pale and sweaty I thought he might barf on me, but I also thought *I* might barf at the fact that I had let a guy who says *Fudge* touch my ass. We were all screwed.

'Quick, help me back up!' I scrabbled against the stone wall with my motorcycle boots, groping with desperate fingers for a better handhold.

'I'm sorry, Alex!' His voice was squeaky with panic. 'I can't!'

'You can't what?'

'I can't get caught with a girl in my room! I can't get in trouble! I'm applying early to Georgetown for engineering!'

'Engineering?' I spluttered furiously. 'You couldn't even unhook my bra! Now HELP. ME. UP!'

5

Father Callahan's footsteps were approaching, snapping twigs in the bushes below. Charlie's barking was rising to a vicious fever pitch, and I was grunting and pulling myself up, reaching out for Colin. I was so close – my hand outstretched –

Suddenly Colin blurted, 'I'm sorry!' and slammed the window down.

Then I really was screwed.

2

The best view at St Mary's Catholic School is from the top floor of the main building, right under the famous golden statue of the Virgin Mary. From there, you can see the whole campus, which is laid out like a cross, with Academic Quad to the north, the well-swept green Girls' Quad of six stone dorms to the east, the identical Boys' Quad to the west, and straight ahead an avenue of pine trees leading down to the shining lake.

Unfortunately, the view inside isn't quite so hot – because it's the principal's office.

It's a place I know all too well. I know the squeaky green leather chairs that stick to the back of your thighs. I know the framed mosaics of saints being martyred in gruesome and bloody ways. I know the smell of old bibles and disapproval. And I definitely know that look on Father Hughes's face; that grim, set-jaw look that makes the old guy from *Up* look like a flirty fireman in a shirtless calendar.

'Well, Ms Heck,' he began, 'here we are, only your second day back on campus, and already I find you in my office.'

'Good to be back!' I said cheerfully. 'I see you put up a new mosaic – *St Agatha on a Bed of Hot Coals*. It really livens the place up.'

Clearing his throat, Father Hughes reached for a square sheet of yellow paper that was also very familiar to me: a St Mary's Incident Report.

'Last night,' the principal pronounced, in his imminent-plague-of-locusts voice, 'you, Alexandra Heck, were found face down in the shrubbery behind St Ambrose Hall. You were uninjured apart from mild scratches and bruises . . .'

Pretty accurate, I thought – and it was nice of Father Hughes not to mention the fact that I'd been found with my miniskirt around my waist, my 'Bow Down Bitches' boyshorts in full view and Charlie the Labradoodle's tongue in my ear.

'. . . and were obviously not in your own dorm at the time of curfew.'

Father Hughes picked up a mahogany stamp from an inkpad. The all-powerful seal of St Mary's. Time to get serious. He held it poised over the incident report and asked, 'Do you dispute the accuracy of this interpretation?'

'No, I do not,' I said primly. I could get serious, too. 'I missed curfew. I don't dispute that.'

Father Hughes lowered the stamp towards the yellow sheet. But, just as the ink was about to make contact with the paper, I continued, 'But I *do* wonder why Colin Nowakowski isn't also here right now.' I gestured to the empty green leather chair next to mine.

'Mr Nowakowski was in his dorm at curfew.'

'With a girl!' I protested. 'Guys and girls are never allowed in each other's rooms! Isn't that in, like, the "hair shirt and chastity belt" section of the school rulebook?'

Okay, I didn't know exactly what I was talking about, seeing as the day they gave me the St Mary's rulebook, I tore the pages out and made 200 origami ninja stars. But I could tell there was a double standard here.

Father Hughes spoke in a calm, measured voice, still holding the stamp above the report. 'Mr Nowakowski did not have a female student in his room at the time of the incident.'

'Because I was climbing OUT of his room!'

'He claims to have no knowledge of you being at St Ambrose Hall that evening. According to Mr Nowakowski, he was studying alone.'

Colin Nowakowski, you little shit-faced liar! I couldn't believe I let his growth spurt trick me. He was still a turd, just now he was a turd with a hipster haircut. And Father Hughes was a turd in a priest collar.

'You know what this is?' I jumped out of my seat. 'This is total friggin' sexist treatment. You Catholics! You're still holding a grudge against Eve and that apple! I mean, what was she supposed to do? Girlfriend was in a nudist garden on a blind date with a dude missing a rib – it wasn't like there were FOOD TRUCKS around!'

Grave, serious and self-controlled as ever, Father Hughes said, 'We are not discussing the Book of Genesis right now, Ms Heck. We are discussing your continual and deliberate disciplinary infractions.'

And, with that, he lowered the mighty mahogany stamp. It pounded the incident report with gravitas. I was officially in trouble again.

Father Hughes searched through the folders on his desk and found my file. I had so many of those bright yellow sheets, I could have wallpapered Big Bird's S&M chamber with them. My very first related to a practical joke gone awry involving the dorm chapel, a can of whipped cream and a prefect's life-sized cut-out of Harry Styles. From there, I had continued to rack up Dress Code Violations, Personal Appearance Violations, Student Safety Violations – you name it.

'Ms Heck,' Father Hughes said, 'we are starting a new academic year – your junior year, an exceptionally important one for your future here at St Mary's and beyond. It is clear from your conduct that my efforts to integrate you as a respectful and productive member of this community have failed. Therefore I felt I had no choice but to call in more . . . impactful . . . reinforcements.'

Exorcism! That was my first thought. Some wild-eyed priest with a tangled beard and six-inch fingernails had been dragged from the wilds of Patagonia to come chain me to the golden Mary statue and chant in tongues until the devil of disobedience was chased screeching from my body.

I was actually pretty excited.

But, when Father Hughes buzzed his assistant to let someone in, the door opened and in walked a cheerful, middle-aged man with a golfer's tan, thinning grey hair and a flashy watch. I groaned and slumped down in my seat.

This wasn't an exorcism – this was worse.

It was my dad.

Nothing explains my feminist rage more than the fact that my very earliest origins were in these privileged white balls. Of course, my molecular rebel self shot out of there like a bat out of Polo Ralph Lauren hell, but still . . .

'Hey there!' my dad boomed, bounding towards Father Hughes for a vigorous handshake. 'Hughie, my man! Good to see you! Look at you in the big office up here – it blows my mind!' Still holding Father Hughes's hand hostage, he turned to me. 'Hey, Al, do you know your principal and I were both Class of Eighty-Nine? Not only that, we're both St Francis Hall men! Fourth floor, right, Hughie?'

'That's right.' Father Hughes smiled briefly. 'You must remember climbing all those stairs to copy my theology homework.'

'There's my excuse,' I piped up. 'Corruption runs in my blood.'

But my dad didn't hear that; he was going on and on about the good old days at St Mary's, and dumb dorm pranks, and some cranky priest who used to make them swim naked in gym class (I'll need at least a minor hallucinogenic to get *that* disturbing image out of my head). Other than squeezing my shoulder and kissing my head carelessly before sitting down, my dad basically ignored me, but he did turn to me to say, 'Would you believe that back when we were students St Mary's was still an all-boys' school?'

'Wow,' I said drily. 'It must have been crazy patriarchal back then.'

Father Hughes was not in the mood to bro out with my dad. He cleared his throat and tried to set a more serious tone, even calling my dad 'Mr Heck' instead of Wingnut, or Captain Blueballs, or whatever his dorm nickname was back in the day.

'Mr Heck,' he said, 'it is clear your daughter is a strong-willed young woman . . .'

Pagan she-demon.

'And an individual thinker . . .'

Spawn of Satan.

'But, as I explained over the phone, it has become clear that my disciplinary actions are no longer effective in your daughter's case. A serious decision must be made.'

'Righto,' said my dad. 'Definitely. Absolutely. Hey, Hughie, is the hockey stadium open? I'd love to see my MVP trophy from Eighty-Nine – do you remember that championship, man?'

From the look in Father Hughes's eyes, I could tell I wasn't the only Heck in the room that he considered a pain in the ass.

The principal asked to speak to my dad alone, so I sat out in the hallway, slumped against the wall, staring at the shut door.

At first, I was pissed. I mean, what the hell? Father Hughes thought his priest-splaining wasn't domineering enough, so he had to fly in my dad to dad-splain, too?

Whatever happened to the good old boarding-school phone chain, where your principal calls your parents and then your parents call you for a really unpleasant Skype that lasts forty-five minutes until you pretend the Wi-Fi dropped out in your dorm? That's how discipline typically goes for boarding-school kids. At least until someone figures out a muggle version of that screaming letter Ron Weasley used to get at Hogwarts.

Then Father Hughes's phrase echoed in my mind: *A serious decision must be made.* I sat up. Hope bubbled up inside me like that science experiment with the Diet Coke and Mentos.

I was getting kicked out.

That had to be it! Why else would the principal fly my dad in? Father Hughes was sick of me, and he was kicking me out. I was leaving St Mary's!

I hurried over to the window and looked down at the bright green quad and the anally retentive flower beds and all the clean-cut little Catholics burning off their sexual frustration with wholesome sports like Frisbee and Wiffle ball. I looked at the grey, prison-like stone walls of the dorms, and the iron doors of the campus chapel, and bid it all farewell. *Goodbye, St Mary's!* Goodbye, 7 a.m. classes and dorm mass and curfew! Goodbye, nuns and priests prowling everywhere, watching my every move! Goodbye, freezing Minnesota winters and ass-kissing A-students who look at me like I'm an ax murderer when I drop an F-bomb!

I was leaving it all. When my dad walked out of that door, I was going with him. Back to California. Back to freedom and burritos and high-speed Wi-Fi and public school where the seniors smoked joints in the parking lot. Back to reality where the only place I ever saw nuns was at the *Sound of Music* singalong at the Castro Theater. Back to the life I was supposed to have, before my parents got divorced and everything got so weird and messed up and off-track.

My dad was gonna walk out of that door, and I was gonna follow him and his golf shorts out of this building and off this campus, and never look back.

I was going home.

The door opened. My dad came out.

'Well?' I asked him.

'Everything's decided,' he reassured me. Then he added, 'By the way, I told your mom I was coming. She said to send her love. Well, actually, she *texted* to send her love – she's on a silent yoga retreat in Big Sur.'

'Wow, the maternal bond is a powerful thing.' I rolled my eyes. 'Now I understand how those moms lift cars off their babies.'

'Hey!' my father cautioned me. 'With all the Pilates your mom does, she'd be able to lift a truck off you in a heartbeat, believe me.'

'Whatever. What's the deal? What did Father Hughes say?'

But my dad was distracted. Strolling over to the windows, he looked down at the quad, smiling.

'Don't you love these summer days before classes start? I remember some killer Frisbee games with the guys from the dorm.'

He turned back to me more earnestly. 'Ya know, Al, the friends you make at boarding school are friends for life. It's an amazing bond. They will always have your back.'

I rolled my eyes again. More of my dad's stellar advice, like the day I got my first period, when he took me out for ice cream and, apparently thinking I was an adult now, started giving me stock tips.

'Did I ever tell you about the secret tunnels?' he asked.

'There's no secret underground tunnel network at St Mary's,' I said, and not for the first time. My dad had tried this urban legend with me before. 'Look, what's the deal? Can we go now?'

He checked his Rolex. 'I wish we had time to hang, but I've got an investors' meeting in Tempe, and I've gotta catch the next flight.'

'That's okay,' I said. 'I can be ready super fast. I'll just throw all my stuff in a duffel bag. Or Mary Kate can pack it up and ship it. Let's go!'

'Alex.' My dad was serious now. 'You're staying.'

My stomach sank. 'WHAT?'

'Honestly, Father Hughes wasn't sure if St Mary's was the right fit for you anymore. That's why he asked me to come. But I think you can do really well here, and I asked him to let you stay – as a personal favor.'

'Those are the kind of personal favors you ask for? Keeping your daughter locked up in Catholic prison two thousand miles away?' My throat was tight, and I was fighting not to cry.

'Look,' my dad said softly, 'I know you're not . . . super stoked to be here.'

Wow, Silicon Valley Ken, props for recognizing a human emotion.

'But your mother and I really believe this place will be good for you. So you're staying and you're seeing this through and you're getting a St Mary's diploma. In this family, we finish what we start.'

Says the divorced dude who did CrossFit for approximately six days.

He kissed my hair quickly and said, 'I've gotta run to the airport or I'll be late. But we'll see each other soon. It'll be Christmas before you know it!'

He hurried off down the hallway. I swallowed hard and called after him, 'You know, most parents who come visit take their kids out to lunch. Or at least to Target to buy an ugly dorm lamp!'

He waved without turning around.

'Fifty bucks?'

But my dad and his golf shorts had already disappeared around the corner.

'Ms Heck?'

Father Hughes was standing in the doorway of his office.

'Will you join me for a moment to finish up our conversation?'

I trudged back inside and plopped down on the sticky green leather again.

'Well,' the principal said, 'it looks like you'll be staying with us until graduation.'

'Apparently,' I said. 'So my dad used to copy your homework back in the eighties, and now he's bullying you into keeping me in school. You should really take one of those peer-pressure pamphlets from the nurse's office.'

'Your father explained your need for structure after some difficult years at home. He made a compelling case. But that's not the only reason I agreed to let you stay. I still believe you have a valuable contribution to make to St Mary's, Ms Heck. Besides –' and here Father Hughes actually smiled – 'as much as this may disappoint you, you are not the first nor the last St Mary's student to be caught breaking curfew.'

'Oh, so that's the problem?' I said. 'I need to be more original and creative in my rule-breaking? *Then* you'll kick me out?'

Clearly, Father Hughes was over me because he didn't even answer. He just pulled out a different file and began making notes. 'You may go, Ms Heck. Have a nice day.'

I jumped up, ripping my thighs from the green leather, and stomped past the wall of mosaics. St Hippolytus, being torn apart by wild horses, had a look of stubborn determination on his face. And I was determined, too. If it would take something shocking and unprecedented to get me kicked out of St Mary's, I would do it. I would do something no student had ever done before – something so anti-St Mary's that Father Hughes would have to send me back to California, even if my dad offered him a million dollars.

As I strode out of the office in my motorcycle boots, I put on my cat-eye sunglasses and mused:

Hmm, I wonder if I can get hold of a blowtorch . . .

3

The Long Huggers were still hugging.

They stood on the front steps of our dorm in the warm August evening with their arms wrapped around each other. Above their heads, fluttering moths circled a yellow light. Her hands were clasped behind his back. His face was buried in her hair. Framed in the entryway of the old stone building, they looked so perfect, their picture should have been in the St Mary's Catholic School brochure: the preppy, clean-cut boy holding the girl with the long brown hair, the crucifixes on their chests pressed together as a symbol of their pure young Catholic love.

Of course, if they did take a picture, they'd have to crop out the braless chick with the purple fauxhawk sticking her head out of the ground-floor window to smoke a clove cigarette.

When I heard the door to my room open, I stubbed the cigarette out on the windowsill and let it drop into the perfectly pruned zinnias.

'Who are you spying on?' It was Mary Kate, my room-mate, coming back from the shower. 'Ooh, are those guys with the southern accents playing glow-in-the-dark Frisbee again?'

She was bundled up in a fluffy white robe with her hair wrapped in a towel. Even though we live in an all-girls' dorm, she would never dare walk the five-foot stretch of hallway from the bathroom with just a towel wrapped around her, like I do. The guys at St Mary's probably have all these horndog fantasies about the girls' dorms after curfew, like we're all pillow fighting in lace thongs, but they would be sorely disappointed if they saw Mary Kate gussied up like an old lady.

Dropping her toiletry bag and shuffling over eagerly in her fuzzy slippers, she leaned across my desk to stick her head out of the window. Then, sounding disappointed, she said, 'Oh. The Long Huggers.'

'I can't believe them,' I said. 'This is only our third night back at school, and they're already Long Hugging again.'

Mary Kate gave me a look. 'This is only our third night back at school, and *you've* already fallen out of a window, gone to the principal's office and gotten another incident report in your file.'

Touché.

'But, seriously, they're ridiculous. Look at this!' I held up my phone, which was on stopwatch mode. 'They've been hugging for *seventeen* minutes! And I didn't even start timing right away. They were out there at least five minutes before the lack of making-out sounds distracted me from my Instagramming.'

'Alex,' Mary Kate said, 'don't be mean. They're so cute.'

'But why do they have to be cute right outside our window?' I asked. 'Why don't they go to one of those private study rooms in the library to not-grope each other? Curfew isn't for another hour.'

Curfew at St Mary's is 9 p.m. on weeknights and 11 p.m. on weekends. Obviously, I'm not too worried about it, since I'm often dangling from windows in a miniskirt around that time, but most students are in their rooms when the dorm priest or nun knocks for bedchecks to make sure everyone is home safe and sober. Sometimes they just barely make it – look out of the window at 10.55 p.m. on a Saturday night and you might spot a tipsy freshman with her shirt on backwards scurrying home before she turns into a Catholic pumpkin.

'But look at the quad tonight! The flowers are in bloom, the stars are out, there're fireflies flickering everywhere . . . It's romantic!' Mary Kate said. 'This is Minnesota. Summer isn't going to last forever. This is, like, a picture-perfect night.'

'It's a St Mary's brochure-picture night,' I told her. 'All they need is a parent-friendly caption under them, like: *St Mary's: Sending your Daughters to the Ivy League with their Hymens Intact Since 1842.*'

Mary Kate gave me her patented death glare. I imagine it's something like the look of fury Anne of Green Gables used to shoot at that buttface Gilbert Blythe when he got between her and her true lady love, Diana Barry, or insulted her kickass ginger mane. My room-mate is a big reader, so she appreciates a good *Anne of Green Gables* reference. What she doesn't appreciate are my dirty jokes.

The Long Huggers were still hugging. Mary Kate towel-dried, combed and parted her long brown hair and began to fix it into two French braids, which she does every night before she goes to sleep. Her French braids are amazing. I've never seen a human being who can braid like Mary Kate. French braids, fishtail braids, inverted fishtail braids . . . seriously, girlfriend could put polygamist sister wives to shame with her skills.

But tonight she braided absent-mindedly, her head tilted to the side, gazing dreamily out of the window at the shadowy, virginal figures on the front steps. 'Do you know they met on their first day here and they've been dating ever since?'

'I think they met on their first day here and they've been *hugging* ever since.' I checked my phone again. 'Nineteen minutes. I mean, are they trying to set a friggin' world record?'

'The Guinness World Record for longest hug?'

'Or the Guinness World Record for bluest balls.'

'Ew, Alex!' Mary Kate stopped mid-braid and stared at me. 'You don't think he's, like . . . *aroused*?'

When she said 'aroused', she dropped her voice to the same awkward whisper she uses when she says 'womb' during dorm mass.

I shrugged. 'I don't know. They've been dating for three years now and I've never even seen them kiss. These Long

Hugs are all the action this kid gets. Maybe a Long Hug is, like, his version of sex.'

Mary Kate shook her head so vehemently her right braid began unraveling. 'No way. He's got a crucifix on. You can't have a crucifix and an ... *erection* ... at the same time.'

'Oh, you can't?'

She seemed pretty certain. 'It's like how the devil bursts into flames if he walks into church.'

'I don't know, Mary Kate,' I said, grinning. 'Shall we test out your little crucifix vs erection theory?'

I turned my laptop around on my desk so the speakers were facing the open window. Then I double-clicked on one of my playlists. Mary Kate, watching over my shoulder, rolled her eyes.

'Seriously?' she said. 'You have a playlist called *Make-out Mix*?'

Clearly, my room-mate has no idea what I got up to when she was away at that young poets' conference last spring.

My Make-out Mix starts off slow – literally, because the first song is 'Slow Hands' by Niall Horan. I turned up the volume to make sure the Long Huggers could hear it outside. But as the music drifted out into the summer night – the slow, regular beat, and Niall's throaty voice offering an erotic rubdown – the Long Huggers didn't even look up from their hug.

Time to step it up a notch, I thought, and double-clicked the next song: 'Truffle Butter' by Nicki Minaj. This one was more uptempo – and the concept behind it is as filthy as hell, but luckily, since I haven't explained it to Mary Kate, she probably thinks 'truffle butter' is a recipe from a celebrity lifestyle blog.

She and I were watching intently through the window, but there was no change in the Long Hug. The Long Hugging Guy didn't slide his hand an inch lower down the girl's back; the Long Hugging Girl didn't press her chest against his any harder; there was not even the slightest hint of a pelvic thrust.

'Maybe they fell asleep on each other,' Mary Kate said, squinting into the dusk. 'They're not moving at all.'

'Well then, I guess we have to wake them up.' I wiggled my eyebrows suggestively.

'Alex . . .' Mary Kate said warningly. 'I think that's enough.'

Ignoring her, I scrolled through my playlist looking for the perfect song. *That's it!* I double-clicked, and music blared out into the night: a throbbing beat and moaning vocals laid over a twangy porn-soundtrack background. It was Khia's 'My Neck, My Back', the dirtiest song I've ever illegally downloaded. '*So lick it now, lick it good . . .*'

'Stop it!' Mary Kate hissed. 'You can't play that!'

'What'd you say?' I cupped my ear, pretending I couldn't hear her over the music. 'Turn it up louder?'

Mary Kate made a grab for my laptop, but I jumped out of my chair. Clutching my computer, I raced around our room, tripping over the motorcycle boots I'd left on the floor and hurdling over Mary Kate's neatly stacked textbooks.

I ran straight into the laundry line of bras I'd hung up to dry and got briefly tangled up, but I never stopped running and, as I ran, I turned the volume up louder:

'*DON'T STOP, JUST DO IT, DO IT . . .*'

My room-mate was in hot pursuit, kicking off her fuzzy slippers, tripping over the hem of her bathrobe, crying out desperately, 'Alex! They're actually gonna hear!'

'Good!' I shouted over the music. 'That's the point!'

'*RIGHT NOW, LICK IT GOOD . . .*'

'It's not just the Long Huggers! What about –?'

She didn't even get a chance to speak the name aloud. But such is the power of this particular netherworld nuisance in a nun's habit that she can materialize at the merest flicker of thought in your subconscious. It happened just as I was climbing to the top bunk, cackling triumphantly over the blaring music with a hot pink bra slung over my shoulder and Mary Kate, red-faced and furious, swatting at me with the belt of her bathrobe: the Knock of Doom at our door.

I immediately clapped my laptop shut. The music stopped. I looked at Mary Kate. She looked at me. We knew that knock – that icy, anal-retentive knock. It could only belong to one person.

And so, communicating silently with our eyes, we did an immediate silent inventory of the contraband in our room. My clove cigarettes were stashed in the hollowed-out pages of my theology textbook; the voodoo doll I'd made of Father Bray was in a winter boot in the back of my wardrobe. Other than that, everything looked normal: Mary

Kate's top bunk was neatly made, with her stuffed penguin, Sir Shackleton, propped up against the baby-blue pillows, and underneath, mine was a mess of sheets and dirty clothes and possibly Ancient Babylonian artefacts buried in there somewhere. So the coast was pretty much clear.

Mary Kate smoothed her braids, retied her robe and went to open the door. She welcomed our visitor in her best chipper, human-equivalent-of-an-American-Girl-doll voice: 'Hi, Sister Hilda!'

Sister Hilda – or Sister Hellda as I fondly call her – is our dorm nun. Picture the Wicked Witch of the West if she ditched the striped tights, wiped off the green BB cream and rode a tornado to an all-girls' dorm in Minnesota because one Dorothy to torture just wasn't enough.

Oh, and did I mention she lives RIGHT NEXT DOOR to us?

'Ms Reagan. Ms Heck.' Sister Hellda poked her giant hawk-like nose into our room. She glared around, taking in me, panting on the bunk-bed ladder and nonchalantly flicking a hot pink bra off my shoulder, and Mary Kate, breathless in her bathrobe. I could sense the pulsating, sublimated rage beneath her wimple.

'Did I or did I not hear loud music from this room? I must have been mistaken because you are both juniors, and *must* therefore know we have quiet hours in the dorm after dinner on school nights.'

'Oh yeah, sorry about that, Sister Hilda,' I said, hopping down from the ladder. 'I forgot to put my headphones in. You know how I love that Christian rock!'

Mary Kate rolled her eyes at me behind the door.

Sister Hellda sniffed. 'Please do not forget again.' Then, with a final scan around the room to make sure there wasn't a condom, crack pipe or unattended curling iron in sight, she said, 'I will see you in fifty minutes for bedchecks.'

'See you then, Sister Hilda!' we chorused sweetly. Before she'd pulled the door even halfway shut, I was flipping her the bird.

4

As always, Sister Hellda had sucked all the fun out of the room. Mary Kate's mood definitely changed for the worse. I was the kind of kid who used to stick Play-Doh up my nose, so I clearly don't give a crap, but Mary Kate hates getting in trouble.

'I seriously don't understand you,' she said. 'We've been back at school three days and you've already broken curfew, gone to the principal's office and had your *dad* fly out here to yell at you.'

'It has been a busy few days.'

'Do you realize what's gonna happen if you get in trouble again?' she demanded. 'You're gonna get kicked out! Expelled. Sent home. Excommunicated.'

'I see that vocab app is really working for you.'

Mary Kate was squinting at me fiercely. Then the realization dawned on her and, when it did, she let out a high-pitched squeak of shock.

'You're *trying* to get kicked out!'

I shrugged.

'What are you THINKING?' she burst out. 'If you get expelled, that's on your PERMANENT RECORD! That's really serious, Alex! You might not get into college!'

'I failed physics last year so I'm not getting into a real college anyway,' I told her. 'I'll probably end up in a nudist commune somewhere picking organic corn.'

'What about your parents? They'll be furious!'

'Believe me, my parents could not give less of a crap.'

'What about ME? If you get kicked out, who am I supposed to room with? They're gonna stick me with that Banjos For Jesus girl on the fourth floor, I know it. Or the Rowers! Oh my God, Alex, I'm gonna have to room with the Rowers!'

The Rowers are two super-buff, six-foot-plus varsity crew girls who live at the end of our hallway. Mary Kate is terrified of them. And, honestly, so am I. They're basically Death Eaters in sweatpants.

'They're gonna bench-press me!' Mary Kate was wailing. 'They're gonna do weird, giant exercise stuff to me, I know it!'

I stood face to face with her.

'Mary Kate, I'm not gonna stay in some *fascist* regime so you don't have to room with people you don't like.' My voice was rising. 'It's been pretty clear from the beginning that I don't belong here, the school doesn't want me here and, most importantly, I don't want to *be* here. So, if I get kicked out, well, GOOD! ST MARY'S CAN SUCK MY MOTORCYCLE BOOTS!'

Suddenly we realized how loud we were being. We stopped, breathing heavily in the new silence. We turned towards the wall we shared with Sister Hellda and listened. Nothing. She was probably down the hall, flagellating someone for leaving their flip-flops outside the door. We looked at each other for a second and hurried over to the window, elbowing each other out of the way to stick our heads out first.

The Long Huggers were still hugging.

I checked my phone. Thirty-one minutes. Then I looked up at Mary Kate. 'Quarter dogs?' I suggested cheerfully.

'Quarter dogs,' she agreed.

Quarter dogs are hot dogs that cost – you guessed it – a quarter. They sell them at the student center the last hour before curfew. I'm pretty sure it's the school's way of getting rid of questionable meat before it expires, but they taste fine, and anything is better than staying in your dorm room finishing that summer essay on *Germinal* (leave it to a French dude to make a book where a bunch of women cut off a guy's dick and parade it around on a stick boring).

We walked down the hallway – tiptoeing past the Rowers' room, like we always do – and pushed open the heavy front door. The Long Huggers were – you guessed it – still hugging, so as we stepped out into the warm August evening, swinging our ID chains on our wrists, we walked in the damp grass to avoid them. I restrained myself from hissing, '*Blue ballssss . . .*' as we passed, but I did flick Long Hugging Boy on the back of the neck.

Mary Kate's attitude had changed. When she'd been gazing at the Long Huggers before, she'd had a sweet, mushy look on her face, like you have at the midpoint of a Nicholas Sparks movie when they're still collecting shells on the beach and no one has been diagnosed with Alzheimer's yet; now the look was a mix of nausea and bitterness.

'The Long Huggers make me sad I don't have a boyfriend,' she explained.

'Everything makes you sad you don't have a boyfriend,' I reminded her. '*March of the Penguins* made you sad you don't have a boyfriend.'

She nodded wistfully. 'Those boy penguins were so nice to those girl penguins.'

Fireflies flickered along our path as we crossed Girls' Quad. In the old stone buildings, lights were on, windows were open and snatches of conversation drifted into the air. We turned onto Academic Quad, and that's when we began to notice the couples. Two by two, hand in hand, their sappy asses were strolling through the summer dusk, all headed in the same direction.

'They're gonna walk around the lake,' Mary Kate said. 'And you know what walking around the lake means.'

'They're in the Mafia and they need someplace dark to dump a body?' I suggested. But, unfortunately, I *did* know what walking around the lake at St Mary's meant.

St Mary's Catholic School is a strange place, full of bizarro superstitions and silly traditions. We even have a campus ghost (more on him later). And, because the school is always trying to brainwash us with all this heteronormative, high-school-sweetheart bullshit, lots of those traditions revolve around love and romance. One of them is that if a guy and a girl (the only kind of couple St Mary's can conceive of) walk all the way around the campus lake, holding hands – without letting go – they're officially boyfriend and girlfriend. But you can't let go – not even for a second. If you do, your relationship is doomed.

I think the whole thing is stupid.

'I mean, the lake is the one dark and romantic place where you could actually feel someone up at this school,' I said. 'And you have to keep one hand out of commission holding the other person's hand?'

'It's tradition!' Mary Kate said. 'Sarah Jane Kelly's great-grandparents walked around the lake before her great-grandpa went off to war! I think it's romantic.'

Cutting across the path of the couples, we climbed the steps of the student center.

'It didn't really bother me last year,' Mary Kate continued. 'But we came back to school and *boom*, it's like everyone's paired off all of a sudden. Everyone's found their soulmate, and I didn't even meet a cute lifeguard this summer!'

'Don't be ridiculous,' I said, holding the door open for her. 'First of all, you don't want to date a lifeguard – checking someone's suspicious back mole for melanoma is not sexy. And, second of all, no one is paired off. It's all in your little romcom-addled head.'

Unfortunately, it wasn't. The student center is always crowded the hour before curfew. Tonight, there were the usual people on laptops, people trying to study but really

32

eavesdropping on other people's conversations, and freshman boys throwing Flamin' Hot Cheetos. But there was also a noticeable number of adorable couples adorable-ing all over the place. Two seniors were splitting a Kit-Kat. In a corner booth, a sophomore boy and giggly girl were taking kissy selfies. And, when we got in line for the hot-dog cart, we ended up behind the grossest couple in the world – HardBurn, a.k.a. Izzie Harding, and T. J. Burns, fellow juniors we hate who started dating after he landed on top of her in a human pyramid collapse. The whole time we were in the quarter-dog line, they wouldn't stop giving each other butterfly kisses, Eskimo kisses and any other kind of politically incorrect kisses they could think of. Seriously. When they stepped up to the cart, they even ordered together:

'We're just gonna share one, please.'

'Half ketchup . . .'

'. . . and half mustard!'

And then burst into a gale of murder-inspiring giggles.

Mary Kate glared at me. *I. Told. You*, she mouthed.

We each got two hot dogs with extra onions ('See?' I told Mary Kate. 'It's good we're not making out with anyone tonight.') and found a table. In between big bites, I tried to reassure Mary Kate about being single, especially after the Kit-Kat couple walked past with a milkshake and two straws.

'I bet most of these people don't even like each other,' I said. 'It's just this whole Catholic pairing-off mentality. I mean, you read a kid enough Noah's Ark picture books growing up and they start feeling like they're a freak show if they're not paw in paw with another aardvark or anteater or whatever.'

Mary Kate wrinkled her nose. 'Are you talking about me? Am I an aardvark or anteater or whatever? Seriously? *That's* the kind of animal I'd be?'

'No, that was just a general statement. You would definitely be one of Taylor Swift's cats.'

Mary Kate lit up. 'Ooh! Which one? Oh, it doesn't even matter, they're both adorable.'

That may have mollified her a bit because we chewed in companionable silence for a few minutes. Sure, we had been screaming at each other less than a half-hour ago, but our relationship had always been like that, ever since we met and bonded instantly during a traumatic freshman dodgeball game. And, by the time we'd finished our first hot dog, she was taking a logical view of her singledom.

'I mean, I understand why I never had a boyfriend before St Mary's. I went to an all-girls' school; I only have sisters and girl cousins; I didn't know any boys. And I was only in eighth grade. Plus, I used to let my mom cut my bangs.'

'Always a mistake. Unless your mom is Zooey Deschanel.'

'But I've been living on a campus full of boys for *two years* now! It's time for me to find a boyfriend.'

'Wait,' I said through a mouthful of hot dog. 'I thought you were waiting till college to get a boyfriend, when you do your junior year in London and meet a shy ginger named Rupert who recites Shakespeare's twenty-ninth sonnet to you.'

'No. That's when I'm gonna lose my *virginity*,' she corrected me – of course lowering her voice on the last word. 'I'm waiting for that, but I'm not waiting for a boyfriend. I'm going to find one this semester.'

I licked ketchup off my fingers. 'You go, girl penguin.'

'I'm serious, Alex!' Mary Kate put down her half-eaten hot dog and wiped her hands on a napkin to indicate the gravity of the situation. 'I am resolved. I am determined. I am making a *vow* here. Before this semester ends, I am going to walk around the lake with somebody.'

Raising my fist, I did my best Scarlett O'Hara impression: '*As God is my witness . . .*'

'Actually, better than that,' she corrected herself. 'I'm gonna do it before the first snow.'

I lowered my fist. 'The first snow?'

'Well, it just gets so cold in the winter,' she said sensibly. 'I don't know if the magic boyfriend-handholding lake thingy works if you're wearing mittens. Plus, it's hard to find guys in the winter. Remember last year how that big snowstorm left a huge wall of snow blocking off Boys' Quad?'

'That actually does make sense.'

'Although,' Mary Kate reconsidered, 'a wall of snow dividing me from my true love *could* be romantic. It could turn into, like, a Pyramus and Thisbe situation.'

'Or a glory-hole situation,' I warned darkly.

She grimaced. Mary Kate had been living with me long enough to know what that meant. 'You're right. Let's definitely make it *before* the first snow.'

35

Humming happily, she finished her hot dog. In her head, I knew she was already choosing which color Sharpie she would use to write her semester vow in her purple planner between *learn 50 new vocab words* and *practice using eyelash curler.*

'You know,' I said. 'With all this climate-change nutsiness going on, and Leonardo DiCaprio driving his Prius around Antarctica, giving homeless polar bears sunscreen, the first snow could be any day now.'

'Well, it's a good thing I'm starting now then,' Mary Kate said. 'You know maybe, instead of trying to get kicked out of school, you should set a semester goal, too. It could give you structure and direction. And something to do besides falling out of boys' windows and being sent to the principal's office.'

'Nah.' A flying Cheeto landed on our table, and I debated throwing it back or eating it. I ate it. 'I'm not really a goals-and-vows person. I'm more a go-with-the-flow kinda gal.'

But, in reality, I did need a plan. My go-with-the-flow attitude hadn't worked so far. I needed something creative and shocking to make sure Father Hughes kicked me out.

And, little did I know, in less than twenty minutes, I would find my inspiration.

It would all come about because of the tampons and the Hint of Lime tortilla chips.

5

Our school store is a mini supermarket stocked with the emergency essentials: first-aid supplies, toiletries, and those microwave brownie bowls you eat to cheer yourself up after you fail your physics final. On our way out of the student center, I paused in front of the store and said, 'Hold on a sec. I've gotta grab some tampons.'

Mary Kate stopped short. Her brown eyes widened. 'In *there*?'

'Uh . . . yeah?'

'*Alex*,' she hissed. 'You can't buy . . . *things* . . . in there. Look who's inside!'

Three guys were heaping gummy worms into plastic bags at the candy wall: a tall, burly ginger Viking, a douchey blond who looked like a prom date from an eighties movie and a skinny dude with shaggy brown hair.

'Undercover tampon police?' I suggested.

'They're *hockey players*.' Mary Kate spoke with hushed awe, as if pronouncing the name of a god capable of striking her down with thunder and lightning.

You have to understand: at St Mary's, ice hockey is a religion. And religion is already a religion here, so that means a lot. I mean, we have a chapel in every dorm. We're forced to go to mass every week. They practically cancel classes every time the pope sends a tweet. But hockey is damn near sacred. At St Mary's, the Holy Trinity is more like a foursome, and the fourth part is a sweaty French-Canadian dude with a dislocated collarbone.

As a result, hockey players get their asses kissed all over campus. Teachers give them extensions on papers when they have away games. Prefects look the other way when they break curfew. And, whenever a really good hockey player who's thinking about playing for St Mary's comes to visit, the students throw these 'recruit parties' in the dorm common rooms with more half-naked teenage girls than the Victoria's Secret fashion show, which the staff pretend not to know about, even though they totally do. It's gross.

'Oh, they're *hockey players*,' I said. 'Pardon me! I didn't realize we were in the presence of friggin' royalty. How dare I even *consider* occupying the same space as these Herculean heroes in order to purchase a product that will staunch the flow of blood from my lowly, non-hockey-playing vagina.'

'Alex!' Mary Kate gasped.

As you can probably guess, my room-mate isn't crazy about the word *vagina*. It doesn't matter how many times I tell her it's the actual, biological, anatomically correct term – she would rather pretend we're all walking around with fabric crotches like rag dolls.

I didn't care. I walked into the school store, strode right past the hockey players with my head held high and grabbed a box of tampons from the shelf. In fact, I purposely picked one of those bright neon, 'Hey, look at me – my nineties throwback color scheme makes your period fun!' boxes. Mostly to attract as much attention as possible and piss off Mary Kate – who had followed me inside after all. (I guess she was still sensitive about that whole Noah's Ark thing. I mean, even Taylor Swift has two cats.)

But little did I know that Mary Kate had no intention of letting my tampons attract ANY attention. 'Okay,' she said, 'now we just need something big . . .'

As she scanned the shelves with her eyes narrowed, I said, 'Um . . . what?'

'Something big!' she repeated, like it totally made sense. Her face lit up. 'Look! Perfect!'

It was a party-sized bag of Hint of Lime tortilla chips.

'They're to cover up what you're buying,' she explained. 'I always buy something big to hide them. The best is when it's summer and the stores are selling beach towels, then you can just wrap the box up completely.'

'You buy a *beach towel* every time you have your period? That is beyond ridiculous! How did I not know this about you? Wait . . .' I frowned. 'I was your room-mate all last year, but I don't think I've ever been with you when you buy tampons. When do you buy tampons?'

'I don't! My mom buys them for me at home and mails them to the dorm.'

I shook my head and shoved the bag of chips back on the shelf. 'Nope. Not happening. I'm not being part of your menstruation-shaming tomfoolery. I have a vagina, I need tampons – get over it.'

Holding my neon tampon box proudly aloft, I went to pay. There was a long line at the register, so I put my tampons on the counter and waited. Then I heard a telltale crinkle behind me: it was Mary Kate with the Hint of Lime tortilla chips.

Out of the corner of my eye, I saw her trying to sneak the chips in front of my tampons. I swatted the bag away. She kept sneaking, I kept swatting, she kept sneaking, I kept swatting, and finally I whirled around, grabbed the bag and snapped: 'It's my period, Mary Kate, not a bowl of guacamole!'

A raucous outburst of dude-laughter rang out – the hockey players were right behind us. They were biting the heads off gummy worms and cracking up. The Ginger Viking had the beginnings of a beer belly that jiggled like Santa Claus's when he laughed, the Blond Eighties Villain had a nasty snigger that made me want to hire Molly Ringwald to slap him in the face, and the Shaggy One was looking straight at me, his dark eyes crinkling with amusement.

Mary Kate looked mortified. I just rolled my eyes and turned my back to them.

That's when I heard it. A breathy, barely audible whisper. At first, I wasn't even sure – I was like Harry Potter in the zoo, trying to figure out if he could really talk to snakes or if he'd accidentally eaten a pot brownie. But no, I *had* heard it:

'*Vagina.*'

The second one was throaty, a little louder:

'Vagina.'

You know this game, right? The vagina game? I definitely do. In fact, I *won* this game on the bus on my eighth-grade field trip to Alcatraz. It's pretty gutsy to shout about genitalia on a teacher-chaperoned visit to a maximum-security prison, but hey, I like to live on the edge. When I played it back then, it was the penis game, but the basic idea's the same. You say *vagina*, someone else says *vagina* a little louder and the person brave enough to shout it the loudest wins. Super mature, right?

'Vagina!' the Shaggy One declared cheerfully.

'VaGINa!' the Ginger Viking boomed in his deep voice.

They were getting louder. The line was still as slow as ever. Mary Kate was cringing into herself desperately – now, instead of using the bag of chips to shield my tampons, she was using it to hide her face.

But me? I was cool, calm and collected. I was choosing to ignore them. Yes, I could have confronted them about their childishness and sexism, but I probably would have just gotten a fart noise in return, so what was the point? Trying to educate a Neanderthal-brained hockey jock is like trying to get your guinea pig to play the xylophone. Yes, they do it on YouTube, but, as every so-called 'beginner' face-contouring tutorial has taught us, YouTube is a magical alternate universe that has nothing to do with reality.

Plus, I didn't want to push Mary Kate over the edge. I could already tell from the way she was pasty and shaking that she was having a flashback to the time her mom asked a bra saleslady if there was anything smaller than an A-cup.

Finally my turn came. I stepped up to the register and said, so clearly and loudly I could have won the vagina game, 'These tampons, please.'

The vagina game hadn't fazed me. The hockey players should have given up, but they didn't. They tried a new tactic. The Ginger Viking began rubbing his big belly and groaning. 'Ughhhh! I have the worst cramps right now.'

The Douchey Prom Blond joined in. He was rubbing his stomach and groaning, too. 'I feel like I'm gonna have a really heavy flow this month.'

'Heavy flow!' the Ginger Viking repeated, and all three of them sniggered.

'You know, ladies,' the Shaggy One stage-whispered behind me, making sure I could hear, 'I've had PMS this week, too. Do you think our cycles are synched up?'

'OUR CYCLES ARE SYNCHED UP!' the Ginger Viking hooted, and all three of them cracked up like it was the funniest thing they had ever heard.

That's it! I couldn't take it anymore. The second the cashier swiped my card, I snatched my tampons and whirled around.

'Sorry, I couldn't help overhearing you guys,' I said in a fake-friendly voice. 'You have your periods this week?'

The hockey players were smirking at each other. Other people in the school store stopped what they were doing, sensing something was about to go down. Mary Kate, blushing bright red from her bangs to her collar, was staring fixedly at the Hint of Lime chips.

'So,' I continued cheerfully, 'I guess you need some tampons, right? Here, allow me!'

I tore the top off the neon box, turned it upside down and dumped the entire thing over the shaggy hockey player's head. Bright pink tampons rained down on him. When the box was empty, I shoved it in his chest, said brightly, 'You're welcome!' and walked out.

Silence. There was no standing ovation – no burst of applause like I deserved. Then behind me I heard a hockey player muttering, 'Dude . . .' followed by the crinkle of plastic wrappers as people stepped on tampons, and lastly Mary Kate stepping up to the cashier and saying in her pipsqueak voice: 'Just these chips, please . . .'

But I was proud. I had made a statement. And this single shining moment of Revolutionary Tampon Frankness had inspired me. If I was trapped in the frozen fortress of celibacy and ignorance that was St Mary's Catholic School, I was gonna melt it down. I didn't know exactly how, but I was going to do something – and it was going to get me expelled. *As God was my witness . . .*

But first I was going to the dorm mailroom to check for a package from Mary Kate's mom. Because I seriously did need tampons.

6

'It may be the first day of school, but we have less than two hundred and sixty days until your Advanced Placement United States history exam. So, if you are not prepared to be dedicated, diligent and determined in your studies, please consider transferring to a less exigent course.'

Dr Cartwright turned her stern gaze pointedly towards me and the shrill St Mary's bell rang.

On that cheerful and welcoming note, so ended the first day of classes of our junior year.

'Ugh, this is gonna be a bitch,' I grumbled to Mary Kate, who was still scribbling detailed notes in the margins of her syllabus. US history was my only advanced class this year, which meant it was the only one I had with my room-mate.

'I think it's gonna be great!' she said, filing her syllabus neatly away. 'Dr Cartwright is supposed to be super smart – did you know she has a PhD in colonial history?'

We stood up from our creaky two-seater wooden desk. Not only were we back in class – we were back in uniform. Mary Kate looked picture-perfect in hers: two neat braids streaming down her back, her crisp white shirt buttoned up to the Peter Pan collar and the hem of her green-plaid skort right at her kneecaps where the school rulebook said it should be.

Yes, that's right, I said SKORT. Those mutant skirt-shorts hybrids your mother used to make you wear so there was no chance of a boy seeing your Dora the Explorer underpants. St Mary's forces us to wear skorts for a similar reason: to keep us non-sexual and vaguely Scottish, like the ginger chick from *Brave*. The actual result? Wedgies. Constant, creeping, Catholic wedgies.

No wonder I've been in such a bad mood all day, I thought, yanking ineffectually at my skort as we started walking.

'AP lit is going to be amazing this year, too,' gushed Mary Kate. 'Sister Carroll and I have the *exact* same taste in books. I'm pretty sure everything we're reading has a secret wife in the attic of a sinister English mansion. Oh, AND!' She interrupted her own babbling to pull out the syllabus. 'Look at this! We're reading *North and South* this year! How long have I been telling people that *North and South* is better than *Pride and Prejudice*?! I mean, of course I love *P&P*, but . . .'

'But what's more romantic than a violent labor dispute?' I finished for her, fishing an old piece of gum out of my messenger bag and popping it into my mouth. *Oops.* Maybe that was actually an eraser. Oh well . . .

Mary Kate didn't seem to be bothered by her wedgie or my sarcasm. She was practically skipping as we went out into the sunshine of Academic Quad, where senior guys were playing Frisbee and senior girls were sprawled on the grass with their knee socks rolled down and their new textbooks flung aside, tanning their legs. She was so pumped about the first day of classes that she even seemed to have forgotten my little tampon tantrum in the school store last night.

'And oh my gosh!' she shrieked right in my ear. 'I forgot to tell you the best part! There's the CUTEST guy in theology. His name is John, and we're going to be sitting next to each other all semester – it's totally fate. Well, technically, it's alphabetical order, but alphabetical order is *part* of fate, right?'

After going over her syllabuses, teachers and potential boyfriends for every class, Mary Kate finally turned to me and asked, 'So how was your day?'

I summed it up in one word: 'Sucked.'

First, I'd overslept, having snoozed my phone alarm four times after Mary Kate left – which meant walking around all day with Einstein-level frizzy hair, a black bra under my white shirt and two different-colored knee socks while trying to sneakily sniff-test my armpits because I couldn't remember if I'd put on deodorant. Then there was the fact that I had to take physics again, and Father O'Brien was the same vector-obsessed phallus as last year.

'And, as if that wasn't bad enough, I walked into remedial algebra and an entire row of hockey Neanderthals called me the Tampon Terror,' I said. 'Man, I really need to study so I can stop being in classes with dudes from that documentary about jock brain damage.'

Mary Kate had stopped short as soon as I uttered the word *tampon*, and now she looked like a deflating birthday balloon.

'Don't worry,' I reassured her. 'I'm sure they'll forget it in two seconds. Brain damage, remember? Plus, the whole tampon thing gave me an awesome idea for our meeting today.'

'Oh right.' She deflated further. 'The meeting.'

'You didn't forget, did you?'

'No,' she said begrudgingly.

'Good. Because I have a BIG idea that is gonna rock everyone's world.'

'Please,' she pleaded with me. 'It's the First Day of School, my favorite day – I have a tiny purple stapler filled with tiny purple staples. Please don't do anything to ruin it. You won't, right?'

'Hello, St Mary's Feminist Club!' I boomed. 'Welcome back!'

The St Mary's Feminist Club was founded almost two years ago by – me. Surprised? I don't seem like an extracurriculars girl, I know. But, as soon as I arrived at St Mary's, I realized what was lacking on campus and took bold action: I founded the Student Alliance for Diversity, Inclusion, Sensitivity and Tolerance.

That club existed for exactly three weeks – which is how long it took our school administration to realize it spelled SADIST.

I changed it to the St Mary's Feminist Club – a name which is slightly more palatable to our priestly overlords – but the school has remained suspicious of the club. Maybe that's why we're forced to meet in this arts building basement room with leaky pipes and suspicious black mold all along the ceiling that will probably lead to a big lawsuit in ten years when we all get miner's lung.

And maybe that's why we only have six members. There's me; there's Mary Kate, who only joined because I told her she could write she was vice-president on her college applications; Robbie Schmidt, a baby-faced sophomore who thought joining a female-centered club would mean he finally got to see a bra strap; Claudia Rosas-Fernandez, a self-absorbed senior whose mother is some hotshot ambassador at the UN in New York; and Sarah and Sophia, giggly sophomore girls I can't tell apart.

Oh – plus our faculty advisor.

'And, of course, welcome back to Sister Georgina!' I added hastily, extending my hand towards the far end of the table where a wizened old nun in a full habit sat under a dripping pipe. Her glasses were so thick it was hard to tell if her eyes were open or closed.

At the time I was founding SADIST, I was working off detention hours as a reading volunteer at the convent by the lake. That's where I found Sister Georgina – half deaf, semi-narcoleptic, and totally unruffled when I read those really racy passages in the Song of Solomon out loud to her. I knew all school clubs needed a faculty advisor and she was perfect.

'I have come up with a fantastic project for us this semester,' I continued. 'Something new. Something bold. Something artistic and daring.'

The faces around the table were watching me intently – except for Sister Georgina, who may have been asleep. Mary Kate looked suspicious.

'We are going to put on the first-ever St Mary's Catholic School production of *The Vagina Monologues*!'

I pulled my well-worn copy of the play out of my backpack and slapped it down on the table. The battered pink paperback was dog-eared and underlined; I'd bought it when I was twelve years old, in a second-hand bookshop in San Francisco. It still smelled like the crushed joint I'd found between the pages. But that was only part of why I'd fallen in love with the play. It was brave, it was revolutionary, it was feminist and funny and original – a masterpiece.

It was also – still – as controversial as hell. *The Vagina Monologues* was everything St Mary's hated. Which is why most of the people in this room had never heard of it. Sarah and Sophia were looking at each other in confusion, and finally one of them spoke up: 'The WHAT monologues?'

'*The Vagina Monologues*,' I repeated. 'Here, pass the book around. Everyone look at it.'

I tried to hand the book to Mary Kate, but she crossed her arms and refused to touch it. So I passed it to Sarah (or Sophia?) instead.

'*The Vagina Monologues* is a totally ground-breaking play,' I explained. 'Eve Ensler wrote it in the nineties. All the monologues are these stories about girls, and women, and sex, and giving birth told from the point of view of their actual vaginas. Eve Ensler gave voices to vaginas, so women would finally be heard.'

Robbie Schmidt was blushing bright red. Mary Kate was still glaring daggers at me.

'I know *The Vagina Monologues*,' said Claudia loftily. She was examining her eyebrows with her phone on selfie mode. 'But I don't think the idea is very modern. I mean, wasn't *The Vagina Monologues* on HBO, like, ten years ago?'

Claudia is not my favorite person on campus. Mary Kate hates her because she uses pretentious words like *meta* and *problematic* in their advanced English class. I hate her because she grew up in New York, and is therefore my main rival for coastal coolness on our Midwestern campus.

'We live in rural Minnesota, Claudia. We're always behind on pop culture,' I snapped.

Until now, I'd been standing at the head of the table. With everyone's eyes still on me, I sat down and leaned towards the other club members.

'Last night,' I told them, 'I was ridiculed by a bunch of hockey players for buying TAMPONS. A necessary feminine hygiene product. And, even worse, they thought the word *vagina* was a punchline. Seriously, it's time to grow up! We need to start talking about this stuff. We need to open up a dialogue about sexual health and taking ownership of our bodies.'

Robbie Schmidt looked like he was about to Schmidt his pants in terror, which told me I was really on to something.

'What does everyone think?' I asked. 'Sarah? Sophia?'

The two girls were still paging through my pink paperback copy of the play. They had tried to pass it to Robbie Schmidt, but he had juggled it like a hot potato and given it back to them.

'Um . . .' S1 began, while her friend looked at her. 'I don't know. I mean, I haven't read the whole thing obviously, but it just seems like they use . . . *that word* . . . a lot.'

I raised my eyebrows. 'Uh . . . *vagina*?'

'It's on, like, every page,' S2 said.

'Yeah, I know,' I said. 'So?'

'It's just kind of . . . intense,' S1 explained. 'It's really intense to actually, like, *say* it that much.'

'Maybe we could do the play, like, without the word?' S2 suggested.

'Do *The Vagina Monologues* and not say *vagina*?' I said.

Around the table, there were a few thoughtful nods and murmurs of agreement.

'Um, it's *the name of the play*,' I reminded them. 'Plus, it's an actual anatomical term!'

'We could say *vajayjay*,' suggested S1.

'Or we could do a big letter V with blank spaces after it,' said Robbie Schmidt.

'It's *The Vagina Monologues*!' I practically yelled. 'Not friggin' Sudoku!'

Mary Kate peeped up like one of the little mice in *Cinderella*. 'Maybe we should just have a bake sale instead?'

This wasn't going the way I wanted. If the play wasn't as offensive and outrageous as possible to Father Hughes, I'd never get expelled.

I would add in a kickline of dancing vaginas if I had to.

'Look –' I tried to stay calm, resting both my palms on the table – 'this is a really important project. I believe in it, and I want you to believe in it, too. This is something I really care about. Seriously. I know I usually don't give a shit about anything – like the dress code, or the school rulebook –'

'Or your grades,' Claudia added helpfully.

I glared at her. 'But I think if we all work together we can make this happen.'

'Um, Alex?' Mary Kate raised her hand out of habit. 'Aren't you forgetting something? If you want to put on an official school event, you need permission from Father Hughes.'

'Psh, we don't need him,' I said. 'We have Sister Georgina here! Sister Georgina!'

A whistling snore emanated from the dark corner of the room. It was pretty cozy back there by the furnace; no wonder Sister Georgina was fast asleep. I crumpled a piece of paper and got ready to lob it at her wimple, but Mary Kate grabbed my arm.

'SISTER GEORGINA!' I called louder, and she started awake. 'CAN YOU APPROVE A SCHOOL EVENT FOR US?'

Sister Georgina, in a rare and unfortunately timed moment of lucidity, recited solemnly: 'Father Hughes has to personally approve all official school events.'

I groaned. *Great.* Sister Georgina's hearing aids had sure picked a great time to kick in. And the friggin' Catholic Church hierarchy – always a man at the top!

'Fine,' I said, boldly taking up the challenge. 'I'll go ask Father Hughes for permission.'

'You?' Claudia looked up from her phone. 'Doesn't Father Hughes hate you? After that whole freaky incident with the Harry Styles cut-out and Father Callahan's dog. I heard they found you wearing the leash.'

'You're conflating two separate incidents,' I told her loftily.

As soon as the meeting ended, Mary Kate cornered me with her mini stapler.

'What exactly do you think you're doing?' she demanded.

'What?' I asked innocently.

'*You know what*,' she hissed. 'This whole project! This whole . . . *Monologues* thing!'

'It's like I said in the meeting! I'm trying to open up a dialogue that will improve our campus community, better gender relations . . .'

'Yeah, right!' Mary Kate wasn't buying it. She was all up in my grill, and now both of us were well aware I'd forgotten to put on deodorant.

'You are NOT trying to improve our campus community. You don't even want to be PART of the campus community. You want to get kicked out! And this is your plan to do that. You know there's no way in . . . heck that we're going to be allowed to perform the . . . the . . .'

Mary Kate fumbled for a G-rated synonym for vagina because there was no chance she was saying the word. Even if the entire International Federation of Gynecologists set her on fire like Joan of Arc and circled around her, chanting, she wouldn't say it.

'. . . a play like that,' she finished instead. 'You know you're gonna get in trouble for it, you know it's gonna create chaos and anarchy, and the worst part is, you're sucking all of us in with you!'

Girlfriend knows me too well. I had to throw her off the scent, or I'd lose my little feminist army right when I needed them the most. So I decided to mix a bit of truth in with the lies.

'Hey!' I said. 'I may hate St Mary's, but I step up when people around here need me. Remember when that freshman in our dorm got her menstrual cup stuck and was too scared to tell Sister Hellda or the school nurse? Who saved the day then?'

That was one hundred percent true. Maybe it's my purple hair, or the cloud of clove cigarette smoke that follows me down to the basement laundry room, but everyone in St Theresa Hall knows I'm the person to come to for non-nun-friendly crises.

'I meant what I said,' I continued. 'There's a lot of stuff I don't care about – how many calories are in a deep-fried Oreo, sports – but I *do* care about gender, and equality, and sexual health. You made your semester vow; this is mine. I'm going to put on the first-ever St Mary's Catholic School production of *The Vagina Monologues*. And I really think it's gonna be good for this campus.'

Mary Kate squinted at me again, for at least a minute and a half. Then, slowly, she tucked the tiny purple stapler away in her backpack. I had at least sixty percent convinced her.

And that meant my cover story was good enough for Father Hughes.

'Well, Ms Heck! Isn't this a pleasant surprise!'

Father Hughes greeted me with a smile as I walked into his office two days later. He extended his hand across his desk to shake mine.

I'm sure it *was* a surprise for Father Hughes to see me walk into his office voluntarily, sober, smiling and in uniform, with my shirt buttoned and everything. I shook his hand and took my seat, discovering that the green leather didn't stick to your thighs when you wore your skort at regulation length instead of rolled all the way up your twat. Huh. Who knew?

'I have a project I want to take on this semester,' I began. 'And I thought, *Hey! Why not go straight to the top? To the man himself?* Well, not *The Man*,' I clarified, indicating the chiseled Jesus with the hipster beard on the crucifix behind his desk. 'But . . . you.'

'That's very exciting, Ms Heck!' Father Hughes's eyes were practically twinkling in his craggy face. He probably thought flying my dad in had finally brainwashed me into the prayer-books-and-pompons spirit of the place. 'We do so love to see our students showing initiative.'

'Well, I was thinking about what you said,' I continued. 'Ya know, about me using my unique perspective, contributing to the school community, all that stuff? And I realized exactly what the school community needs.'

Dramatic pause. I took a deep breath and then held my hands out to Father Hughes like I was offering him a gift.

'St Mary's Catholic School presents *The Vagina Monologues*.'

The twinkle in Father Hughes's eyes dimmed. The lines in his face hardened to stone. Silence. We stared each other down over the desk for a good minute or more before he cleared his throat and spoke.

'That certainly is . . . creative, Ms Heck. And I appreciate your giving thought to the artistic enrichment of the school. But I'm afraid it will not be possible.'

'Oh yeah?' I crossed my arms. 'And why is that?'

'The content is simply too mature,' Father Hughes said. 'May I remind you that some of our students are only thirteen years old?'

'And a thirteen-year-old is too young to say *vagina*?' I balked. 'A thirteen-year-old came OUT of a vagina thirteen years ago!'

'Parents entrust us with students in their formative years, and St Mary's takes that responsibility very seriously. Which means strictly scrutinizing any content featuring inappropriate language or sexual situations.'

'Vagina doesn't necessarily equal sex,' I informed him. 'Vaginas are for lots of other things! Vaginas are for giving birth, for the miracle of birth! Vaginas are for . . .'

Smuggling drugs? Okay, not a great example.

'Besides,' I continued, 'whatever happened to the First Amendment? You may think I don't listen in US history, but I know I have the right to free speech.'

There! I sat back in the green leather chair in triumph. No way even Father Hughes could fight that one. Sure, the dude isn't cool enough to have *Hamilton* memorized, but he knows that free speech is a basic, unalienable right of all human beings – even human beings in frozen Catholic teen exile.

'That is true,' Father Hughes acknowledged, folding his hands on his desk. 'You do have a right to free speech in the public domain. But St Mary's is a private institution. Not only a private institution, but a private *Catholic* institution. And we have a moral mission to promote Catholic values. The school would not devote time, energy and its name to a project that promotes different values – for example, sexual activity outside the confines of Holy Matrimony.'

'That's not what the play's about!' I burst out. 'The play is about being comfortable with your body and yourself and your own identity, and not feeling weird and icky and shameful just to be a friggin' human being every day! But you would have no idea because you've probably never heard of the play before I walked in here! You're just home cracking open, like, the Book

57

of Revelations again – "Ooh, can't wait for those four horsemen to come. They sound really neat!'"

'I am aware of the play,' he said tersely, his jaw tight. 'And I believe it is an adult work of art inappropriate for the students of this institution. However . . .'

I looked at him suspiciously.

'While we do not have an unlimited right of free speech on this campus, we *do* have a democratic process. You may put this to a petition, Ms Heck.'

'Petition?' That was a word almost as surprising on this campus as *vagina*.

He nodded. 'Students have the right to petition the administration. If you collect five hundred verified student and faculty signatures, you earn the right to bring your suggestion to committee, and we will seriously reconsider *The Vagina Monologues*.'

'Seriously?'

'Seriously,' Father Hughes confirmed. 'You'll find the right to petition on page eighty-one, section A of the student handbook.'

Dammit. The student handbook again. I would really have to unfold some of those ninja stars. Or steal Mary Kate's.

But a petition – I could do a petition! I'm definitely a petition girl. I've got righteous political fervor. I went to, like, twenty different injustice marches back in San Francisco, with killer signs, too. I can rock the hell out of a petition.

'Well, good!' I stood up. 'Then I look forward to seeing

you back here. Me and my five hundred signatures.'

Father Hughes stood up, too. 'I look forward to it, Ms Heck.'

I extended my hand across the desk and gave him my best ballbuster, steel-toed-motorcycle-boot handshake of determination. I knew he didn't think I could do it – but, even after dozens of disciplinary meetings in this office, I was pretty sure Father Hughes had no idea what he was dealing with when it came to me.

september

7

Parents! Are you worried about your teenagers? Do you feel the world is just too *sexy* these days? Do you suspect your teenage child's hormones are out of control? Have you feared there's nothing you can do to fight the horny and inevitable tide of biology?

Well, rest easy, parents. There's a simple way to kill the mood: just send your kid to a St Mary's school dance.

On Saturday night, after our first week of classes, Mary Kate and I strolled into the cafeteria. I turned to her and walked backwards like a school tour guide.

'Welcome, you sexy young thing! To your left, you will see the giant, bloody crucifix that gives our venue its special Spanish-Inquisition ambience. To the right, observe the line of cranky nuns and priests. Notice their lips pursed in disapproval, their eagle eyes fixed on the dance floor. Fun fact: under those habits, they're armed with Super Soakers of Holy Water to extinguish the satanic fire that will erupt should your bare knee brush an inch of generic boy khaki on the dance floor. And, finally, inhale the irresistible aroma of stale French fries, lest you should forget for a moment that we are, in fact, in the school cafeteria. As Marvin Gaye would say, *Let's get it on!*'

It was 7.30 p.m. The dance had begun half an hour ago, and it was still painfully awkward. Even though speakers were blaring a Katy Perry song with every other word bleeped out (fuckin' St Mary's censorship – what do you even bleep out in a Katy Perry song? 'Cupcake boobs'?), no one was on the dance floor, and the sexes were completely separated. The girls were clustered in little groups, swapping lipgloss. The guys – ninety-nine percent of whom were dressed in blue button-down shirts and khaki shorts – had staked out the snack table, where they were throwing tortilla chips at each other and shaking up cans of soda.

'It doesn't look like anyone's really mingling,' Mary Kate said.

She had unbraided her hair so that it rippled down her back like a Disney mermaid's, and was wearing a short dress she probably thought was sexy. In reality, she's so cute and tiny that she looked like a fourth-grader on school picture day.

I, on the other hand, am so curvy that everything looks slutty on me: I could wear Sister Hellda's nun's habit and all I would look like is a sister of the Kardashian order. So I was rocking kind of a rebel look with jeans, a vegan leather tank top, and my hair moussed and gelled into what MK calls my 'lady fauxhawk'.

'Oh my gosh!' Mary Kate said. 'Look who it is! Theology John!'

'Who?'

'That cute guy from my theology class! Remember?'

'Ohhh. That guy who you cried about because he heard your stomach growl during a pop quiz?'

'No, Alex!' she snapped impatiently. 'That was Biology Bobby. That was freshman year! This is my *current* class crush.'

'Sorry, sorry!' I held up my hands to excuse myself. 'I haven't been studying my flashcards. Which one is he?'

Any other girl would have told me he was the one in the blue button-down and khaki shorts. Instead, this was Mary Kate and, when Mary Kate lusts after someone, she becomes oddly specific.

'Five foot eleven, cinnamon-brown hair parted on the left, two feet to the right of the tortilla chips, between that senior James with the rosacea and the ginger who burped in your face on the bus back from the sophomore laser-tag trip.'

'Ahhh,' I sighed. 'Another magical St Mary's social event. All right – c'mon, let's go say hi to him.'

I started to cross the dance floor towards Theology John (okay, let's get real, the bowl of tortilla chips) when Mary Kate grabbed my hand. She looked horrified.

'Say *hi* to him?' she squeaked.

'Well, I thought that would be a good first step. But, if you'd rather pinch his ass, by all means go ahead, girl-friend. Way more original.'

She ignored that. 'Alex, you NEVER say hi to a guy first!'

'Says who?'

'I just read this book on caveman psychology that says women shouldn't make the first move.'

'You're taking dating advice from Neanderthals now?'

'It's biology! Men are genetically programmed to hunt, to chase. As long as we don't approach them, they'll run after us.'

Where does she get this stuff? Is she secretly swapping seduction tips with the chain-smoking housewives from *Mad Men* under beauty-shop hairdryers? Personally, I think this whole idea that people should stick to archaic, stereotypical gender roles is bullshit.

'Okay, how about this? We don't say hi, but we DO stand near him.'

And the tortilla chips and Dr Pepper.

Mary Kate carefully weighed her decision. Finally, she agreed. 'I mean, how can he know he has to chase me if he doesn't even *see* me? But we're just gonna stand near him. We are NOT making the first move.'

So we set up camp near Theology John, who, in my eyes, was a pretty generic preppy dude with floppy brown hair – other than the fact that he was wearing boat shoes with no socks, a sin which, to my agnostic eyes, should rank *waaay* higher in the Ten Commandments than all that nonsense about boning your neighbor. He was standing in a circle with a bunch of his bros, who I'll call the Apostles. Most of them were dressed like him, also in blue button-downs and boat shoes without socks, and the only remarkable thing about the group was that the Cherry Cokes they were drinking smelled like rum. They had somehow found a senior with a fake ID and paid him to get them alcohol. That, or the Jesus of the group had performed that water-into-wine miracle.

I figured it wouldn't take long for Theology John to notice Mary Kate. I mean, he was drinking so his pretty-girl radar would kick in any second, right?

Unfortunately, I had ignored one crucial detail: the guys were talking about hockey.

Crap on a crucifix, I thought. *We're gonna be here all night!*

'C'mon, Mary Kate,' I whined. 'Can't you make SOME kinda move? You don't have to say hi to him, just . . . brush up against him.'

'No.'

'C'mon, a little brush!'

'No!'

'Nudge?'

'No way.'

'Spank? Slap? Wet willy?'

Mary Kate did not even dignify those suggestions with an answer. She just gave me a look.

'If I make the first move, I throw off the power balance in the relationship,' she explained. 'He's emasculated and forced into a passive position, and has no incentive to make any moves. We never make any progress, and the relationship is stalled in one place.'

I looked at the snack table we'd been standing next to for thirty-five minutes now. 'Yeah, you wouldn't wanna be stalled in one place.'

My next tactic was sneaky. Inch by inch, millimeter by millimeter, I forced Mary Kate closer to Theology John. It was a really careful, calculated move on my part – like when I used to covertly nudge the pointer-thingy on the Ouija board at my eighth-grade sleepovers to spell out messages from my friends' dead grandparents. Patient, subtle, devious. Now Mary Kate and Theology John were practically butt to butt, but he still didn't turn around.

I can't take this anymore! By now we had listened to ten bleeped-out Rihanna songs, three bleeped-out Ed Sheeran songs (really?), and musically relived the entire relationship and break-up of Selena Gomez and Justin Bieber. I couldn't stand around all night with Mary Kate playing the coy Jane Bennet to Theology John's Mr Bingley in boat shoes. There was a senior somewhere with a flask of rum that could actually make this night interesting, and I was going to hunt that sucker down.

So I took action. I reached out and shoved Mary Kate.

She stumbled backwards into Theology John, who lost his balance and sloshed the contents of his Cherry Coke can all over the front of his blue button-down. Luckily, seeing as what was in the can smelled very little like Cherry Coke, Theology John was confused about who had bumped into whom. First, he looked around, flushed and nervous, checking for teachers. Then he noticed Mary Kate and was super apologetic.

'Oh man, are you okay?' he asked her. He inspected her clothes, holding his dripping can away from her. Then he looked at her face. 'Hey, wait, aren't you in my theology class?'

'Oh, am I?' She tilted her head to the side like a golden retriever puppy, her best 'adorably puzzled' face. 'I think you might be right! Do you need a tissue? I think I have one . . .'

As she began pulling tissues and wipes and stain spray out of her purse like a boy-crazy Mary Poppins, I thought, *My work here is done.* So I walked away. I had some mingling to do.

If you're a girl at a St Mary's social event, probability says you will be hit on by at least three guys named Pat.

My first Pat that night was a guy I already knew. Pat Number One and I had gym together freshman year – an early-morning class that *he* spent running endless laps around the track with the obsession of a lab rat, and *I* spent eating Pop-Tarts on the high-jump mat. So we're not exactly best buds. But Pat is a super-friendly dude so, when he spotted me alone at the dance, he bounced over like a human pogo stick.

'Hey, Alex! What's up? How was your summer?'

Pat Number One is a rubbery beanpole with an overbite that makes a cheerful whistling sound when he talks.

'Good, Pat.' I craned my neck back to look up at him. 'How about you? What'd you do this summer?'

'Oh man! I ran a *marathon*!' His enthusiasm showered spit down on me. 'The training was intense but *awesome*! I got up at four a.m. every day and started with push-ups and a protein shake, then . . .'

Pat Number One is nice and all, but I stopped listening pretty fast. To me, people talking about exercise is pretty much white noise. 'Ten miles ... shin splints ... whey protein ...'

Tuning out, I let my gaze wander across the dance floor, where a bunch of sophomore and junior girls were bopping around innocently like extras in a 1960s beach movie. I checked on Mary Kate, who was still talking to Theology John, giggling and twirling the ends of her long, ripply hair.

When I tuned back in, Pat Number One was saying, 'Hey! You wanna make out?'

Wait – what? How did we get from marathon training to hooking up?

'Uh ... no thanks, I'm good,' I said.

'That's cool!' Pat Number One said cheerfully, undaunted and just as bouncy as ever. He was practically bobbing up and down like a life-sized birthday balloon. 'We can keep it platonic! Friends are great! Hey – we could be exercise buddies!'

That was when I left. I'm not offended by someone asking to slip me the tongue at a party, but there's no way in hell they're making me do sit-ups. THAT is taking things too far.

After I had gone to the bathroom, chatted people up in search of smuggled rum, failed and returned to the snack table, I met Pat Number Two.

Now Pat Number One may have been too optimistic for me, but Pat Number Two was sadder than the Twitterverse when One Direction broke up. The first thing he said to me when he approached me by the soda was: 'You probably don't wanna talk to me.'

Pat Number Two was obviously a freshman. He was doing a fairly good job blending in – he even had a blue button-down on – but I could still tell he was a freshman. There's no hiding that scared-rabbit look in your eyes and the rash on your neck from unnecessarily shaving with a five-blade Mach razor when your face is smoother than Elle Fanning's ass.

So I tried to be nice, even though, to be honest, he was right – I probably didn't want to talk to him. I introduced myself and asked where he was from.

'Lubbock, Texas,' he said, and added sadly, 'Twelve hundred thirty-eight miles away.'

The kid was seriously homesick. But the weird thing was, instead of bumming me out, his melancholy made me get oddly enthusiastic about St Mary's. Hey, what can I say? I'm a contradictory person.

'Don't worry, you're gonna love it here!' I chirped reassuringly. 'I bet you've met a lot of cool people already!'

He shook his head. 'I don't know anyone. I ended up at this dance by accident because I got lost trying to find the library.'

'You'll make a whole bunch of friends!' I lied. 'And this place is awesome! I mean, sure, the dorm rules are anal-retentive. And homework's a bitch. And people *are* crazy competitive – like last year, in the PSATs, this kid started giving me crazy eyes during the math section, and I thought he was gonna stab me in the thigh with his pencil. Yeah, everyone can be a little nuts here. Not as nuts as the weather, though! Have you ever lived through a Minnesota winter? We're talking apocalyptic, *Game of Thrones*-style winter here . . .'

As I was talking, Pat Number Two's eyes grew wider and more terrified until it looked like he was about to number two himself.

'NO!' I panicked, realizing that my uncustomary cheer had trailed off into my usual bitter but witty sarcasm and I was traumatizing the kid. 'No, it's totally awesome! I mean . . . we have Fajita Friday!'

And I gave his scrawny freshman self a comforting hug. He sniffled into my bare shoulder for a few seconds – then, as we pulled apart, his wet eyes lit up and he asked, 'Hey! You wanna make out?'

To be fair to both Pats, the atmosphere had taken a turn for . . . well, *sexy* would be too strong a word. More like horny and sweaty. Now that it was after nine o'clock, a lot of the older, crankier nuns and priests had left and gone back to their rooms to put on hair shirts and pray for our sinful souls. Mostly the semi-cool chaperones were left – like Father Dan, the youngest dorm priest, who plays guitar for us on school retreats. It was darker, someone had put on an R&B song with no bleeped-out words and the dance floor was filling up. Couples were clinging to each other, and Theology John's friends had finished their rum-spiked sodas and were cruising for anyone to grind their khaki shorts against. All the rum breath and sweat and khaki-boner friction had made the room so hot and steamy that the windows were completely fogged up. As I stared at the windows in gross, horrified fascination, I saw a kid reach up and smear his handprint across the condensation in a clear homage to Kate Winslet and the sex-in-the-car scene in *Titanic*.

I laughed. Then I saw who it was.

'Well, well, well,' he hailed me. 'The Tampon Terror!'

It was the Shaggy Hockey Player – the one I'd dumped tampons on. He was perched on the ancient radiator under the window, swinging his legs.

'You know,' I told him, swaggering over, 'when you make ignorant jokes about a woman's body, you just prove to everyone around that you've never actually touched one.'

He put his hand to his chest in mock offense. 'I'll have you know I can get one of those plaid skorts unbuckled in thirty-four seconds.'

I leaned in. 'I wouldn't brag too much about what you can get done in thirty-four seconds.'

He laughed, throwing his shaggy head back.

'But it doesn't matter,' I said airily. 'You Neanderthals actually ended up giving me a great idea.'

'Oh yeah? What's that?'

'I am going to put on the first-ever St Mary's Catholic School production of *The Vagina Monologues*.'

He barely raised an eyebrow at my bold statement. Then he shook his head and said calmly, 'No you're not.'

'Excuse me?'

'You'll never be able to put on *The Vagina Monologues* here. You can't pull it off, trust me. Last year the Drama Club got *Beauty and the Beast* censored because the vice-principal didn't like the "overtones of bestiality".'

'*Beauty and the Beast*? Disney's *Beauty and the Beast*?' Shit.

'Wait,' I said. 'How do you know about the Drama Club?'

'I know many things, Young Grasshopper. So, if you need some assistance with *The Vagina Monologues*, I may be able to help you out.'

'How are *you* gonna help me? Get a bunch of your baboon friends to come body-paint VAGINA on their chests and cheer us on?'

The hockey player shrugged. 'Maybe there's more to me than baboonery. Wanna find out?' And he patted the empty space next to him on the radiator.

Okay, I know, I know. Hockey players are total creeps. But you have to understand that I'd just been quasi-groped by an overemotional freshman and had Pat Number One offer to show me his Fitbit. I was in a weird frame of mind.

I sat down.

'By the way . . .' The Hockey Player wiped his window-steamy hand on the front of his khaki shorts and held it out to me. 'I'm Pat.'

'Oh Jesus,' I groaned.

And that's how I – *officially* – met Pat Number Three.

After I'd introduced myself, Pat studied me for a long minute, crossing his arms over his blue button-down and narrowing his eyes. I raised my eyebrow questioningly as he stared at me, and finally he asked: 'What color is your hair?'

I reached up and defensively ruffled my purple fauxhawk.

'The color is called Violet Beauregarde,' I told him.

'Ah.' He waited a minute. Then he said, 'Well, aren't you gonna ask me?'

'What?'

'What color *my* hair is!'

'You don't dye your hair!'

He shrugged. 'So what?'

'Okay.' I rolled my eyes and gave in. 'What color is your hair?'

'Scrumdiddlyumptious Chocolate Bar Brown.'

I laughed. I couldn't help it. A triumphant smirk curled up one side of Pat's mouth.

'Hey.' He nudged me and pointed to the row of black-clad chaperones under the bloody crucifix. 'Kiss, Marry, Kill – priests only. Go.'

'Psh,' I scoffed. 'Way too easy. Kill Father O'Brien as revenge for failing me in physics last year. Marry Father Joe because he's a thousand years old and friggin' adorable. And obviously kiss Father Dan. He's the Bieber priest!'

Pat agreed. 'He gets me a little hot with that guitar, I'll tell you.'

'Although . . .' I reconsidered. 'I probably *should* say kiss Father John-Paul.'

'Why's that?'

'Because he's seen my nipples.'

'Me too!' Pat said, wide-eyed like he was amazed at the coincidence. 'What's your story?'

'Freshman year, Andrew Naylor's room, strip poker gone awry. You?'

'He lives down the hall from me, so he pretty much sees my nipples every time I go take a shower.'

I shook my head in mock disapproval, thinking of Mary Kate's floor-length robe. 'Strutting down the hallway in a towel. You brazen hussy.'

Pat leaned so close to me that his breath was hot on my ear. 'Who said there was a towel?'

A shiver shot through me, from my lady fauxhawk down to the heels of my motorcycle boots, and suddenly I could feel all the flushed heat of that trapped breath and sweat and sex. *Ugh, come on, ovaries!* I groaned inwardly. *Don't get it up for a jock!*

Suddenly – speaking of horny people – we were interrupted by the giddy whirlwind in ballet flats that was my room-mate.

'ALEX! ALEX!'

Mary Kate pushed her way through a clingy, moist couple on the dance floor who were *not* leaving room for the Holy Spirit. Her face was glowing with excitement – okay, and sweat – and there was one perfect curl draped over her shoulder that she'd been twirling obsessively while talking to Theology John. Her Flirting Curl.

'Guess what?' she bubbled. 'Theology John asked me to take a walk. What do you think that means?'

'Mary Kate, I'm not going over this again. Why do you think I bought you that *Birds and the Bees* picture book?'

'He's waiting for me by the snack table,' she gushed, staring at him, starry-eyed. 'Doesn't he look *sooo* cute?'

'Oh yeah. Sexy ankles.'

Then she turned back to me urgently for confirmation. 'So he definitely wants to make out, right?' She blew air into my face. 'How's my breath?'

'Good from over here,' Pat chimed in, and Mary Kate, embarrassed, clapped a hand over her mouth.

'Oh my gosh! I didn't see you!' she said, but was still all in a tizzy and turned back to me. 'But I'm scared we're gonna get in trouble.' She glanced back at the chaperone wall nervously. 'Do you think any of the nuns will notice that we're leaving so close together?'

'I think they have bigger fish to fry,' I told her.

On the dance floor, a senior guy had just ripped open his shirt so violently that a button flew off and hit a girl in the eye. It was kind of like a scene from *The Hulk*, if the Hulk had a pasty, concave chest with three hairs on it. The kid was clearly drunk – and Sister Hellda had spotted him.

As Sister Hellda dragged Pasty Hulk off the dance floor, presumably for an exorcism, Mary Kate saw her chance. Here was her shining moment for love, for romance, for clumsy Catholic over-the-shirt and in-the-vicinity-of-the-khakis fondling! In a magical daze, like Cinderella, all sparkly-eyed from whatever fairy dust those sweatshop mice had sprinkled on her, Mary Kate began to make her way over to Theology John . . .

Then the cafeteria blew a fuse.

The lights went out. The music shut off. A loud cheer went up, everyone shouting and whistling in the dark. There's nothing St Mary's kids love more than a blackout.

Luckily for us, it happens pretty often, thanks to the fact that our school's electrical wiring – like its values system – dates back to the Dark Ages. This has its advantages and disadvantages. I mean, sure, there's a high risk of us running screaming out of burning buildings with our hair on fire. But there's also those ninety precious seconds of co-ed pitch-blackness, a rare chance for all these sexually repressed kids to finally let loose and feel each other up a little. People were bumping and grabbing and giggling, and I'm pretty sure I heard at least one khaki zipper being unzipped.

A calm voice – Father Dan, the Bieber priest – was calling out, 'Everyone be cool! Let's chill, everyone, shall we?'

My heart was speeding up from the thrill of the velvety darkness, the sweaty bodies of strangers around us, the unknown . . . Suddenly I was intensely aware of the heat of Hockey Player Pat's body beside me, his leg pressed against mine on the radiator. His hot breath was on my cheek; my hand fumbled in the dark and I found his sweat-softened collar; my fist closed around it; I pulled him towards me . . .

And the lights came back on.

I reared back in horror and jumped off the radiator. Now my heart was pounding in panic – even though Pat

Number Three was still cute with the lights on. That only freaked me out all the more. *What the hell do you think you're doing, Tampon Terror? You were about to kiss a hockey player!* Sure, I'd kissed a lot of people in my day – every guy in my seventh-grade health class without a retainer, a girl the summer before sophomore year, the hipster cashier at Urban Outfitters for a ten percent discount on a crop top. But a hockey player? That was way too far! I had to get out!

But it was a zombie apocalypse in the cafeteria. When the lights come on at a St Mary's dance, shit gets scary. Suddenly you're face to face with the guy you've been making out with and it's NOT that cute indie kid from jazz band, but the buck-toothed turd who always asks for more Spanish homework.

But, when you turn to flee, you find yourself swept up in a stampede of horror-stricken faces, bloodshot eyes, crushed in a mob of clammy pale bodies. Everywhere you turn, everyone is pushing and shoving, desperate to bolt from the bad decisions they made in the dark.

'IT IS TEN FORTY-FIVE P.M.,' Sister Hellda announced. 'ALL STUDENTS MUST RETURN TO THEIR DORMS. STUDENTS, PLEASE FILE IN AN ORDERLY FASHION BACK TO YOUR DORMS . . .'

I pushed and bobbed and weaved and briefly considered squatting to crawl through the legs of the girl in front of me and tunnel to freedom. But I was stuck – wedged in a bottleneck, crammed in a crush of sticky bare arms that smelled like sweat and Axe body spray.

But somehow Mary Kate had wormed her forceful little way through the mass of disheveled sinners, because out of nowhere she popped up in front of me in an advanced state of panic, with eyes as big as an anime character's.

She blurted out, 'I think John is DEAD!'

'What?' I said. 'What happened?'

'John who?' came a voice from behind us. It was Pat Number Three, who thanks to the zombie crush was still right behind me, and was now sticking his cute dumb nose in our business.

'Theology John!' Mary Kate shouted at him in frustration, then turned back to me. 'I lost him when the lights went out! We were supposed to meet by the snack table, remember? But, when I went over, he was lying behind the table, passed out!'

'Well, it's Theology John,' I said. 'Wait three days, he'll probably come back to life.'

'ALEX! I'm serious!'

'Hold up,' Pat intervened. 'Is this John O'Connell we're talking about? Junior? Tall, kinda boring?'

'Yes!' shouted Mary Kate, who was yelling everything impatiently in her panic.

'Oh yeah, I know him.'

'What do you know about him?' my room-mate demanded.

'He lives in my dorm. And I'm not too surprised he passed out.'

'Does he drink a lot?' Mary Kate frowned suspiciously.

'Nah. He probably drank tonight because he's super shy around girls.'

'Aw!' She clasped her hands to her chest in adoration.

'But, every time he has one drink, he either pukes or passes out.'

'Oh my gosh!' She whipped her head towards me in alarm. Damn, this really was an emotional roller coaster for the girl.

'Of course,' Pat continued, 'I *could* go help him . . .'

'Yes! Yes!'

Pat looked at me and grinned slyly. 'For your room-mate's number.'

'What?' I said. 'No way!'

'ALEX!' Mary Kate shrieked. 'HE COULD ACTUALLY DIE!'

'Okay, fine!' I said, just to calm her down. Pat tossed me his phone and I put my number in, grumbling, 'I can't believe I'm giving a hockey player my number.'

I threw the phone back at him, kinda hard, but he caught it easily with one hand as he reassured Mary Kate.

'He'll be fine. I'll get him back to the dorm.'

With that, Hockey Player Pat was off, weaving easily between the tight-packed groups of people and even leap-frogging over a dude's back.

'See ya, Alex!' he called back over his shoulder.

I shouted back, 'What was your name again?' hoping my sarcasm resonated even over a mob of the horny undead.

*

Outside the air was cooler – at least for me. For all those Catholic nerds burning with shame about the butts they had groped in the dark, not so much. Everyone straggled off towards their dorms, hanging their heads in regret. The lucky few who had shared that flask of rum stumbled.

Mary Kate trudged.

'Aw, come on,' I told her. 'It's for the best. You can't date a guy who drinks – not even one drink. You get loopy on cough medicine. What you need is a nice, friendly, substance-free dude who's scared to touch your boobs.'

And, right on cue, that dude arrived – in the form of a curly-haired, smiling senior with big front teeth who popped up seemingly out of the ground like a cheerful whack-a-mole.

'Good evening, ladies!' he chirped. 'Would you care for an escort back to your dorm?'

I saw the green pin on his polo shirt and groaned. Campus Safewalk.

Campus Safewalk is so dumb. What's the point of it? It's not like we're in a Syrian war zone. We're on a closed campus in rural Minnesota with hawk-eyed nuns and priests and probably surveillance cameras everywhere. The most insidious threat on this campus is the athlete's foot in the third-floor showers.

Plus, this dude was way too Catholic hippie for my taste. He had one of those chunky wooden cross necklaces and the sandals that always make me think of Jesus, even when they're strapped to the feet of a long-toed pagan at a San Francisco death-metal festival.

'I think we can walk the seven hundred feet to our dorm without getting tied up with nunchucks and held for ransom,' I told Jesus Sandals. 'Thanks anyway.'

But then I saw that Mary Kate was gazing into his sweet, dimpled face. She turned to me with pleading eyes.

Fine! I guess I had to give in. Mary Kate had had a rough night: she'd already lost one crush with terrible footwear.

We set off towards Girls' Quad, across the dewy grass, the smell of late summer flowers in the air almost dissipating the scent of BO from the clusters of giggling people. So in the end Mary Kate had her romantic stroll – in fact, the three of us did, the little Holy Trinity of Mary Kate, Jesus Sandals and me.

8

Academic Quad was festooned with bright signs and balloons. Juniors and seniors in green plaid were bustling around tables that were arranged in a giant semicircle on the grass, clipboards in hand, chattering to each other with lively and anal-retentive enthusiasm.

It was Club Fair Day.

For most St Mary's students, the September Club Fair is the time to shop for extracurricular activities. For my room-mate, it was the time to shop for a boyfriend. Even though Mary Kate hadn't asked for his number or seen him again since, our meeting with Jesus Sandals – whose name turned out to be Caleb – had awakened her sense of infinite possibility and optimism.

'Look! Model UN! There's always cute guys in that – we should set up next to them,' Mary Kate said as we turned onto the quad. She was leading the way, practically skipping in her penny loafers. 'No, wait! Mock Trial! Cute guys in *suits* . . .'

'Just pick a table,' I told her, dragging behind, weighed down by the big shopping bag of school supplies I was carrying. Somehow I always get stuck carrying stuff with Mary Kate, just like when I ended up putting our futon together with that little Barbie-sized screwdriver. 'I want to get down to business.'

'Hmm . . .' she pondered thoughtfully, her crazy brain calculating angles and wind velocity and the golden ratio and absolute distance from every attractive guy on the quad. Finally, she pointed decisively. 'There. Let's take that one. Model UN is on one side, and there's an empty table on the other side, so if someone good shows up we can call them over.'

'Fine.'

Dumping the shopping bag on the table, I yanked out a neon-yellow poster and unrolled it. In big purple letters, it read:

SUPPORT *THE VAGINA MONOLOGUES*!
SIGN OUR PETITION!

Mary Kate groaned. 'You can't put that up at our booth! The Club Fair is for recruiting club members, not signing petitions!'

'We already have a bunch of club members.' I pulled a roll of duct tape out of the bag.

'We have SIX club members. Plus, every teacher in the school is gonna be here! You can't put that sign up! There'll be nuns!'

Tearing off a piece of duct tape with my teeth, I slapped it on the sign, securing it to the front of the table.

'Yup,' I said. 'Every teacher on campus is gonna be here, and almost every student. And we need five hundred signatures to move ahead with this thing, so we really need to capture people's attention.'

'Alex!' Mary Kate hissed. 'There are guys here, too! Smart guys who are involved in extracurricular stuff! You're gonna scare them away!'

'If they don't want to support *The Vagina Monologues*,' I said, placing our clipboard on the table, 'then to hell with them.'

'Well, I'm leaving then.' She snatched up the rainbow-colored pens she'd brought with her. 'I'll just go recruit freshmen with the *Literary Magazine*. I'm a member of eight other clubs, you know.'

'Yes, but you're not an *officer* of those clubs. Thanks to me and my nepotism, you're vice-president of *this* club, even though you're just a junior.'

Sulkily, Mary Kate surrendered and began unpacking her pens again, arranging them in ROYGBIV order next to my clipboard. We had just finished setting up when we heard an irritatingly cheerful voice.

'Hey, Alex! Hey, MK!'

Coming towards us was what looked like a Valentine's Day parade float: pink balloons that seemed to hold up a huge white smile. As she got closer, we could make out the freckled face and red hair of my campus nemesis, the girl who embodies everything I hate most about St Mary's: the irrepressible perkiness, the do-gooder Girl Scout facade, the deep-seated sexual repression.

It was Katie Casey.

'Fuck my tits,' I groaned under my breath.

Mary Kate hit me. 'Stop it! Katie's really nice!'

'No, she *acts* nice. She's *really* Kim Jong-un in a scrunchie,' I said. 'And why is she calling you MK? Like you two are best buds or something.'

'We are friends! We had health class together freshman year.'

'Watching a video about abstinence together doesn't give you, like, a bond for life.'

Katie Casey stopped at the table next to ours, breathless. She wore a pink T-shirt from a breast-cancer walk, and rubber charity bracelets all up her arm, and was carrying two trays of pink cupcakes.

'Do you girls mind if I set up here?' she asked.

'Actually . . .' I began, as Mary Kate chimed, 'Sure, no problem!'

I glared at Mary Kate.

Katie Casey unrolled a white poster, sending a shower of pink glitter over both our tables. It read:

SAVE YOUR HEART club!
We're waiting for marriage!

Grrr! It took all my self-control not to tear the poster to pieces. Virginity pledges are the worst. Encouraging young girls to hand over ownership of their sexuality to some disembodied deity? Basically, these girls are denying

87

themselves any kind of physical pleasure until they get a promise ring from some turd in pleated khakis who learned about female anatomy from cartoon prostitutes in *Grand Theft Auto IV*. That can't possibly lead to anything bad, right?

As usual, Katie Casey was oblivious to the righteous hatred for her simmering under my skin because she was chatting with us, all freckly and smiley, her ponytail bouncing, asking how our summers were, what classes we were taking. 'And what's the St Mary's Feminist Club up to this semester?' she asked.

'Actually, something really exciting,' I told her. 'We're putting on the first-ever St Mary's Catholic School production of *The Vagina Monologues*.'

'Wow!' she chirped. 'I don't know too much about it, but I've heard of it! Definitely exciting!'

Oh, is it? I thought. I decided to test her.

'Yeah, the school doesn't want us to,' I continued. 'The *school* thinks the play goes against Catholic values and promotes premarital sex. But we're collecting signatures to support the show.' I held out our clipboard and pen enticingly. 'Would *you* like to sign?'

For a moment, our eyes met, both narrowing in the bright sunlight of the quad.

Then she said, 'Sure!' And she took the pen and signed.

See? Mary Kate mouthed over her head.

Yeah, yeah, I know what you're thinking – *This girl seems really nice! I would totally buy Santa Claus wrapping paper from her – or elect her as a benevolent dictator! I mean, the world today needs strong leadership, right?*

But I was suspicious. There was a reason she was using our actual club name instead of referring to us as *those lesbians in the basement* like everyone else did. The girl had an ulterior motive.

'You know,' she said thoughtfully, peeling the plastic wrap off her cupcake tray, 'we should collaborate on something this year. I think Save Your Heart and the Feminist Club could do something really amazing together. I mean, so many of our concerns overlap – we're both mostly female clubs talking about sexuality and choices . . .'

'I actually think we have pretty different takes on a lot of issues,' I said. 'Like choices, for example. Because we're – you know – *pro*-choice.'

'Right!' she chirped. 'But there's definitely common ground there. Like, for example, we were brainstorming this whole weekend festival – maybe you guys could get involved? It's all about sisterhood –'

I cut her off. The last thing I needed to hear about was one of Katie's knit-your-own-chastity-belt craftathons. And how dare she compare her little cult to my Feminist Club?

'No, thank you,' I said clearly. 'We're focused on our own projects.'

'Okay! No worries!' Katie Casey responded, undaunted. She held up her cupcake tray. 'Want one? They're red velvet!'

Honestly, her cupcakes looked friggin' amazing. But, up close, I saw they were decorated with crosses. Crosses made of white-chocolate chips, but crosses nonetheless.

Mary Kate graciously accepted one and took a big bite. 'Mmmm, cream-cheese frosting.' She made pointed eye contact with me to rub it in. 'This is *delicious*.'

But I would not eat those Virgin Cupcakes. It was a matter of principle. Sometimes you have to sacrifice a sugar rush to stick it to a misogynistic society.

And there was no way in glitter-covered hell Katie Casey would ever get involved with the Feminist Club.

'Support *The Vagina Monologues*! Stand up for free speech and sexual equality at St Mary's!' I was shouting.

'Join Save Your Heart! Experience friendship and fellowship, and dedicate your purity to the Lord!' Katie Casey was chirping.

'Wow, Finland! What an interesting place! What is the social and political history of the country like?' Mary Kate was gushing in fascination. (She was talking to the cute, big-eared kid from Model UN.)

A scrawny, wide-eyed freshman girl, whose backpack was bigger than her, stopped in front of our booths. She looked up at me and took in my purple hair, my righteous fury and the neon vagina sign. She looked at Katie Casey and took in her welcoming smile, her glitter and her cupcakes.

She signed up for Save Your Heart.

The freshman throng had arrived at the Club Fair. This was their second week on campus. For the first few days, they had been paraded around en masse by perky leaders – among them Katie Casey – who took them on campus tours and taught them the school fight song and indoctrinated them into all the green-plaid bullshit that surrounds us.

For the next week, the freshmen had stayed clumped in one big, scared herd like gazelles, all wide eyes and skinny legs, bolting in terror across the quad at the sound of church bells, terrified of missing curfew.

Two weeks in, they had evolved from gazelles into meerkats: still nervous, but starting to break off into little cliques, venturing out beyond their holes and sniffing around. And, for the meerkats, today's Club Fair was a big step forward. Today was the day each one had to look inside and ask: *Who am I going to be?* An uber-competitive brainiac demolishing fellow brainiacs in the Debate Club? A sports masochist rowing across the lake until they puked blue Powerade? A goody-goody sweating desperate enthusiasm on the cheerleading team?

Or, just possibly . . . a feminist rebel fighting for the right to stage *The Vagina Monologues* at St Mary's?

Or . . . not.

It didn't seem very likely, at least at the start of the Club Fair. My vagina sign definitely attracted attention, but not the good kind. Well-behaved girls with their white shirts buttoned all the way up were scared of it and didn't know where to look; they cried out in relief when their eyes fell on Katie Casey. 'Oh look, *cupcakes*!' And, just like that, they hurried past.

Baby-faced freshman boys spotted my sign, blushed bright red and scurried away to see if the rumors of a Video Game Club were true. And mid-pubescent assholes with gelled hair nudged each other, pointed and snickered.

My only hope lay with the bolder girls: the groups who prowled with their plaid skorts already rolled up around the waist to make them shorter. 'Hey!' one of them pointed. 'Feminist Club! Emma Watson's a feminist. I *love* Emma Watson.'

'Yeah, but when she became a feminist she chopped her hair off. I can't do that. I have my dad's ears.'

'You don't have to!' I protested, jumping into their conversation. 'Feminists don't always chop all their hair off!'

The girls stared at my purple fauxhawk.

'I mean, I did,' I continued. 'But not everyone does. Look at my room-mate!' I yanked Mary Kate away from the Model UN table by one of her long braids and put her on display. 'She looks like Laura Ingalls Wilder! And she's vice-president of the Feminist Club!'

'I don't support *this*, though.' Mary Kate pointed to the sign.

Next to us, the Save Your Heart booth was mobbed. Katie Casey was chattering about Save Your Heart's activities for the year: 'We're going on a retreat with the amazing Father Dan, we're doing a bake sale to raise money for the Crisis Pregnancy Center in Minneapolis, we're playing minigolf . . . Our first meeting is this Wednesday – and we'll have snacks!'

The little freshmen in the front row were all whispering, 'Let's join!' 'That sounds *sooo* fun!'

Glaring at them, I grumbled to Mary Kate, 'I swear, the lemmings on this campus would take part in a witch-burning if there was pizza afterwards.'

'She was smart,' Mary Kate said. 'We should have thought of cupcakes.'

'We don't need cupcakes! We have freedom of expression and the First Amendment on our side!'

'Well, she's on her second sign-up sheet already – or is it her third?' Mary Kate squinted. 'And our sheet is practically empty.'

'It's not empty! There's my signature . . . your signature . . . Katie Casey's signature . . .' I mumbled over that one. 'And those two sophomore guys! Remember? Seymour . . .' I read the names more carefully and dropped the clipboard on the table with a disappointed clank. 'Seymour Butts and Anus McFarty.'

Mary Kate gave me a smug look.

I grabbed her green pen and set to work trying to transform Seymour Butts and Anus McFarty into legitimate signatures.

'It's definitely her third sign-up sheet,' Mary Kate reported. 'And it's almost full . . .' She craned her neck to look past all the people, and then suddenly squeaked, 'Oh my gosh! Look who it is!'

'Another virgin?' I suggested sarcastically.

And . . . I was right. But not just any virgin. The current virgin of the month on Mary Kate's Virgin Cuties Calendar.

It was Caleb, old Jesus Sandals himself. He was gliding towards us across the quad, hovering flawlessly an inch above the green grass.

I'm kidding. He was walking like a normal human being, except for those fucking sandals.

When he got to the Save Your Heart table, he maneuvered himself around the crowd and gave Katie Casey a big hug.

'Of course they're friends,' I groaned.

'He's coming over here!' Mary Kate hissed.

Caleb had spotted us. Maybe it was the radioactive glow of Mary Kate's ovaries, beckoning him like some kind of boy-crazy bat signal.

'Hey, Mary Kate! Hey, Alex!'

'Hi!' Mary Kate was breathless with excitement. 'How's it going, Caleb? Did you just get here?'

'Yup.' Caleb tilted his head towards the campus chapel on the north side of the quad. 'I was just squeezing in a little pew time first.'

Pew time? I scoffed inwardly. *More like puke time! And cover your toes, bro.*

'What are you guys up to?' he asked.

'We –' I began my declaration, but Mary Kate, who was scrambling in front of our table to cover up the raging neon vagina sign, cut me off.

'Oh, just signing people up for . . . this project Alex is doing,' she said vaguely. 'It's not really anything. I'm just helping her because I'm her room-mate.'

'Yeah, ya know, all that "honor your neighbor" stuff,' I chimed in.

94

Mary Kate swiveled to shoot burning daggers out of her eyes at me. Then she turned back to Caleb, instantly assuming the dewy glow of a Disney princess. 'What about you?'

'Actually, I'm here with my band,' Caleb said. 'We're trying to recruit a new bassist, so we thought we'd put on a little show.'

'Your band?' I raised a skeptical eyebrow. I couldn't exactly picture Caleb in guyliner and leather pants, shredding the electric guitar.

'Yeah! The Beatitudes! We're one of the Catholic acoustic rock groups on campus.'

There's more than one Catholic acoustic rock group at this school? Jesus. Literally. Jesus.

'So cool!' Mary Kate gushed. 'Are you guys gonna play now?'

'Yeah! You should come watch – if you can take a break.'

My room-mate waved her hand dismissively. 'Oh, Alex doesn't need me. She's doing great on her own.'

'Oh yeah,' I said sarcastically, holding up the clipboard. 'Five whole signatures, including Seymour –'

'Bye!' Mary Kate said hurriedly. As she skipped off beside Caleb, I heard her ask, 'So do you write your own songs, too, or . . . ?'

Mary Kate had officially ditched me. For a man in sandals.

Maybe Laura Ingalls Wilder was giving up, but not me. And I was rewarded because, mere minutes later, a freshman badass came along. Well, maybe not a badass yet, but she had black nail polish on, which at St Mary's indicates badass potential at least. She spotted the sign and, instead of fleeing, she lingered.

'Hey, what's up?' I called out in a friendly but calm voice, trying not to spook her, using some tricks from a video Mary Kate showed me of a family who tamed wild chipmunks to eat Cheerios out of their hands.

'Hey.' She smiled and made eye contact.

Good sign.

'So are you interested in social issues?' I asked.

I figured 'social issues' was a pretty general term, which could encompass anything from voting rights to the fiery world panic about antibiotic-resistant gonorrhea.

'Yeah, for sure.' She came closer and read my sign. 'So you guys are doing *The Vagina Monologues*?'

'We are! I mean, we want to. And you could help make it happen – all you have to do is sign your name.' I held out the clipboard.

She took it, and I saw a henna tattoo on the inside of her wrist. *Jackpot!* Then, suddenly, she wavered. She looked at the mostly blank page, including the scribbled green mess that was *Seymour Butts* on the third line, and handed back the clipboard, withdrawing her hand so her white uniform sleeve covered her tattoo.

'Actually, I don't know if I should,' she said. 'My parents don't even let me watch PG-thirteen movies. If they saw my name on this . . .'

Don't let her slip away, Alex! Close the deal! Sweet-talk her, Alex! Woman up and sweet-talk her ass into a signature!

96

'Your parents won't see your name on this,' I told her. 'Because guess what? *Your parents aren't here.* I know it's weird to try to comprehend that when you first go away to boarding school, but you're basically an adult now. No one can tell you what to do.'

A look of wonder came into Henna Wrist's eyes. Amazement – an epiphany: she was on the threshold of adulthood. Of independence. Of total liberty. She had just taken the clipboard when a balding priest stopped at my table.

'Ms Heck!' he called out. 'Please do not forget to submit your summer reading reports. When I said extension, I did *not* mean two weeks.'

'Yeah, sure, Father Flanagan, I will,' I grumbled dismissively, then turned back to the girl. 'What I'm saying is this. No one can tell you what's right and what's wrong. This is your time to grow, to develop your own social conscience. You need to make your own decisions now!'

'Ms Heck!' Sister Hellda strode over. 'Please do not forget to sign your substance-free dorm pledge. As you know, the pledge is *mandatory*, and I will need it under my door, *tonight*.'

'Yeah, I know,' I growled. I whipped back to Henna Wrist, who was looking doubtfully at the clipboard. 'My point is,' I continued feverishly, 'YOU are your *own* person, and –'

'Dress code, Ms Heck,' Sister Carroll admonished me in passing. 'Please keep *all* buttons buttoned.'

'GODDAMMIT!' I burst out, and Sister Carroll chastised me drily.

'First Commandment, Ms Heck.'

'You know what?' I snatched the clipboard back from Henna Wrist. 'Just go. Everything I said was a lie. You can't make your own choices, you are not free, no one is free, freedom is an illusion and Jean-Paul Sartre was full of crap. Just go!'

She went. She never signed the petition. But I did spot her a little later browsing brochures at the Philosophy Club table, and I like to think I had something to do with that.

Hardly anyone stopped by after that. I heard a girl with a unibrow and crucifix earrings hiss to her friend, 'That's *obscene.*'

'Obscene?' I spluttered. 'Your face is obscene! Get some tweezers!'

Then, through the crowd strode a figure all in black with a long, menacing shadow of doom behind him: Father Hughes. Really, the Darth Vader theme music should be playing to warn people when he's coming.

'Hello, Ms Heck!' he greeted me. 'Your poster caught my eye. Very . . . bright.'

'I made it to grab people's attention.'

'And how is your petition coming along?'

I quickly turned over the clipboard. 'Fine. I'm guessing you won't be signing it?'

'Unfortunately, I cannot sign school petitions as the petitions are – technically – addressed to me.'

'And unfortunately, unlike the table next to me, I can't bribe you to sign with a red-velvet Virgin Cupcake,' I said.

Father Hughes sighed and crossed his arms. He studied my neon vagina sign for a long moment. Then he said, 'Ms Heck, may I give you some advice?'

I feigned surprise. 'How novel and exciting! Please do. I'd love your input.'

'I cannot help but notice you are collecting signatures by yourself. If you are truly passionate about this project, why not look for an ally who shares your interest, and can support your efforts? Your club could team up with the Drama Club, or with the *Literary Magazine*. I know Ms Chan, the new teacher in the art department, has an interest in modern theater – an ally of this type could help you try to achieve your goal, or brainstorm a more realistic way to share the message you are passionate about conveying. Some kind of . . . compromise.'

Oh *hell*, no.

'Compromise? You want me to compromise? Well, guess what? The values of freedom and sex positivity and feminism have been *compromised* on this campus for too long. I'm putting on *The Vagina Monologues*. I don't need an ally; I'll put on a one-woman show if I have to, and –'

All of a sudden, my words were swallowed up in a roaring hurricane of sound – hoarse shouts and the stomping of feet. Onto the quad rushed a human tidal wave – fifty whooping, cheering, clapping, shirtless dudes. A tsunami of man-nipples and lanky limbs and bony Adam's apples thundering towards us.

'Oh balls,' I groaned. 'The hockey team.'

In case not everyone could recognize the smell of jockstraps as quickly as I could, they began shouting: 'ST MARY'S VARSITY HOCKEY RULES! EVERYONE MAKE SOME NOISE FOR S.M. HOCKEY!'

It was chaos. Everyone screamed in excitement.

'THIS IS THE YEAR WE WIN NATIONALS! ST LUKE'S IS GOING DOWN! THE TOOTHLESS BEAST IS GOING DOWN! S.M. HOCKEY RULES!'

The freshmen were dazzled. They surged towards the shirtless rock stars in the center of the lawn. Father Hughes strode forward, too, trying to keep order. He and everyone else were swept away by the thundering crowd as the marching band sounded the all-too-familiar opening notes of the St Mary's fight song: '*Dum-DUM-dah-dah . . .*'

Disgusted, I shook my head, shielding my eyes from the blinding white flesh and scraggly body hair. 'And my *sign* is obscene?' I protested loudly.

Then I looked around and realized I was talking to myself. Everyone was crowded in the center of the quad, singing the fight song and clapping their little hearts out. There was no one at the Model UN table to my left – and, intriguingly, no one at the Save Your Heart table to my right. The little minion who had been minding the store while Katie Casey went off for more sign-up sheets had bounced off, giggling, to ogle the topless hockey players. Now the table was empty. Unguarded.

So of course I had to go through their shit.

I snatched up their clipboard, which had a strip of tape across the top reading: JOIN SAVE YOUR HEART and a thick sheaf of papers clipped to it. I flipped through the pages – sign-up sheet after sign-up sheet, all covered with names and email addresses and dozens of little smiley faces. I looked back at my clipboard, which had SUPPORT *THE VAGINA MONOLOGUES* BANNED BY ST MARY'S on the tape across the top, and a single sign-up sheet clipped to it, with five signatures. In the end, I'd managed to turn Anus McFarty into Angus McCarthy – to show we had the support of the fictional students of Scottish-Irish descent on campus. But still it was practically empty. Pathetic. I turned back to the Save Your Heart clipboard, then shook my head and told myself, *No. You shouldn't.*

Then something caught my eye – a bumper sticker they were handing out, which had a little pink present with a bow and read: *Your purity is a gift for Jesus.*

I glared at the bumper sticker, then I grabbed their clipboard, tore off three of their pages and added them to my own clipboard. I looked up – everyone else was in a big circle with their arms around each other, singing in harmony. No one had seen me. So I reached over and stole a cupcake, too. I stuffed it in my face with savage satisfaction.

It was pretty fucking delicious.

9

Mary Kate was in love.

Before you get too excited, you should understand my room-mate's version of being 'in love'. Last winter, a freckled barista at the student center coffee shop gave her extra whipped cream and she sneaked a secret picture of him for an app to see what their future babies would look like.

But actually – and I can testify to this – Mary Kate and Caleb were hanging out on a regular basis. Although at St Mary's the term 'hanging out' has a more sneaking-into-the-locker-room or fondling-on-the-futon connotation to it, and that was NOT what was going on with them. Their first three dates consisted of: milkshake mass on a Sunday morning, working the snow-cone machine at a scholarship fundraiser and painting fences for local senior citizens.

For their fourth date, Caleb asked her to his dorm common room to watch a movie. Now, in St Mary's speak, 'watch a movie' definitely has a dirty connotation. I've gone to at least five different common rooms to watch

Baby Driver, and I didn't even know there was a car in it until the fourth time. So, after Mary Kate left on Friday night, I wondered, *Should I have given her the sex talk?*

Nah. I mean, this is Mary Kate we're talking about. Girlfriend got her sexual awakening from that kid in *The Secret Garden* who can talk to birds. So I figured my room-mate was safe with Caleb and his Jesus Sandals.

And I was quickly reassured when she walked in five minutes before curfew, smiley and glowy, but with her school shirt still buttoned up to the top.

'So what movie did you guys watch?' I asked her, pulling out my earphones and sitting up in the bottom bunk. I'd shoved all my dirty clothes into my army duffel, but never actually got around to doing laundry, so I was using it as a backrest.

Mary Kate sighed happily as she slipped off her loafers. '*American Experience: The Pilgrims*.'

I wrinkled my nose. 'That educational thing about the uptight people with the big buckles and smallpox?'

Mary Kate sighed happily again, watching her own glowing face in the mirror as she took off her cardigan and folded it lovingly over her arm. 'Yes.'

Okay. Nothing to worry about.

Then, one Sunday night, Mary Kate arrived late to dorm mass with big news.

Mass had already started. All the St Theresa Hall girls were gathered in our dorm chapel in sweatpants and pajamas, the opening chords were sounding on the chapel piano, and the overzealous freshman choir member who was always too intense about banging her tambourine was banging her tambourine. The incense was burning and Father Dan was about to make his entrance. I looked around, frowning. Mary Kate wasn't going to miss mass, was she? She never missed mass! Especially not with Father Dan – he was the Bieber priest!

Tambourine Girl had already pounded and rattled her way through a full verse when Mary Kate scurried into the chapel, flushed, her hair loose and rippling. She crossed herself rapidly with holy water, grabbed a hymnal and slipped into the crowd beside me.

'Where were you?' I hissed.

'I was with Caleb,' Mary Kate whispered. 'And guess what? He's asked me to walk around the lake with him!'

This was what Mary Kate had been waiting for. This was like Elizabeth Bennet and Mr Darcy finally exchanging that chaste peck on the lips after six agonizing episodes of letter writing and blue balls in tight trousers. Only Mary Kate hadn't been forced to wait that long – she had practically achieved her semester goal already, and it was only September.

As the opening hymn ended and we all sat cross-legged on the chapel carpet, Mary Kate was practically trembling with excitement. When Father Dan asked us to bow our heads and pray silently, she held up her hymnal for cover and, eyes sparkling, asked me: *'Hey, do you think I should take a selfie stick?'*

*

'Do I look okay?' Mary Kate asked for the thousandth time.

It was Friday night, the night of her lake walk with Caleb, and she was finally ready. It had taken us two hours to prepare her; we'd even missed Fajita Friday for it. First, I'd talked her out of taking a selfie stick by reminding her you needed two hands to use it, which had convinced her right away. There was no way she was letting go of Caleb's hand. No way. They were getting all the way around that lake.

Then picking out her outfit took at least forty-five minutes, which is a ridiculous amount of time considering almost our entire joint wardrobe consists of school uniforms, gym clothes and a cowboy hat, a feather boa and a Yoda mask left over from Halloween last year.

Clearly, she went with the Yoda mask.

Just kidding. Although that would have been amazing.

She stood on Girls' Quad in her pink cardigan and navy dress with pockets, plus my fox-print tights for a touch of whimsy. Her hair was loose and she was practically bouncing with excitement.

'You look perfect,' I reassured her. 'Go with God. Almost literally.'

She squeaked, twirled and skipped across Girls' Quad, where the September sunset revealed the tips of the trees turning gold. Watching her go, I felt suddenly sentimental. *My little Mary Kate, all grown up.* In my head, I still pictured her as the tiny, terrified fourteen-year-old with big brown eyes I'd met during that deadly freshman dodgeball game. I had always felt like a big sister to her, even though we're the same age.

And, actually, I was kind of a big sister to the whole dorm, as I was reminded as soon as I walked back into St Theresa Hall.

'*Alex!*' came an urgent hiss from the stairwell.

I went and looked up. 'Preeti?'

Preeti I actually know, unlike a lot of the younger girls who come to me for help. She was my freshman buddy this year. She pulled me up the stairs into her dorm room. The dresser doors were flung open and her clothes were all over the floor. 'My room-mate found my weed!' she cried.

I put my hands on her shoulders. 'Okay, calm down.'

'It was in here – a little bag – it was *definitely* in here. Now it's gone. My room-mate must have found it!'

'Who's your room-mate? Is she cool?'

'Annie! Annie Rubio! The choirgirl! The one who's super into the tambourine!'

'Tambourine Spanker is your room-mate?' I said. 'Oh man, she is *not* cool at all.'

'I KNOW!' Preeti wailed. 'She's gonna tell Sister Hellda!'

'No, no, we'll figure this out,' I said. 'Hey, wait! This could actually work to our advantage! What if she's SO not cool that she doesn't even know it's weed?'

Preeti wavered. 'Maybe . . .'

'Yes! She found something weird in a little plastic bag, she didn't know what it was, she's suspicious. But it could be anything! It could be oregano!'

'Oregano?' Preeti rolled her eyes. 'What am I, Papa John? What would I be doing with oregano?'

I shook my head, thinking rapidly. 'No, wait! I've got it!'

I sprinted downstairs to my room, grabbed something and ran back up. When Preeti saw it, she frowned. 'A sleep mask?'

'Yup.' I found the seam of the purple silk sleep mask and began tearing it open. 'Sometimes it comes in handy to have a mom whose entire parenting style consists of sending me healing crystals and other bullshit from ashrams two thousand miles away.'

The sleep mask split and a handful of herbs showered to the floor as Preeti stared.

'Lavender and chamomile!' I said triumphantly. 'So make sure to tell your room-mate the little bag she found was just *soothing herbs* to help you sleep. If she could walk in and find you meditating, that would definitely help.'

'Okay, okay,' Preeti said, biting her thumbnail. 'And if it doesn't work?'

'If it doesn't, you tell Sister Hellda you never smoked weed before, but you were super stressed about being away from home for the first time. Use the word *overwhelmed* a lot. That way they'll send you to the school counsellor instead of Father Hughes.'

Preeti nodded obediently and started anxiously picking up her clothes. Before I left, I paused and watched her.

'And you know . . . you can go see the school counsellor anyway,' I added gently. 'I mean, I just go there to skip gym class and play with that Zen garden sand thingy. But she could probably help.'

*

Phew, I thought as I flopped onto the futon in my dorm room, *being selfless is exhausting!*

With a whole Friday night ahead of me, I should have done something productive – like wash my duvet cover, study my Spanish verbs, or hide Sir Shackleton in my bra drawer and leave a ransom note on Mary Kate's pillow made with cut-out letters from her *Seventeen* magazine. Instead, I found myself scrolling through my phone to find the first text I'd gotten from Hockey Player Pat, which said,

> Hey, how's your vagina doing?

And then a follow-up message that said:

> (. . . and yes, this is my opening
> line to every girl I text)

I hadn't replied at the time. I preferred to watch that grey bubble with the dots pop up as he drafted the next message then withdrew it, savoring the sadistic pleasure of torturing him.

But now, I had to say, I was tempted. And bored.

> My vagina is going full steam
> ahead, whether Father Hughes
> wants it to or not.

It was only a few minutes before Hockey Player Pat replied:

> I'm sure Gwyneth Paltrow would
> be very impressed with you and
> your steamy vagina.

Then the grey bubble with the dots popped up and I found myself watching it, holding my breath, until he sent the next message:

> . . . and so am I.

I grinned like an idiot, glad that Mary Kate wasn't here to see it.

> The only thing steamier than
> Gwyneth's vagina are the windows
> at a St Mary's dance.

Pat wrote back right away.

> If Father Dan had whipped out his
> guitar, it would have gotten even
> steamier.

I found I was typing back right away, too:

> And then you would have had to
> get topless in front of Father John-
> Paul again . . .

Just then I heard a noise at the door and a key turning in the lock. *Shit! Sister Hellda!* The dorm nuns have copies of our room keys, and I was sure mine was storming in because her tingling spidey-sense had told her I was on the verge of sending a dirty text.

But then the door opened and it was Mary Kate. She was back way too early from her lake walk and she looked small and sad in the doorway.

'What happened?' I asked her. 'How'd it go?'

Without answering, she came in and let her little patent-leather purse drop to the floor instead of hanging it on its assigned hook. Not a good sign.

I frowned. 'Caleb didn't . . . like, try to pressure you into anything, right?'

Mary Kate sighed and sank onto the futon. 'No,' she said finally. 'Caleb is a good person. A . . . really good person.'

I sat next to her and put my hand on her knee. 'I'm sorry,' I said, and then waited a sympathetic beat before suggesting, 'Cup Noodles?'

Mary Kate leaned her head against the futon and nodded. 'Chicken flavor, please.'

Clearly, my room-mate needed some TLC. I wrapped Mary Kate in a furry blanket, tucked Sir Shackleton next to her on the futon and microwaved her Cup Noodles. As she clutched the warm cup, she began to tell her story.

'We met up at the Victory Fountain. Caleb was wearing a baby-blue polo shirt and he looked *soooo* cute. So we start walking to the lake and, before we even get there, just while we're going down those stone steps, he takes my hand already. Then he tells me he has something super important to talk to me about, and I'm thinking – *This is it! This is it!'*

She clutched her ramen to her chest with a look of bittersweet nostalgia, like she was that sassy old lady remembering banging Leonardo DiCaprio on the *Titanic* back in the day.

'Then we came around that bend, you know where the lake turns . . .'

'Sure,' I said. 'Where you can see the seminary.'

A seminary, as I learned freshman year (and I'm proud I actually remember), has nothing to do with semen. Nothing at all, because it's a priest house where all the priests who don't have rooms in the dorms with us live together. It would make the most boring reality show ever.

For the first time since she walked in the door, Mary Kate looked me in the eye. 'Right,' she said meaningfully. 'The seminary. Then he said he had something to show me . . .'

By this point, I was really tense. What does a kid like Caleb take you into the woods to show you? His schlong? A lower-back tattoo of the loaves and fishes?

'. . . and he let go of my hand.'

To demonstrate, she held up her pale empty palm.

'And I'm thinking, *It's ruined! We're not holding hands! We're not boyfriend and girlfriend now!* But I'm trying to keep calm. I'm reminding myself that it didn't have to happen tonight, that we have all the time in the world. We may not be boyfriend and girlfriend yet, but we have our whole future ahead of us to get to know each other, to date, to get romantic . . . And then I looked up and he was pointing to the seminary.' Mary Kate's face darkened. 'And he said, "That's where I'm going next semester. I'm moving in."'

She stopped dramatically with doom in her eyes and waited for my reaction.

'Huh?' I wrinkled my nose in confusion. 'He's moving into the seminary? What, is he doing an internship? Doesn't he have a dorm room? How is he even allowed to live there? Can't you only live in the seminary if you're a priest?'

Mary Kate was staring at me. Suddenly the realization hit me.

'WHAT? He's becoming a PRIEST?'

'He said he wanted to tell me first because we "share such a special friendship".' Setting aside the Cup Noodles, she swaddled herself in the blanket and slumped down gloomily on the futon.

'What the hell?' I was raving. 'But he's so young! He's not even old enough to drink! What does he do about the communion wine? Wait – can he get us wine?'

Then I saw how upset my room-mate was, so I wrapped my arms around her. 'Sorry,' I said sympathetically. 'I know you really liked him.'

There was a moment of silence. Then I just had to ask.

'Was he wearing his Jesus sandals to walk around the lake?'

Mary Kate sighed heavily. 'Yeah.' She stood up. 'I guess I should have known.'

*

My loyal troops were gathered in our Feminist Club meeting room, and they were pumped.

Okay, pumped may be an overstatement. Robbie Schmidt was trying surreptitiously to smell-check his pits without anyone seeing. Sophomores Sarah and Sophia, whichever one was which, were watching him and giggling. Claudia was trying out different eyebrow pencils on the back of her hand, and Mary Kate was reviewing her French verb flashcards.

So they weren't pumped exactly. But they were all here, and they were *about* to be pumped because *I* was about to make a big announcement.

Even with the stolen signatures from Save Your Heart, I had come nowhere close to the 500 I needed to petition St Mary's for an official school production of *The Vagina Monologues*. But, undeterred, I had decided to take the project in a new – and interesting – direction.

'Ladies and gentleman!' I barked. Then I realized how heteronormative and gender binary that was. What about 'my loyal followers'? Too Mussolini?

'People!' I boomed finally. 'I have a very exciting announcement to make. It's a little daring, it's a little bold, but I know you joined this club because you are daring and bold . . .'

Robbie Schmidt broke out in a sweat; there was no hope for his armpits now. Sophia and Sarah giggled. And Mary Kate interrupted me as soon as I opened my mouth to speak again.

'Um, Alex? Shouldn't we wait for Sister Georgina?'

I looked down the table. Sister Georgina's usual seat in the back corner was empty. Honestly, it was a bit weird. As spaced out as Sister Georgina was, she had never before failed to show up for her weekly nap in the mildewy dungeon that was our meeting room. But I was too jazzed about my idea to care.

'As I was saying, we are gonna do something bold. Something daring. Something controversial, unprecedented, revolutionary – even incendiary! We are going to – What the hell are YOU doing here?'

The door had opened, interrupting my speech and my momentum, and, when I saw who it was, I had blurted out the first thing that came into my head.

Mary Kate looked up and gasped. 'Alex!' Her face was dead white. Panicked, she stood up immediately and – I swear to God – did a little curtsey. It was awkward, but no one laughed because everyone was frozen in terror.

Father Hughes had just walked into the room.

Sometimes I forget that not everyone at St Mary's has this whole playful, antagonistic, Sherlock–Moriarty thing going on with Father Hughes like I do. For most of them, he's an awe-inspiring figure they only see at a distance, looming over them from his giant pulpit during mass or assembly, making big, thunderous pronouncements from God and the school board. Me, I see him on the regular. The principal's office is my second-best hang-out on campus, after that secret smoking area on the roof of the science building.

'Hello, everyone,' Father Hughes greeted us. 'I have some news to share with you. Sister Georgina will no longer be serving as faculty advisor to the St Mary's Feminist Club.'

'Wait, WHAT?' I spluttered in astonishment. Then I burst out accusingly, 'You killed her, didn't you? You killed her so you could take her spot here and spy on us!'

'Alex!' Mary Kate gasped again. She was sitting down now, but perched tensely on the edge of her seat, trembling.

Father Hughes took it calmly, though. 'No, Ms Heck. Happily for all of us, Sister Georgina is in good spiritual and physical health. She is, however, in her later years and in need of a rest – as perhaps you've noticed? So she has decided to take her retirement down at a Catholic retreat center in Florida.'

'Retirement?' I balked. 'What does a *nun* have to retire from? Don't you retire the day you check yourself into the convent and sign away your lifelong right to lipgloss and –'

This time I cut myself off before I put my foot in it too badly. The only reaction from Father Hughes was to raise a single grey, stern eyebrow.

'We will search for a new faculty advisor who is an appropriate fit for the Feminist Club. In the meantime, in order that your meetings may continue without inter-ruption, I will be serving as a substitute. But please –' he looked around pleasantly and smiled at the sweaty, twitch-ing group – 'do not let me distract you. Just continue as planned. Pretend I'm not here.'

Pretend you're not here? Sure, no sweat. This was just like back when I was in tween therapy during my parents' divorce and the perky therapist with the home-made earrings used to have me make macaroni picture frames while asking me oh-so-casual questions and secretly analyzing my use of the glue stick for signs of psychopathy.

But I had brazenly continued with my satanic crafting back then, and I just as brazenly plowed onward now. Was it going to be difficult to execute a plan to shock and offend Father Hughes when he was in the room where we were planning it? Yes. But was I going to be daunted, surrender, or – worst of all – decide to act appropriately and behave myself in front of a priest? Oh hell, no!

'We,' I declared, 'are going to put on a *non-school-sanctioned* production of *The Vagina Monologues*.'

Silence. Tense, buzzing, uncomfortable silence.

'Um,' Mary Kate ventured. 'Don't you think that might be a bit . . . difficult? Like, for example, the first step, which would be finding a place to put *on* the play. As I understand it –' she kept glancing down the table towards Father Hughes, but not making actual eye contact – 'you can only book a campus venue for an official school event . . . approved by the principal.'

She turned again to Father Hughes, who was writing in a notebook. We all looked at him. He looked up. 'That is correct,' he confirmed calmly.

'Well, okay, yeah, sure. That's *technically* correct,' I continued, undaunted. 'That's the way things have always been done. But *we* are doing something new here. Something unprecedented. And unprecedented actions require unprecedented methods. And you know what?'

No one was looking at me, but I didn't care.

'You know what?' I repeated. 'I think, when we visit those venues, we are going to find some authority figure on this campus who supports us. *Some* authority figure on this campus who is open-minded, and progressive, and feminist, and not a stodgy, backward-looking philistine with a big biblical staff up his –'

'Alex!' Mary Kate interrupted me sharply, her face bright red. She looked around in panic, then, in frantic relief, pointed at the clock. 'Look what time it is!'

'All right,' I growled reluctantly. 'Fine. But just let me say that I will be starting a search for a campus venue for *The Vagina Monologues* tomorrow, and I know we're going to find a great place to make this happen.'

I sat down. There I was, at the head of the table, president of the club, determined to put on *The Vagina Monologues* and get myself expelled. There was Father Hughes, across from me, meeting my eyes, determined to stop me. Two strong wills facing off. Two gunslingers in the Wild West, and this campus wasn't big enough for the both of us.

But, in all honesty, I had thought the mounting tension was pretty much in my head – until it became too much for Robbie Schmidt, who suddenly groaned, leaned over and threw up on his backpack.

10

Monday after classes I set out on a mission: to find a venue for *The Vagina Monologues*. Mary Kate came with me – which surprised me at first, until she explained her latest tactic in the Great Boyfriend Search.

'I call it my Theory of Proximity,' she told me as we strolled through campus with our best cat-eye sunglasses on and our knee socks rolled down. Minnesota was giving us one last blast of summer in late September, and it was giving Mary Kate hope that, even though Caleb had ditched her for a house full of priests, she could still achieve her semester goal. 'If I want to meet a guy, I need to be *around* guys.'

'Is this in any way related to your crazy fantasy where you get stuck in an elevator with your crush and end up making out?' I asked.

'The Elevator Axiom is directly related to the Theory of Proximity, yes,' Mary Kate acknowledged. 'But this is bigger than that. I need to be everywhere. I need to be out and about. I'm gonna see and be seen, baby! Ooh . . .' She lowered her sunglasses. 'Look, those guys are out playing badminton again. Maybe on our way back we should join in and actually learn to play instead of admiring their butts as usual.'

'Mary Kate, FOCUS!' I said. 'The man butts of St Mary's will have to wait. Our first stop is Mendoza, which is the fanciest venue on campus. So we need to walk in there like we own the damn place.'

The Mendoza Banquet Hall is evil Spanish-Inquisition-glamour at its finest: stained-glass windows, long mahogany banquet tables, silver candlesticks Jean Valjean would kill to get his grubby little hands on. It's so fancy that we peasants whose parents pay a mere $50,000 a year for us to attend this school are rarely allowed inside. It's mostly reserved for visiting Republican senators who vote against birth control.

Mary Kate was in awe as she tiptoed along, trying not to scuff the shiny mahogany floors with her penny loafers.

'Wow,' she breathed in wonder, looking up at the vaulted ceiling. 'It's like Hogwarts in here.'

'Yeah, meanwhile, they keep our dorm at just above freezing in the winter and charge us a dollar per tampon in the arts building bathroom. But we can't think about that right now.' I tried to smooth my shirt, which had more wrinkles than a Shar-Pei's ass. 'Remember, we own the place!'

Unfortunately, we did not own the place. We did not even manage the place. The woman who did sat in the back office, wearing a long black habit and silver crucifix, and writing with a shiny silver pen.

'Alex!' hissed Mary Kate, stopping suddenly as we approached the office and grabbing my arm. 'She's a nun!'

'Very good, Mary Kate,' I said. 'What clued you in – the *I'm Married to Jesus* bumper sticker across her forehead?'

'No, I mean, she's a *nun*. You can't say the . . . the *V-word* . . . to a nun!'

'I already said *vagina* in front of Sister Georgina! You were there!'

'Sister Georgina is deaf – this one could hear you!'

'She HAS a vagina!' I said. 'You've got a vagina, I've got a vagina, and guess what that nun has under her habit? Well, probably some really ugly but comfortable granny panties, but also a vagina! So I'm not gonna walk around pretending we're all Barbie plastic below the waist.'

And, with that, I strode into the fancy office and declared proudly: 'I would like to book the Mendoza Banquet Hall for a performance of *The Vagina Monologues* by the St Mary's Feminist Club.'

Sister Marietta – her name was engraved on a gold plaque on her desk – blinked a few times in surprise at a purple-fauxhawked badass bursting into her office.

'Pardon me, what was that?' she asked.

'We are putting on *The Vagina Monologues*,' I stated even louder, my voice echoing to the vaulted ceilings. I could feel Mary Kate cringing into herself beside me.

'I see . . .' Sister Marietta narrowed her eyes, looking from me to Mary Kate. 'And this is an official school event? Approved by Father Hughes?'

'Well . . . *technically* . . . no.'

She shook her head. 'The venue can only be booked for official school events. Unless . . .'

Her tone changed and she opened a green leather ledger on her desk. I saw that it had a bunch of long columns of numbers in it – like a medieval version of an Excel spreadsheet.

'We are willing to make certain exceptions in the case of a good cause,' she explained. 'For high-volume fundraisers in particular.'

'Whoa, whoa,' I said. 'Hold up. So we're not technically allowed to use the banquet hall, but we could *bribe* you to use it?'

Sister Marietta frowned. 'We do not accept bribes. However, we do welcome certain events that will donate a portion of their proceeds. The money is given to charity.'

'Oh yeah.' I rolled my eyes. 'It looks like a real soup kitchen in here. I'm surprised Mother Teresa's ghost isn't in the corner taking selfies with Michelle Obama.'

'Thank you anyway!' Mary Kate interrupted brightly. 'I think we're gonna look for someplace that's . . . a better fit.'

'All right then.' Sister Marietta smiled and closed her green leather ledger. 'I'm sorry the space didn't work out for you.' She opened a drawer. 'Would you girls like some rosary beads? They were blessed by His Holiness the pope.'

'How much do they cost?' I sneered.

'We'll take two!' Mary Kate said hastily, and grabbed two strands of rosary beads and draped them around her neck. 'Thank you very much.'

On our way out, I stomped my motorcycle boots to scuff the polished floor all the way to the door, my steps echoing to the three-story ceiling.

'I can't believe it!' I fumed. 'The greedy-ass Catholic Church! Centuries of tricking dim-witted peasants into handing over their cash, and they're still at it! Did Anne Boleyn's cleavage do all that work for nothing?'

'Maybe Sister Marietta would have made an exception,' Mary Kate suggested, 'if you hadn't said THE WORD.'

'Mary Kate.' I gritted my teeth. 'You may have grown up in the Midwest, where your school library censored the Harry Potter books because of satanic overtones, but I grew up in San Francisco. My babysitter was the drag queen from the local dildo shop. I am not scared to say *vagina* to a nun. I will NEVER be scared to say *vagina* to a nun.'

I marched to our next destination: the library with the Latin inscription over the double doors. No way was I backing down! I was gonna stride right in there and declare my plans for *The Vagina Monologues* loud and proud. It didn't matter if the Virgin Mary herself was in charge!

That was until I met Sister Rose.

The community room of the library – a place I'd never been before, since I do most of my studying by Googling stuff on our futon in front of trashy reality TV – was bright and sunny, with a big quilt spelling out LOVE on the wall. Perched at the desk like an adorable cuddly gargoyle, four foot nine if she was an inch, was Sister Rose.

When she saw us, a smile lit her kindly, wrinkled face, her blue eyes twinkled and she held up a bowl of butterscotch candies.

'Hello, dears! Welcome! Would you like a candy?'

Mary Kate took one. I was too distressed. Because all of a sudden I couldn't speak. What was wrong with me? I'd lost my nerve. Yes, I had sworn that I was a badass bitch who'd drop an F-bomb in front of the whole singing convent from *The Sound of Music*, but . . . but this nun! This little fun-sized nun! She was so cute! She even SMELLED cute, like chocolate-chip cookies and soap. She was like my grandma, without the passive-aggressive comments about my cartilage piercing!

Finally, I cleared my throat and managed to speak.

'Hi!' I began. 'So we . . . we want . . . we were wondering . . .'

Seeing me falter, Mary Kate smiled. She popped the butterscotch candy in her mouth and crossed her arms, ready to watch me squirm.

'Yes, sweetheart?' Sister Rose tilted her head to the side. Even more adorable – like a puppy with one floppy ear.

'We're going . . . we were hoping . . . to put on a little show!'

My ears burned. I refused to look at Mary Kate.

'Oh, how wonderful!' Sister Rose cooed. 'What is your show about?'

'I . . .' I balked. I faltered. I stalled. Finally, I turned to Mary Kate in desperation.

She looked up at the quilt on the wall. 'Love!' she said. 'Wouldn't you agree, Alex?'

I nodded.

Don't hate me. This Sister Rose is kryptonite to badasses, I'm telling you. A hepatitis-ridden gang leader could swagger into that community room and in five minutes flat she'd have him sitting on the carpet singing 'Itsy Bitsy Spider'.

'How perfect!' Sister Rose beamed. 'Everything we're doing at the library this semester has a theme: *Jesus Loves the Little Children*. Do you think your show would fit in with that?'

I considered. 'Um . . . I think there's a pretty gnarly birth scene . . .'

'I don't think so.' My room-mate cut me off briskly. 'Thank you anyway! Maybe next semester.'

This time, I accepted the rosary myself. But, as we stepped out of the library into the bright sunshine of the quad, I handed it to Mary Kate, who added it to the growing collection around her neck. She was starting to look like the most chaste chick at Mardi Gras.

'Friggin' nuns!' I growled. 'How come there are so many on this campus? They're everywhere! It's an infestation!'

'I kinda like it,' Mary Kate said. 'It reminds me of *Madeline*.'

'*Madeline*,' I scoffed. 'I hated that book! All those girls in that perfectly straight line. Friggin' fascist propaganda!'

'Yeah, but how cute were their little hats?'

'THAT,' I warned her darkly, 'is what they said about the Blackshirts.'

As far as Mary Kate was concerned, our search was done. *The Vagina Monologues* was canceled. Now it was time to go back to the badminton boys . . . right?

Wrong.

'There's one more place,' I said. 'One more venue on campus.'

'What?' Mary Kate frowned. 'Where?'

I turned sharply right and she stopped short.

'Nope.' She crossed her arms over her rosary beads, planted her little loafers on the pavement and refused to take one more step. 'No way.'

'Come on!' I said. 'Look at it! It's beautiful!'

McLaughlin Hall is one of the oldest buildings on campus, with a turret, Gothic stained-glass windows and a wrap-around porch. It had been transformed into a theater almost a hundred years ago.

'Wouldn't this be a killer venue?' I continued. 'This place was a boys' dorm back in the day. Think about it: all those years of repressed male virgins huddled together, weeping under cold showers in this building . . . It's a total symbol of the patriarchy. Then we come along and turn it on its head by performing a ground-breaking show about the female anatomy on its stage! It's such a badass rebel move!'

But there was one very important fact about McLaughlin Hall that I was forgetting. And, when I say fact, I mean the kind of 'fact' you would find on Wikipedia after a bunch of middle-school boys insert dick jokes into the *Frankenstein* entry.

'Alex,' Mary Kate said seriously. 'It's *haunted.*'

She pointed to the bronze plaque by the stained-glass entry doors. It had a carving of a man's head on it, like all the bullshit sexist coins in this country except the Susan B. Anthony and Sacajawea ones no one ever uses. Below the head was inscribed:

ICHABOD 'THE ICEMAN' WILLIAMS: 1895–1912

The Iceman is our campus ghost. Yes, I know how dumb that sounds. He was also a real-life St Mary's legend. Ichabod Williams was the star player on the 1912 St Mary's ice hockey team. A week before the big national championship game, he stayed out late and missed curfew. In those days, if you missed curfew, the priests locked you out. So Ichabod was forced to sleep on the steps of his dorm – McLaughlin Hall – on an icy February night and he caught pneumonia. On his deathbed, he gathered his hockey team-mates around him and gave them this big emotional speech about how he would always be with them and they needed to win that championship. 'Win it for me,' he croaked meaningfully. 'Win it for the Iceman.'

They won the championship, and the Iceman died. Now he haunts this hall. Supposedly.

'That whole story is complete bullshit,' I told Mary Kate.

'No, it isn't! It's true! My guide told me when I took the campus tour here!'

'The school perpetuates the myth on purpose. They want to scare you so you don't miss curfew. Like, *Oooh, get home on time or you'll die of pneumonia! Don't stay out late or the Iceman will get you!*'

Mary Kate shook her head stubbornly. 'He's real! So many people have seen him! Clare Crowley had to stop practicing Irish dance in the basement because the Iceman was always banging around down there!'

'Mary Kate, you're taking five advanced classes,' I reminded her. 'You're way too smart to believe in a ghost! You need to stop buying into all this St Mary's bullshit. The lake walks and the purity rings and the paranormal activity. You're better than that.'

'I don't know.' She looked up at McLaughlin Hall anxiously. 'I started reading English Gothic novels at a very impressionable age. I think I have Brontëan Stockholm syndrome.'

'You're seriously refusing to go in that building with me? What happened to your Proximity Theory? Go everywhere? See and be seen? What if your future boyfriend is waiting inside?'

'I don't want a *ghost* boyfriend!' she told me, in a *duh* tone of voice, like I was the ridiculous one. 'Although –' she looked back at the bronze plaque – 'the Iceman was actually pretty cute.'

Nope. Too much. I was not going to stand here arguing with a girl wearing multiple rosaries about the sex appeal of her ghost boyfriend.

'Okay, that's it. See you later, Mary Kate,' I said, and climbed the steps.

The inside of McLaughlin Hall was beautiful, too. It had been converted from a dorm to a theater in the 1920s, right in that amazing art deco, *Great Gatsby*, more-is-more time period I love. A big gold chandelier, plush green velvet seats, elaborate curlicues on the balcony overhead – when I first walked in, all I could do was look around in awe.

Then I began to notice how dark and empty it was. The red velvet curtains were open and the stage was pitch-black.

'Hello?' I called out.

My voice echoed. No answer. Not even a nun in the place.

When you go to boarding school, you're never alone. There's always a million people around, even when you don't want them there – like when you're washing your Wonder Woman G-string in the laundry-room sink. Everywhere you turn, there's another dope in a green-plaid uniform. So, when there's *no one* around, it gets a little creepy.

I found myself tiptoeing down the soft-carpet aisle to the stage, looking cautiously from side to side. Suddenly I stopped. I'd heard something. I froze and listened hard. *Sssssss.* A soft hissing sound. I spun around; it sounded like it was coming from behind me. I waited a beat, then decided it was probably the radiator. The old-ass St Mary's radiators are always hissing and banging. No big deal. I kept walking down the aisle, focusing on trying to remember which Shakespearean cross-dressing play we'd watched on this stage last year.

Then I heard it again. Louder this time. *SSSSS*. A hiss – no, wait. Not a hiss. The sound came again, echoing to the three-story ceiling of the empty theater, and that's when I realized: it was a word.

'*Iceee . . .*'

No way. Not possible. Don't be a dumbass. That is NOT a ghost. It's just your overactive, horror-movie-stimulated, slightly tobacco-addicted subconscious being a little bitch and playing tricks on you. Thinking quickly, I tried to remind myself what my freshman psych teacher told us about your mind creating imaginary scenarios when you're scared, but all I could remember was that Greek dude who clawed his eyeballs out after he accidentally hooked up with his mom, and that was NOT comforting.

'*Ice . . .*'

Okay, that is DEFINITELY a word! I was sure of it. And it had come from the balcony above me because clearly the Iceman, who always kept his skates on the ground when he was alive, could fly now. Because he was a ghost. He was a ghost, and he was after me. I sprinted down the aisle, my heart racing, goosebumps prickling under my plaid skort. Shit – wait – what was I doing, running towards the stage? Once I got there, I'd be trapped! Was there some kind of trapdoor in the stage I could use? *No, don't go through the trapdoor! The trapdoor leads to the Iceman's underground lair! Wait, does the Iceman have an underground lair? Is the Iceman like the Phantom of the Opera? Is he gonna force me to sing really high-pitched duets with him? No way am I getting out of this alive!*

Then the hiss, which had become a whisper, which had become a word, became a sentence: '*The Ice . . . man . . . COMETH!*'

I screamed. I screamed at the top of my lungs, and my scream echoed through all three stories of the theater. I was sure it would shatter the light bulbs in the gold chandeliers. Then, over the echo of my scream, there was another sound: laughter. Boyish, smug, self-satisfied laughter.

Up in the balcony, a lanky kid with shaggy brown hair was grinning at me. As I watched, he hopped the balcony railing, hung from the lower bar for a minute with his khakis sliding down his ass until I could see most of his green-plaid boxer shorts, then dropped a good ten feet to the carpeted aisle below. That's when I recognized him: it was my little text buddy, Hockey Player Pat.

He landed perfectly and stood up with lazy grace. He was wearing his uniform, but his shirt tails were untucked, his tie loose, his collar open at the throat. I was surprised he was wearing his uniform at all. Most athletes wear their grey varsity sweatsuits all the time just because they're allowed to, strutting around campus, all smug with jock privilege and looking down on us green-plaid peasants. But Hockey Player Pat was plenty smug in green plaid. There was an irritating smirk on his face and annoying crinkles around his eyes when he laughed.

He was laughing at me.

'You believe in the Iceman!' he hooted.

I bristled. 'I do not! The Iceman is typical St Mary's fear-mongering, Catholic, superstitious bullshit, and I would NEVER believe in him! It! Whatever!'

'You *screamed*. You seriously screamed! That was the best thing EVER!' Pat was laughing so hard he was actually holding his stomach.

My heart was still racing, but I wasn't going to let him know that.

'Yeah, I screamed,' I said. 'I screamed because I didn't think there was anyone in here, then some creep in the balcony started hissing at me! That's why I screamed! It was adrenaline – that was survival instinct! And what the hell are you doing here anyway?'

'You know,' he said, looking at me from under his shaggy brown hair, 'you're cute when you're mad.'

'Excuse me?' I spluttered. 'Are you kidding me? *You're cute when you're mad?* Do you realize how ridiculously sexist that comment is?'

'No, it's not,' Pat said. 'I would say that to a guy. I say that to guys all the time. You know our center, Lundqvist? Six foot three, three hundred pounds, ginger stubble? He's adorable when he's mad. Of course, when I tell him that, he kicks me in the nuts, but I'm usually wearing a cup at the time, so it's all good.'

I rolled my eyes. 'What is it with guys and their nuts? You're all so friggin' obsessed with your testicles. You think a "kick in the nuts" is, like, this exquisite, unearthly pain that no little female birdbrain could possibly understand. Try getting a pre-menstrual purple nurple from Sabrina Becker in the eighth-grade locker room.'

'Sabrina Becker.' Hockey Player Pat shook his shaggy brown head sympathetically. 'She sounds like a real asshole.'

He hopped up onto one of the theater seats and perched on the back of it, setting his boat shoes on the armrests. He looked perfectly at home in this empty, creepy place. I frowned.

'What *are* you doing here?' I demanded suspiciously, suddenly remembering our conversation at the dance about *Beauty and the Bestiality*. 'Don't tell me you're a jock who does theater. That's way too *High School Musical*.'

'I don't actually *do* theater,' he clarified. 'I'm one of the student stage managers. You need a fog machine or a follow spot, I'm your man. And, if you're trying to put on … for example … *The Vagina Monologues* at the McLaughlin, I could probably help you with that, too.'

Unlike most people on this campus, Pat didn't stutter, cough or falter over the word *vagina*. And, without his obnoxious jock crew around, he didn't shout it as a punchline, either.

But I still didn't want his help.

'We have multiple venues we're considering right now,' I informed him haughtily.

'Yeah, right.' Hockey Player Pat grinned, and his eyes crinkled up again. 'You're such a liar. I bet every single place you walked into, the nun running the joint heard the word *vagina*, tossed you some rosary beads for your burning pagan soul and shut the door in your face. I bet the McLaughlin is your last chance.'

'As a matter of fact,' I said loftily, 'it is not.'

Okay, it was. Unless you counted the demonic black-hole abyss under Sister Hellda's habit as a performance space.

'No problem then.' Pat jumped down from the chair, put his hands in his pockets and strolled up the center aisle, whistling. 'If you don't want my help, no sweat. I'll be sure to check out the show wherever you have it!'

His relaxed attitude was driving me nuts.

'It's not like you could help us anyway! Apparently, you can't even moonwalk down your dorm hallway on this campus without official approval from Father Hughes, and I don't think I'm gonna get away with forging his signature again. Although I am a boss at it.'

Still sauntering away from me, without turning around, he said, 'What about the second weekend in November?'

'For what?'

'For *The Vagina Monologues*.'

The second weekend in November was perfect.

'What are you talking about?' I demanded. 'Are you saying you can get approval from Father Hughes? Friggin' hockey players!'

'I can't get Father Hughes to approve *The Vagina Monologues*,' he admitted. 'But! There is an event that already *is* approved, which will be taking place in this very theater the second weekend in November. And it's looking for more shows to add to the line-up. And I think *The Vagina Monologues* would be just perfect.'

I rolled my eyes. 'Yeah, right. You're so full of shit.'

Hockey Player Pat shook his head solemnly. 'I swear,' he said. 'On the soul of the Iceman.'

Two days later, I was in the language lab, tits-deep in a riveting dialogue between Maria and José about the climate of Mérida, when I was suddenly interrupted by a perky 'Hey, Alex!'

My nemesis, Katie Casey, was kneeling next to my computer, her apple-pie happy face smiling up at me. I took my headphones off.

'Pat told me to come see you!' she said.

'Pat?' I frowned.

'Pat, the student stage manager at McLaughlin? Where we're putting on the Save Your Heart Festival in November?'

'Oh, Hockey Player Pat! You know Hockey Player Pat?'

Wait, the Save Your Heart *what*?

'Wait, the Save Your Heart *what*?' I said out loud.

'The Save Your Heart Festival? In November? That we're putting on in McLaughlin?'

Wow, this chick was really a champ at that Gen-Z speech pattern where your voice goes up questioningly at the end of your sentences.

'We're planning a bunch of different activities, but we still need more events, and a show focused on women would be SO great – I thought so when you mentioned it at the Club Fair! Remember? So, when Pat told me you guys were having trouble finding a venue, it sounded like fate!'

Now I remembered Katie mentioning this whole festival thing. Some kind of chastity testimonial where everyone got onstage and vowed never to look down in the shower. Obviously, Hockey Player Pat was trying to mess with me.

'Look, thanks for coming to talk to me,' I told her. 'I'm sorry you wasted your time, but I think Pat orchestrated this whole thing as a joke. And, to be clear, we will *not* be working with you guys on *The Vagina Monologues.*'

Undaunted, Katie Casey smiled. 'No worries,' she said brightly. 'If you change your mind, just come knock on my door – St Anne Hall three-oh-five!'

'*¡Señorita Heck!*' snapped Sister Lucia, glaring at the headphones around my neck. '*¿Está escuchando?*'

Katie Casey popped up. '*Lo siento, Sor Lucia – tuve que preguntar algo a Señorita Heck. Ya me voy.*'

Sister Lucia's perpetual frown literally turned upside down. '*¡Sin problema, Señorita Casey!* I hope to have the pleasure of seeing you in another one of my classes soon!'

I glared at Katie Casey as she bounced out of the library, her swinging ponytail wafting the scent of strawberry shampoo in her diabolic wake. I hated her more than ever. She had power, she had the love and approval of the St Mary's administration and faculty – and she had the McLaughlin Theater.

Which meant I had to come up with a new plan.

October

11

'HELLO, FEMINISTS!' I boomed across Academic Quad.

The bold fall colors of the campus in October matched my bold spirit and my color scheme for the day. Planting my motorcycle boots right in front of the Virgin Mary statue, I flung my arms open wide, showing off my red T-shirt, which read **VAGINA** in big black paint letters across my boobs. 'Are we ready for this?'

Undaunted by the fact that no venues on campus would let us put on the *Monologues*, I had decided to move on and pursue it in a different way. Who needed those crusty old venues anyway? They were all haunted by that church smell of incense and anal-retentiveness. Not to mention the ghost.

No, instead I had come up with a new approach. We were going to bring *The Vagina Monologues* direct to the people – raw, shocking and unfiltered.

We were doing a *Vagina Monologues* flash mob.

And, to my surprise, all the members of the Feminist Club had actually showed up. All six of us.

'I've been leading everyone in vocal warm-ups,' Claudia informed me. I had told everyone to dress in red, and she was in it from head to toe – a red beret, red lipstick and pointy red flats. 'Everyone repeat after me: "red leather, yellow leather, red leather, yellow leather . . ."'

'We made our shirts like you did,' Sarah or Sophia told me. 'See?'

S1 on the left was wearing a red sweatshirt that said THIS IS WHAT A FEMINIST LOOKS LIKE, with an arrow pointing to the left. S2 on the right was wearing a nearly identical red sweatshirt that said THIS IS WHAT A FEMINIST LOOKS LIKE, with an arrow pointing to the right.

'Switch places,' I told them.

They switched places. Then one of them turned to Mary Kate, who was standing a couple of yards away, fiddling with my phone. 'Hey! She's not wearing red.'

Actually, Mary Kate *was* wearing red – I had made her an identical version of my T-shirt, with **VAGINA** in big black letters. But she had her green St Mary's fleece zipped to her chin to cover it up.

'C'mon, Mary Kate,' I had tried to coax her on the way over. 'We are about to do something amazing. Something shocking and revolutionary. Everyone else is excited about it! Claudia's excited about it!'

'Of course *Claudia's* excited about it,' she had said. 'This is exactly the kind of thing Claudia likes.'

I frowned. 'What do you mean by that?'

'Oh, you know ... standing in the middle of the quad, shouting and waving your arms desperately like a chronically spoiled only child who always has to be the center of attention.' Mary Kate smiled sweetly at me. 'No offense.'

In the end, Mary Kate had threatened to ditch the flash mob for a chance at romance and Nutella with the French Club's Crêpes and Conversation afternoon, and we had come to a compromise.

'Mary Kate's gonna film us,' I explained. 'We're gonna upload it afterward for the whole world to see!'

'You are?' Claudia whirled around. She hurried over to Mary Kate. 'Upload on what? Instagram? YouTube? Wait, can you link my channel on there?'

After I had unzipped my backpack, distributed copies of the play to everyone and rearranged Sarah and Sophia, who had switched places again, it was my turn to boss Mary Kate around.

'Can you see all of us?' I called to her. 'Make sure you can see all of us. Wait – what should we call the video? *Pop-up* Vagina Monologues *Shocks Catholic School*? *Rad Feminist Flash Mob Rocks Conservative Campus*?'

Mary Kate was holding my phone uneasily at a distance from her body, like it might secretly be a Transformer that would spontaneously erupt into a tractor-trailer with python teeth. She looked around the quad anxiously. 'Let's just get this over with,' she urged me. 'We'll figure out the name after.'

'Right,' I agreed. 'I'm sure we'll have an OMG moment that will make it go viral. We'll name the video after that.'

Clearing my throat, I cracked the spine on my second-hand *Monologues* and found one of my favorite passages. I told everyone the page and they turned to it, too. Maybe Mary Kate was right about my only-child Napoleon complex or whatever she'd said, but I had a feeling this was going to be great.

'THE CLITORIS!' I boomed.

Then I heard it.

It started with the low *bum-bum-bum*, which at first I thought was my own heart racing with adrenaline and excitement. But no, it grew louder, shaking the quad like an earthquake – a bass drum. Then the *rat-a-tat-tat* of the snare drum, and a big crash of cymbals set off a sweeping explosion of music – horns blaring, flutes and piccolos twittering . . .

Then I saw it.

The sun glinted off big brass tubas and enormous white drums – a whole green army in green hats with gold tassels, marching in unison, a hundred pairs of shining shoes pounding the grass of the quad: the St Mary's Marching Band.

'They're heading straight towards us!' Sarah or Sophia exclaimed.

'I'm turning the camera off!' Mary Kate called out to me.

'No!' I protested, waving my arms. 'Keep filming!'

'I CAN'T EVEN HEAR YOU!' she shouted back.

'The Stars and Stripes Forever' was blaring at us, full volume, only fifty feet away now. But gamely I turned to face the approaching onslaught full-on, and gestured for the others to do the same.

'I BET YOU'RE WORRIED!' I screamed. Turning around, I glared at S&S, who were huddled together, staring at the marching band, mesmerized. Robbie Schmidt was hiding behind them, his fingers jammed in his ears. He had dropped his copy of the *Monologues* in the grass. Only Claudia, thrusting forward her red chest proudly, joined in:

'WE WERE WORRIED. WE WERE WORRIED ABOUT VAGINAS . . .'

The band was enormous – it seemed to be multiplying, like some kind of clone army instantaneously duplicating row upon row of green soldiers in tasseled hats and shiny shoes. A dozen flutes, a whole row of thundering bass drums, a brass phalanx of tubas and trombones. Thirty feet away, twenty feet away . . .

'They're not stopping!' S1 called out in alarm. Robbie Schmidt bolted, a streak of red across the quad, and Sarah and Sophia scurried after him. Claudia broke away from me and started twirling and pirouetting in front of the marching band, making wide sweeping gestures with her arms, still holding the *Monologues*. Her interpretive dance version of the play probably. Or just an excuse to show off her belly-button piercing.

But me? I was still standing. I would not be silenced.

'WE WERE WORRIED WHAT WE THINK ABOUT VAGINAS!' I declared. 'AND EVEN MORE WORRIED THAT WE DON'T THINK ABOUT THEM!'

Fifteen feet away . . . louder, bigger, brighter, the deaf-ening blast was right in my face now.

'MOVE, ALEX!' Mary Kate shouted hoarsely to me. She had scurried to safety on the side of the quad with the others, but she was still filming as she pleaded with me.

'You're gonna get crushed in the stampede, Alex! HAVEN'T YOU SEEN *THE LION KING*? THIS IS HOW MUFASA DIED!'

I ignored her. *Hold your ground, Heck*, I told myself, planting my feet in determination, tightening every muscle in my body. *You are a badass bitch with righteous principles, like that suffragette who threw herself in front of the king's horse. HOLD YOUR GROUND!*

The band brought 'The Stars and Stripes Forever' to a crashing, thunderous finale – I could still hear Mary Kate, sounding very far away, calling out to me – but the band was not slowing down – they transitioned into the infamous St Mary's fight song – those dreaded first notes rang out – *dum-DUM-dah-dah* – I was standing my ground, stand-ing my ground – I closed my eyes and thrust my book in the air and shouted one last hoarse cry right into the bell of a giant tuba, '*THE VAGINA MONOLOGUES* FOREVER!' – but the marching band and the music swallowed me and my battle-cry whole.

Everything went dark for what felt like several minutes. When I woke up, I was sprawled on the ground. Blinking in the sunlight overhead, I saw Mary Kate's face. I pulled myself up and groped in the damp grass to find my battered copy of *The Vagina Monologues*, which had been flung several feet away. The sound of the fight song was fading away, and, turning my sore neck with a sharp pain, I saw the marching band in the distance, streaming on towards the hockey arena. Robbie, Sarah and Sophia were still huddled together in the bushes, and Claudia was leaping and twirling on the trampled quad.

'Are you okay?' Mary Kate asked me, brushing off my red **VAGINA** shirt.

'What happened?' I asked. 'Did I get run over? Did that tuba take me out? Man, those dicks! I hate the marching band! They ran right over me and kept marching! Fascism in action! Now I can sue the school, and that will *really* piss off Father Hughes!'

Mary Kate looked at me for a long moment.

'What?' I asked her.

Wordlessly, she turned my phone around and showed me the end of the video. There I was alone – damn, my hair looked good! – standing strong in my red shirt, facing down the marching band. There was the army of green clones, ten feet away from me, five feet away, and then –

The tiny me in the video shrieked in terror, flung the book aside and dived head first into the grass on the side of the quad.

The marching band, unobstructed and unbothered, marched on.

'I took a dive?' I blinked in disbelief at the phone screen, and my shoulders slumped.

Mary Kate took the phone back and started typing. 'What are we thinking for the name of the video? *Cowardly Feminist Flees Marching Band*? *Marching Band Quashes* Monologues?'

I groaned. 'There goes my OMG moment. I couldn't help it, though! My body betrayed me!'

Mary Kate's face lit up. 'I've got it! *Feminist Fail*!'

It was after midnight on a Tuesday when a soft but urgent knocking on our door woke me up. I'd only fallen asleep an hour before, after a long night of writing a physics lab report while simultaneously playing *Mega Dead Pixel* on my phone, and I groaned as I dragged myself out of bed. Swiping my phone to flashlight mode, I saw that Mary Kate was asleep, neatly tucked in with Sir Shackleton, her face smeared with a blue face mask.

'I know you like to think you're all delicate and sensitive and all that shit,' I grumbled at her. 'But, if we were in *The Princess and the Pea* right now, those royal assholes could shove the Pyramids of Giza under your waterbed and you'd still be snoring away.'

Opening the door, I saw a blonde chick who lives on the third floor of our dorm. She also happened to be one of Katie Casey's Save Your Heart girls. For obvious reasons, she and I weren't friends. But this wasn't the first time a girl in this dorm had shown up at my door in the middle of the night with a crisis. Homesick chicks, chicks who were drunk for the first time, once a girl who thought she'd lost a baggie of Ritalin between her butt cheeks.

Like Preeti, everyone in St Theresa Hall knows I'm the one to go to for the stuff you can't say to a nun or your room-mate.

Which is why, as soon as I opened the door, this girl blurted out: 'I just had sex.'

'Congratulations,' I grumbled, yawning.

What was this girl's name again? Maggie? Meggy? Whoever She Was was still in her uniform, but her pea coat was open, her blouse was unbuttoned, and she was turning her pink rubber Save Your Heart bracelet around and around on her wrist.

'I think I did it wrong,' she whispered.

'I had Kama Sutra Ken and Barbie. Trust me, any way you did it is fine.'

'But what if I get pregnant?'

'Wait.' I blinked and rubbed the crust out of my eyes, trying to register what she was saying. 'Did you not use a condom?'

'No.' Maggie-Meggy's anxious mouth was smeared with lipgloss. 'We didn't have one.'

Oh Jesus, I thought.

This whole midnight emergency thing was getting old. Staff at St Mary's are paid full-time to supposedly look after our physical and emotional well-being – meanwhile, here I am, the black-sheep fairy godmother of the dorm, saving girls from all kinds of real shit and all I got was a cake once from a hungover freshman with SORRY ABOUT THE VOM spelled out in M&M's.

'So you had unprotected sex,' I said.

'No, not exactly.' The girl hesitated. 'We did use . . . *something*.'

'What? Pill? Diaphragm? Sponge?'

'A balloon.'

'A BALLOON?'

'One of those long, skinny balloons you make balloon animals with,' she continued in her hushed, anxious whisper. 'He's a volunteer clown at the children's hospital.'

I couldn't help myself; I had to ask. 'Did it FIT?'

'Well, he did keep saying it was tight,' she admitted. 'But I thought he was talking about my . . . you know . . .'

'Vagina? You can say it. You had a balloon animal knocking on your cervix tonight, so you can say the word *vagina*.'

The girl was gnawing anxiously on the silver cross around her neck.

'Okay, okay,' I said, trying to pull myself together. This was important. 'We need to take action. Balloons are not condoms. You need Plan B. You need an STD test . . .'

She looked horrified. 'He doesn't have STDs! He's a volunteer clown at the children's hospital!'

'Oh right, I forgot,' I said. 'That's why clowns wear those big shoes, SO THEY CAN RUN AWAY FROM AIDS!'

A door down the hall opened and I realized how loud I'd just been. Luckily, it wasn't Sister Hellda – just a girl shuffling towards the bathroom in her robe and bunny slippers. But I pulled Maggie-Meggy into our room just in case, and spoke in a whisper.

'Listen, you're in the third-floor wing, right? I'll come get you right after classes tomorrow. We're going to Planned Parenthood.'

'There's a Planned Parenthood here?'

'Well, near here,' I said. 'Or not that near actually . . . After we scale the fence and sneak off campus, we'll have to walk a mile to the interstate, and possibly sell our bodies to some truckers to get the rest of the way. But we're going for STD testing anyway, so it'll be fine.'

Maggie-Meggy was too panicked to even notice I was joking. She just nodded obediently, and when I opened the door she scurried off – a little uncomfortably, which wasn't too surprising, given she was probably dealing with post-balloon vaginitis.

St Anne Hall 305.

That morning, Maggie (it was Maggie) and I had made a successful trip to Planned Parenthood. Well, we would still have to wait forty-eight hours for the blood tests to see how successful the trip had actually been, but Maggie was at least a lot calmer. Of course she had frozen up and turned bright red the minute it came to explaining to the nurse that she'd rounded the bases with a helium penis the night before, which meant I had to pretend she was a Bulgarian exchange student and I was her translator, but all's well that ends with free birth control. Now she was back at our dorm, relaxing in her room, easing her discomfort with cranberry juice and a romcom marathon.

And I was here, in front of a door: St Anne Hall 305.

Even Katie Casey's door was annoyingly perky. A cartoon penguin decorated her nameplate and friendly messages were scrawled all over the whiteboard in pink marker: *Movie night downstairs at 8* and *Don't forget milkshake mass!* and *I ♥ you! – Sarah.*

I did not want to be here. But my mindset had changed since Katie Casey and I had spoken last. Until yesterday, I'd thought I needed to put on *The Vagina Monologues* to get kicked out of St Mary's. But now I realized I needed to put on *The Vagina Monologues* BEFORE I got kicked out of St Mary's. After all, once I was gone, who were girls like Maggie going to turn to? I needed to act now and start spreading some knowledge. Mary Kate may call me a selfish only child, but when you realize there's young people around you having unprotected sex with amateur clowns, it's a wake-up call, lemme tell ya.

The cartoon penguin was staring me down. I really wanted to just turn and go. But I reminded myself: *Alex, this afternoon you trekked nineteen miles to a Planned Parenthood with a girl who thinks 'Spermicide' is Spider-Man's evil twin brother. This whole thing is bigger than just you.*

I sucked it up. I took a deep breath and I knocked.

When the door opened, Katie Casey's freckled face lit up with a huge smile.

'Alex!' she trilled. 'What a nice surprise! Here, come in!'

'No,' I said quickly. If I didn't ask her immediately, I'd lose my nerve. Plus, I was pretty sure that cartoon penguin was covering the entrance to a hellmouth.

'I don't have a lot of time, but I wanted to ask you something important.' I took a deep breath and spat the whole thing out quickly. 'I wanted to ask if you were still okay with doing *The Vagina Monologues* as part of the Save Your Heart thing. Because, if you are . . . I want to do it.'

Katie Casey's smile deepened, dimples showing in her freckled cheeks.

'Of course!' she chirped. 'I'd love it! We'll actually be talking about the festival at our meeting tomorrow, in the health classroom at four. Can you come?'

I nodded, setting my jaw in determination. 'I'll be there.'

'Great!'

I turned to go, but, just before Katie closed her cheerful door, I called out – 'Hey, Katie?'

'Yes?'

I swallowed the stubborn lump in my throat. 'Thanks.'

The next afternoon, as I turned the corner in the science building, I saw Pat strolling down the hallway with his duffel bag slung over his shoulder.

'I heard the good news!' he greeted me. 'Save Your Heart presents *The Vagina Monologues*.'

That smug smirk curled up the side of his mouth, and I could tell from the twinkle in his eyes under his shaggy bangs that he had most definitely played matchmaker between me and Katie Casey to fuck with me. And honestly I was kinda impressed. Not that I would ever tell him that.

'You surprise me, San Francisco,' he continued. 'I gotta say, you're a bigger person than I thought.'

'I *am* a big person,' I snapped. 'I am a HUGE person. I will have you know, I saved a girl's life this week.'

'Oh yeah? What happened to her?'

'She had sex with a balloon.'

Pat burst out laughing.

'Shut up!' I told him. 'That's serious! She could have gotten, like, exploding helium uterus!'

'Well, in that case, I'm glad you were there. And, if my bringing you and Katie Casey together can prevent one single future case of exploding helium uterus, I'm honored to be part of such a noble cause.'

He brought his hand solemnly to his chest. I rolled my eyes. 'What are you doing here anyway?' I asked. 'Did Father Hughes make all the hockey players join Save Your Heart to head off a green-plaid crabs epidemic?'

'I was talking to Katie,' Pat said. 'I've got practice, so I can't come to the meeting today, but I'm gonna be helping with stage-manager stuff for the festival. So you and I will be seeing a lot of each other, San Francisco.'

Ugh! He already had a nickname for me. Annoying. And annoying, that little twinge I felt behind my belly button when he smiled at me . . .

Before he sauntered away, he leaned in and whispered in my ear, 'By the way, you're just in time for prayer circle.'

An explosion of pink assaulted me as soon as I stepped into the room. A pink SAVE YOUR HEART banner, the ever-present pink balloons (does Katie Casey fart helium or something?) and a platter of pink cookies on the desk. The health classroom was where we had our super-progressive and illuminating abstinence-only sex education unit freshman year, so the bookshelves were filled with *The Abstinence Workbook* and *My Body, My Bible*, and there was a big poster of two ugly 1980s teenagers in acid-washed mom jeans that said: WE'RE WAITING . . . IS THAT COOL WITH YOU?

And . . .

'*Friggin' hell*,' I whispered under my breath.

There was an actual prayer circle going on. Katie Casey and her little lemmings were sitting cross-legged on the floor in a circle, holding hands, along with their faculty advisor, Ms Hyde, the nervous young teacher who had taught us sex ed with those clueless Catholic workbooks.

'Alex!' Katie called. 'Come join us!'

And I did. I walked in and sat down, right between Katie Casey and Ms Hyde, who looked like a human pink cupcake, plump and flushed. I took their hands. I bowed my head. I joined the prayer circle. And the whole time I was reminding myself of one very, very important fact:

I was using Katie Casey.

While, to the casual observer, it might seem like I was compromising my values by allowing *The Vagina Monologues* to be airbrushed with pink glitter as part of the Save Your Heart Festival, that wasn't true. Really, I was being sneaky. I was using Katie Casey's squeaky-clean, G-rated, Heidi the Mountain Girl facade to smuggle my radical feminist message into St Mary's. She was my Trojan horse. Or non-Trojan horse – you know, because of the whole celibacy thing.

'So, Katie!' I said when the circle had broken up and the virginity minions were helping Ms Hyde put the desks back. 'We're all good to go, right? Green light? *The Vagina Monologues* is full steam ahead?'

'Well . . .' Katie was smiling as always. 'I went to see Father Hughes this afternoon . . .'

I wagged a playful finger at her. 'I bet he was happy to see you!'

Of *course* Father Hughes was happy to see Katie Casey. She's probably his favorite student. I mean, she gets good grades, she's never in trouble, she's always helping people – give the chick a blue pashmina and a carpenter boyfriend and she's the Virgin friggin' Mary.

'Well, he was SUPER happy about our collaboration!'

Of *course* Father Hughes was happy about our collaboration. He probably thought Katie Casey's chastity fairy dust would rub off on me.

'So there's just *one* little hurdle left,' she concluded.

Until that moment, I had been floating along on a smug river of self-congratulation. Now my ears perked up. 'Uh . . . what?' I said. 'What little hurdle?'

'Just . . . Father Hughes wants us to get approval on the edited version of the text before it's performed,' Katie said.

'The edited version?'

'Well, I didn't think you'd have time to put on the *whole* play,' Katie explained. 'So Father Hughes suggested we –

or you, I guess – come up with an edited version to be approved by Father Vincent.'

My heart sank into my motorcycle boots. See, there's this whole priestly pyramid of authority at St Mary's. Father Hughes is the big enchilada at the top who gives the go-ahead to projects and events, and then the vice-principal, Father Vincent, handles the nitty-gritty details: the who, what, where, when and how. Or – in this case – the 'how naked' and 'how many F-bombs'.

'It's fine!' Katie reassured me quickly. 'It's just, the thing is . . .' She gave a nervous, tinkling laugh. 'Father Vincent isn't *quite* as cool as Father Hughes.'

Yeah, no kidding. This was the guy Pat said got his priest panties in a twist over *Beauty and the Beast.*

'So are you saying . . . I have to create a version of *The Vagina Monologues*, a play full of cursing and radical nineties feminism, that's acceptable to a guy who is *less cool* than Father Hughes?' I said.

'Just that little hurdle,' Katie Casey insisted. 'And then we're all good!'

She went back to her fondle-free flock, and I, in front of all the pink balloons, the abstinence books and the too-cool-to-fool-around poster couple, said: 'Fuck.'

12

Before I got to St Mary's, I'd never really interacted with a priest or a nun before, and they really freaked me out. Did they have superpowers? Did they have X-ray vision? Could they see through my green-plaid uniform to my leopard-print thong and the tattoo I regretted from the summer before freshman year?

Soon enough, like everything else at St Mary's, priests and nuns became a minor annoyance that I mostly ignored. What were they but more authority figures, just like all the camp counsellors, detention monitors and Girl Scout troop leaders I had sassed, ignored and disrespected for years?

And actually – as much as I hate to admit it – a few of the priests and nuns on this campus are kinda cool. My freshman theology teacher even took the whole class out to Dairy Queen for my birthday. But the vice-principal is not one of them. Father Vincent is the most awkward human being alive. Every conversation with this guy is like a sex talk with your dad.

And, to no one's surprise, Mary Kate was not thrilled to be accompanying me to discuss *The Vagina Monologues* with him.

'I can't believe you're making me do this,' she fumed, stomping brown leaves with her little loafers as we crossed Academic Quad towards the main building with the golden Mary statue on top. It was definitely October. I was wearing a vegan leather jacket I'd found in a San Francisco thrift shop, and Mary Kate had her green St Mary's fleece tightly wrapped around her and her arms crossed against the cold.

'Come on, I need you!' I said. 'You're intelligent, you're insightful, you're articulate. Plus, look at you. You're friggin' adorable! You're like that YouTube video of Teddy the Porcupine eating corn on the cob. Who's gonna say no to that face?'

I reached out to pinch her cheek and she slapped my hand away.

'You better do all the talking. This was your idea – this is your issue. I am not saying a word.' She shoved her finger in my face. 'And I am most definitely not saying THE WORD. I'm serious. I'm not in the mood.'

She really wasn't. Teddy the Porcupine had claws. If I was bumping into obstacles at every turn, trying to put on *The Vagina Monologues*, Mary Kate seemed to have hit a brick wall in her boyfriend search. She was still sitting next to her original target, Theology John, in class, but he was shy and silent. In over a month since the dance, when they had been on the brink of a St Mary's make-out, they had had exactly one interaction: she asked him for a pencil (even though she already had one), and he looked away, blushed and shook his head. As far as romantic milestones go, that was about negative twelfth base.

'And FYI,' she continued, 'if Father Vincent doesn't agree with you, I'm not fighting. At best, I'm sitting there for silent moral support. At worst, I'm taking his side. Because guess what? I'm ON his side. I'm glad Father Hughes told you no when you first asked him! I DON'T think this . . . play . . . is appropriate to perform on campus, when some freshmen are thirteen. I am anti!'

'Well, you shouldn't be,' I told her. 'Body shame affects all of us – especially you. Think about all your anxiety about your growling stomach and your sweaty armpits, and making your mom send you boxes of tampons. Remember the freshman swim test when you thought you had a camel toe in your one-piece so you made me walk in front of you and do a nip slip to distract everyone? I wouldn't have had to do that if society hadn't ingrained body shame into you.'

'I know you now,' Mary Kate said darkly. 'You would have nip-slipped anyway. You would nip-slip at the Vatican.'

When we arrived at his office, the vice-principal was standing in the doorway, waiting for us, nervously rubbing his dry palms together. As soon as he saw us, he tensed up and began awkwardly nodding and bowing like a socially inept scientist greeting his robot girlfriend.

'Hello, Ms Reagan!' he said, then cleared his throat (*ehem*). 'Hello, Ms Heck! How is our semester? Is our semester all right?'

Twitching anxiously, he jerked out a mechanical hand to invite us into his office. We sat down, and he coughed and cleared his throat and sat down, then stood back up to pull in his chair, then sat back down and coughed and rubbed his dry palms together again.

'Well – *ehem* – I suppose we should discuss the ... *ehem*, project ... you've come here to ... discuss.'

No way was this guy saying *vagina*. He didn't even like using his own job title because it had the word *vice* in it. Like, you got the idea that if you said *bra strap* in front of him, he'd just melt into a pile of mortified goo.

So of course I had printed out our edited version of the play with **VAGINA** in size-1,000 bold font on the front. When I handed it over, he blinked rapidly and cleared his throat about six times. He continued clearing his throat at regular ten-second intervals as he read, with Mary Kate literally on the edge of her seat, her own copy of our edit trembling in her hands, and me also on the edge of my seat, my copy clenched in my fist, ready for a fight.

We had worked for the past two days to create a shortened version of *The Vagina Monologues* to perform at the Save Your Heart Festival by picking and choosing ten different monologues. In the spirit of open-mindedness and generosity, I had let Mary Kate choose five. She had chosen the five with the least sex and cursing. And, actually, I'd sucked it up and picked the five I thought were the best fit for St Mary's, even though they weren't the most shocking. Ever since Maggie had come to me, terrified, in the middle of the night, I'd realized that the most important thing was to get *The Vagina Monologues* seen by as many of these abstinence-only ignoramuses as possible, even if it meant giving an inch to the administration.

Which is why it was extra frustrating seeing the vein bulging in Father Vincent's forehead as he read, and realizing that even this PG-13 version wasn't gonna fly.

Clearing his throat again, the vice-principal set down the pages.

'While I appreciate the literary merit and the, er, postmodern experimentalism of the – *ehem* – work,' he began, 'I must express my concern that the Catholic moral mission of the school and content of the – *ehem* – work are not exactly aligned. I believe we must make significant changes. If we do not succeed, we must abandon the – *ehem* – project altogether.'

Mary Kate shot me a look. I ignored her.

'Can you tell me what it is exactly you have a problem with?'

'Well . . .' Father Vincent pushed his wire-rimmed glasses up his beaky nose. 'In the first place, there is the issue of – *ehem* – language. As I'm sure both of you are aware, our school rulebook prohibits spoken and written profanity . . .'

Yeah, sure, but the school rulebook also prohibits getting to second base with your bio tutor on a lab table, and that went out the window for me freshman year.

'We are molding young minds here,' Father Vincent continued, blinking rapidly. 'Our aim is to enrich them with the language of the Scriptures, of Shakespeare, of the Ancient Greeks. As St Augustine once wrote –'

'We can cut out the F-bombs,' I said.

'Alex!' Mary Kate hissed.

Father Vincent tugged at the white collar around his neck and swallowed uncomfortably.

'Well, the – *ehem* – language would have to be modified or, in certain cases, eliminated altogether, which would be quite difficult when one takes into account the ratio of acceptable phrasing to unacceptable phrasing. But, in addition, this extract contains many . . . *ehem* . . . elements that are . . .'

'Revolutionary? Informative? Ground-breaking?' I suggested. 'A refreshing way of reappropriating the female anatomy, which for far too long has been objectified by the patriarchal male gaze and alienated by the Madonna–Whore dichotomy?'

The word *whore* triggered a full-minute fit of coughing and wheezing in the vice-principal, like someone had just sprayed Justin Bieber's cologne in his face. I was staring him down, my arms crossed challengingly across my chest. Mary Kate was gnawing at her cuticles, her little knees knocking together under her plaid skort.

When Father Vincent began to speak again, his voice was strained and high-pitched.

'As you know,' he began, 'St Mary's embraces the Catholic Church's teaching that a genuine and complete expression of – *ehem* – love through . . . physical – *ehem* – means – *cough, cough* – requires a commitment to a total living and sharing together of two persons in marriage. This is the reason students who engage in – *ehem* – sexual union – *cough, cough, cough, ehem* – are subject to expulsion. And, of course, we as a school would never want to – *ehem* – support a production that would celebrate or encourage "activities" – *ehem, ehem, ehem* – such as – *ehem, ehem, hack, hack, cough, cough, cough* . . .'

Then he broke down completely into a hurricane fit of hacking – phlegmy, lung-rattling coughs, as if he was trying to hawk up Satan himself from his lungs. I was kind of bummed about it. What activities was he talking about? I really would have liked to know what a guy with a lifelong chastity vow imagines we're getting up to. Like, just crazy, animalistic, green-plaid orgies in the math classrooms at night?

Father Vincent yanked a drawer open and fumbled with shaking hands for a cough drop, which he unwrapped hurriedly and popped into his mouth. But, when he started to speak again, his voice was barely a wheeze, and Mary Kate, perched precariously on the edge of her seat and clearly terrified he was about to be carried away by another asphyxial spasm, cut him off.

'What if we get rid of all the offensive language?' she burst out.

'Wait, what?' I said. 'I said we can cut the F-bombs, but –'

'*All* the curse words, and anything else offensive!'

What the hell was Mary Kate doing? I hadn't agreed to this! Cut out 'anything else offensive'? Oh hell, no! Vagina Sudoku would have been better than this!

But clearly she thought she was on a roll. Now she was flipping rapidly through the pages, ruthlessly throwing phrase after brilliant phrase out the window because of a 'shit' or a 'hell' or a 'screw'.

'The word at the bottom of page two . . . the phrase at the top of page three . . . page four, the whole last paragraph . . .'

Father Vincent must have thought she was on a roll, too, because his cough had slowed. He leaned back in his chair, sucking his cough drop and following along, turning the pages of his copy and nodding thoughtfully.

'So that just leaves . . .' Mary Kate flipped back to the cover, which had the big, bold **VAGINA** on it. 'Well, obviously, there's the . . .'

'*Ehem, ehem –*' Father Vincent leaned forward in his chair again.

'THE NAME OF THE PLAY!' Mary Kate shouted. 'We'll change the name of the play!'

'Mary Kate!' I cried.

But Father Vincent's coughing had subsided. Mary Kate turned towards him anxiously.

'We could just call it *The Monologues*.' She looked over at me and made this *c'mon, keep it rolling* gesture to urge me to get on board. 'Or something that gives credit to the author, and puts the focus on her! *An Extract from Eve Ensler*! That's perfect!'

Father Vincent was quiet. Mary Kate had apparently silenced the Damning Sinners Cough of Disapproval. But she had torn up *The Vagina Monologues* beyond recognition. It wasn't even *The Vagina Monologues* anymore! It was *The NON-Vagina Monologues*. I had no words. So I fixed her with my best hardcore-metal death stare.

At first, she looked back at me and gave a little shrug like, *What could I do? I'm Teddy the Porcupine!* But then she turned to Father Vincent and gasped in horror.

His face was purple, his hands clutched his throat, the rooster-veins in his neck straining as he tried to speak – or cough – or anything.

'Oh my God!' I shouted, jumping up so fast I knocked over my chair. 'HE'S CHOKING!'

He was struggling to stand up now, leaning over his desk, still gripping his throat desperately. 'Oh my God!' I kept yelling, 'Oh my God!' and Mary Kate was yelling it, too, and there was no time to notice or care if the six crucifixes on the walls were flipping us off for taking the Lord's name in vain.

I started to run around the desk to Father Vincent, but then I remembered his assistant, Brother John, was right outside the door and turned around and leaped over my chair to go get him, but my brain was screaming, *There's no time! There's no time!* I was running frantically over to the closed door, grabbing the door handle, but then turning back (*There's no time!*), racking my frantic brain for what I'd learned in freshman health class. Choking, choking, what did you do when someone was choking? Pound them on the chest, right? No, pound them on the BACK! Or roll them on their side? *No, that's an overdose!* All I could remember from freshman health was Scottie Frost tongue-kissing the CPR dummy, and that was absolutely no fucking help and super gross, too. *Why don't you EVER pay attention in class?* I raged at myself inwardly. *See how it bites you in the ass!*

I sprinted to the door again and grabbed the handle – but, just then, I heard a hacking sound behind me. I turned to see little Mary Kate with her arms wrapped around Father Vincent and her fists in his stomach, and him spluttering all over his desk, and then – glistening like a wet, spitty diamond – the cough drop.

There we were, all of us, staring at the cough drop, me damp with panic and pit stains, Mary Kate with her arms still wrapped around the wheezing, trembling vice-principal, like they were posing for the world's worst prom photo. Carefully, she let go of him and withdrew her arms in the slowest, most uncomfortable way possible, like a socially awkward sloth.

After we'd all sat down again, Brother John had brought the vice-principal a cup of water and he'd taken several slow sips, he seemed to look at us in a new way. And, by that, I mean his socially awkward self actually made eye contact: he looked at Mary Kate for a long moment, then me.

'Obviously, I believe all things are in the hands of . . . our Lord God.' He raised his eyes briefly towards the ceiling. 'And therefore I cannot believe it was an accident that you two were in my office this afternoon. It is clear you are quick-thinking young women, of good judgment . . .'

(He looked more at Mary Kate when he said that, but that's fair.)

'And therefore . . . I believe you can be trusted to go ahead with this project,' he said, then added quickly, 'with the modifications Ms Reagan suggested, of course.'

Silent, still in shock, we stood up at the same time. After we left his office, we stopped and stood on the fifth-floor landing and stared at each other. Mary Kate's brown eyes were in full Bambi-in-headlights mode. She looked down at her hands and I saw they were trembling violently. Then I looked down at *my* hands and saw they were trembling violently.

'You saved his life, Mary Kate!' I said in astonishment. 'How did you know how to do that?'

'I did it once before,' she said, sounding dazed. 'I used to babysit this hyper kid who was addicted to Sour Skittles.'

We just stood there, looking at each other for another minute, as if in gratitude for life itself, then turned and slowly started down the five flights of stairs.

13

The school semester was in full swing now, and all of St Mary's was buzzing about one thing. (Unfortunately, it was not *The Non-Vagina Monologues*; without the key word, it lacked a bit of pizzazz.) One larger-than-life zeitgeist figure dominated every conversation: Dominic LeClair, the Toothless Beast.

Who was Dominic LeClair? The star hockey player of St Luke's Catholic Boarding School – St Mary's biggest hockey rival. St Luke's was an all-boys' school, a super-harsh and competitive one where guys were always getting busted for throwing weaklings into an icy river and causing them to almost die of hypothermia. Last year, they beat us in the varsity hockey championship, and there was one reason why: an amazing freshman hockey player from Quebec named Dominic LeClair.

Dominic LeClair is ferocious. The reason he's nicknamed the Toothless Beast is because he's famously missing three front teeth – and in hockey, just like in a second-grade class picture, the most badass person has the fewest teeth. For Dominic LeClair, hockey is a game of human bumper cars. After he played against us in the championship game last year, three of our players had concussions, and two Zamboni machines were needed to clear all the blood off the ice.

Dominic LeClair was basically on the same level as Satan on our campus. After we lost the championship, a guy in St Francis Hall even made a life-size model of LeClair in a hockey jersey and they all carried it down to the lake, chanting, and set it on fire and threw it in, like one of Mary Shelley's fever dreams or something.

But now, in October of our junior year, everything changed. It was the start of hockey pre-season, and all across the rapidly chilling tundra of the Midwest, hockey players were beginning practices and 5,000-calorie, protein-packed diets in order to inflict maximum bodily harm on each other. All varsity hockey players, that is, except Dominic LeClair. The Toothless Beast was not practicing with the St Luke's team. And, according to rumors, it was because he wanted to transfer to another school: St Mary's.

All of a sudden, the switch flipped. Everyone loved Dominic LeClair. And, everywhere you went, someone was talking about him.

'I hear the Toothless Beast drinks a raw-egg milkshake every morning to build muscle,' I overheard one guy tell another in the line in the cafeteria.

'I hear the Toothless Beast dislocated his shoulder during a game and snapped it back into place himself in the penalty box,' a girl hissed to a guy behind me in detention.

'I hear the Toothless Beast's left elbow is registered as an assault weapon in Hennepin County,' a girl informed her friend as they jogged past me on the track in gym class.

'You know what *should* be registered?' her friend said. 'His butt. I love hockey butts.'

Mary Kate and I, picking our way across the muddy quad on the first sunny day after a big rain, were not discussing the Toothless Beast. We were coming back from a meeting about the play, and she was blaming me for the failure of her boyfriend plan.

'If I wasn't spending so much time on YOUR semester goal, I would have achieved mine by now,' she said.

'Mary Kate, this is a worthy cause,' I reminded her. 'And you of all people should be into this!'

'Me?' she squeaked. 'Into the *Monologues*? Why?'

'Because this is *literature*, Mary Kate. You love books, and reading, and all that crap! We are about to bring an award-winning piece of literature to life.'

My room-mate shook her head and refused to look at me. All around us on the quad, rosy-cheeked students in green fleeces were playing freeze tag and football and kicking soccer balls through piles of wet autumn leaves.

'You know,' I said casually, 'we're not the only creative people to be the victims of censorship. The word *vagina* has played an important role in literature for centuries now. Do you know the original version of Shakespeare's most famous sonnet? *Shall I compare thee to a summer's vagina? Thou art more lovely . . .*'

Mary Kate just shook her head again, but I could see the corner of her mouth twitch.

'Or Hemingway! Good old Hem's first drafts were littered with vaginas.' Putting on a deep, manly voice, I began to narrate: *'My vagina was warm and wet. It ate good bread and hard cheese and sour wine. The mountains were far from my vagina, and tall . . .'*

Mary Kate smiled in spite of herself. She still hated the word *vagina* and refused to say it no matter how much I tickled her or bribed her with Oreos, but she couldn't resist anything to do with classic literature.

'Jane Austen?' she suggested.

My hoity-toity English voice, with a pinkie sticking out: *'It is a truth universally acknowledged, that a single man in possession of a good fortune, must be in want of a vagina.'*

Mary Kate was having fun. She was walking backwards, facing me, like a tour guide, throwing out names –

'Faulkner!'

'My vagina is a fish, my vagina is a fish, my vagina is a fish . . .'

Suddenly, as we were strolling along the bright quad, an object came hurtling through the air towards us. I looked up. Mary Kate looked up, too, but the sun blinded her and the next second it was already too late – a football smacked her in the forehead, and she crumpled to the ground.

'Oh my God!' I gasped, throwing myself down on the wet grass next to her. For a split second, I thought – and hated myself for thinking – that this was some kind of punishment from God for trying to put on *The Vagina Monologues* at St Mary's. It seemed fitting for such a jocky school that the punishment should come in the form of a football instead of, like, locusts or a hurricane of virgin blood.

'Oh crap, oh crap!' came a voice from above me.

Someone else had rushed over – a really tall, tan senior with big biceps bulging through the sleeves of his uniform polo shirt and a shaved head that emphasized his bright blue eyes. He squatted in the mud next to me and asked Mary Kate, 'Crap, are you okay?'

She was okay, luckily. Her eyes were open, and she had already reached down to make sure the flap of her plaid skort was covering the weird granny-panty shorts underneath. She was okay, but she was muddy, she was shaken and – most of all – she was *mad*.

Pushing herself up off the ground, ignoring the hand I held out to help her, mud-splattered and trembling all over, she stood and drew herself up to her full height.

'I'm so sorry, seriously,' Football Dude said, reaching out tentatively to brush some mud off her skort. She slapped his hand away, so I have no idea why he decided it was a good time to make a dumb little joke.

'At least it wasn't your nose, right?' he said, then laughed this dumb-jock stuttering laugh: '*Heh-heh-heh-heh.*'

When she looked up, her face, which had been pale with shock a second ago, was furiously red. Tears of rage gave her eyes an evil gleam like she was the Predator or something, and she blew up completely.

'My NOSE?' she shouted. 'At least it wasn't my NOSE? What am I, some beauty-pageant contestant who thinks

Hiroshima is something you eat with miso soup? My NOSE? You hit me in the HEAD! Do you know how much my *brain* is worth? I can factor a quadratic equation in the time it takes you to sniff-check your armpits! I speak *Latin*, JERK!'

It was pretty entertaining to watch this six-foot-two jock back away in fear, his hands up in surrender, almost tripping over an errant Frisbee as Mary Kate shouted at him and poked her finger into his chest. My only small note of criticism: it would have been way better if she'd said, *I speak Latin, BITCH!* But this was Mary Kate after all.

'Sorry! Really! I'm sorry!' Football Dude stuttered, terrified. 'I didn't mean to!'

Mary Kate backed off, fuming, but it was almost a full minute before he dared to ask, gesturing cautiously from a distance, 'Uh . . . could I maybe have my . . . uh, football, please?'

'Oh, you want your football?' Mary Kate said. 'You want your FOOTBALL?'

Huffing angrily, she snatched the ball up off the ground and Football Dude immediately raised his hands to protect his face, sure she was about to beat him over the head with it. Instead, she took a step back, raised her arm and hurled it with all her might. All of us looked up in wonder, as if Amelia Earhart had just taken to the sky, and shielded our eyes to watch Mary Kate's football arc miraculously across the quad in a shaft of sunlight.

'Holy crap!' Football Dude breathed, his blue eyes bright with astonishment. 'That was a perfect spiral!'

Then he turned to my room-mate, who hadn't even looked to see where the football had gone. She'd just hurled it and forgotten about it, and was now brushing mud off her skort.

'I'm gonna remember you,' he promised, pointing a finger at her.

Mary Kate was still in huffy mode, so she just folded her arms, looked Football Dude right in those blue eyes and said, 'Well, I hope I remember *anything* now that you've hit me in the head. If I get even ten points less than a perfect verbal score on the SAT this spring, you're getting sued.'

But Football Dude just stared at her admiringly for a minute before jogging off to retrieve his ball.

I was staring at her, too. 'Mary Kate!' I said. Where had she possibly learned to throw a football like that? Did she secretly have some bionic robot bicep under her extra-small fleece that NASA scientists had engineered? And, if so, why was she always asking me to finish blow-drying her hair when her arm got too tired?

As she turned towards me, the red flush of anger drained from her face and she blinked a few times, dazed. Her fists unclenched. She was coming back to reality after her rage blackout. She looked at me, then at Football Dude jogging away towards Boys' Quad, and asked: 'Wait. Was that guy, like, really cute?'

That week, Fajita Friday in the cafeteria was overshadowed by excitement about the Toothless Beast and the possibility of him bringing his hockey butt to St Mary's. Buzz was at an all-time high; people were chattering loudly at every table, and, between that and the sizzling of the fajitas, it was surprising we even heard the voice call from across the cafeteria:

'HEY, YOU! HEY, GIRL WITH THE KILLER ARM!'

We turned and saw Football Dude waving at us enthusiastically.

'Oh no!' Mary Kate panicked. 'It's that sexy man who almost gave me a concussion!'

'And you're "the girl with the killer arm",' I added. 'Who would've thought? I had my money on "the girl with the Jane Austen tattoo".'

'COME OVER HERE! COME SIT WITH US!' Football Dude was smiling and beckoning to us, so Mary Kate and I grabbed forks and napkins and, gripping our trays tightly, made our way through the busy dinner crowd.

Football Dude was sitting with a bunch of other jocks. Clearly, they were all varsity athletes and they'd just come from practice. They were wearing the official St Mary's grey varsity sweatsuits and drinking big glasses of blue Powerade; the guys had shaved heads and the girls had messy buns on top of their heads. Football Dude – his name was Michael – introduced us to everyone and said to his friends, 'This is the girl I told you about.' Then he turned to Mary Kate. 'Hey, I was hoping I'd run into you. There was something I wanted to ask you.'

'Yes,' Mary Kate said immediately, breathlessly, gripping the edge of her seat. 'Whatever it is, yes.'

'So we all play on this team,' Football Michael began. 'Ya know, just a casual weekend league with other St Mary's teams, guys and girls together, for fun. Not tackle football – we wear flags.'

'Wait,' I interrupted him. 'You guys do two-a-day varsity practices all week, then on the weekends you play *more* sports? For fun?'

The whole table frowned at me in confusion and nodded, like *duh*.

'Uh . . . cool,' I said.

'But the quarterback on our flag team just got injured,' Football Michael told Mary Kate. 'And we have a big game next weekend. Do you think you could step in?'

Mary Kate, still gripping the seat, sat there frozen. Her mouth was slightly open, but she didn't know what to say. She looked at me.

Mary Kate! I tried to convey my message with a pointed look. *Do not do this! Do not play sports at St Mary's! REMEMBER DODGEBALL, MARY KATE!*

Now our telepathic room-mate connection is strong, but right now Mary Kate was distracted. Her eyes had wandered back to the beautiful, symmetrical face of Football Michael and she couldn't look away.

'It's so crazy,' he was saying. 'I meet you and you throw that incredible pass and, like, *two* days later, our quarterback gets hurt. It's, like, meant to be!'

'Meant to be,' Mary Kate repeated, starry-eyed, and I groaned inwardly. I'd lost her.

'So,' Football Michael finished, 'will you play?'

'Sure!' she blurted out. 'That would be fun!'

'Yes!' He reached across the table to high-five her, then told the others, 'Seriously, this girl has a killer spiral.'

Mary Kate looked around with a pleased smile on her face, and noticed that one of the girls at the table had her arm in a cast. 'Oh, were you the quarterback?' she asked politely.

The girl looked down at her arm and scoffed dismissively. 'Oh no. This is just a sprain. I'm *definitely* playing in next week's game. Lauren's the quarterback. She's still in the infirmary. You know how uptight those nurses are about concussions!'

'Right . . .' Mary Kate trailed off, frowning at me worriedly. Then, as all the jocks shoveled meat into their mouths and guzzled blue Powerade, she made a new attempt at conversation: 'So what's your team name?'

The six-foot-five guy at the end of the table, who was tearing the meat off a chicken wing, answered with his mouth full: 'The Bonecrushers.'

'Oh!' she squeaked. 'That's nice . . .' Looking down at her plate, she delicately rearranged the peppers on her tortilla like she was arranging lilies for the Dowager Countess's flower show.

Clearly, this conversation needed some help, and Mary Kate needed some distraction. I didn't know what hardcore jocks usually talked about, but there was one fail-safe topic at St Mary's right now, and I went straight to it.

'So what do you guys think of the Toothless Beast?' I asked. 'Pretty awesome that he's thinking about transfering, right? Hopefully we get him on our team.'

But the reaction wasn't what I'd expected. A few of the athletes nodded and muttered, 'Yeah, cool,' but Football Michael wasn't too amped about it.

'I don't know,' he said. 'I mean, yeah, he's good for a sophomore, and he's an improvement over the team we have now . . .'

'The team we have now?' Chicken Wings was crunching loudly with his mouth open – and I'm pretty sure he was eating the bones. Well, now I knew where the team name came from. 'Total weaklings, man. BS.'

'I hate to say that they didn't even deserve to *be* in the championship last year,' said the girl with the sprained arm, who was using her good hand to dump hot sauce all over her fajita. 'But they really didn't.'

'Yeah, I mean, we'll see how he does. Hopefully, he's put on a bunch of muscle weight over the summer,' Football Michael said. 'I just wish his playing was more –'

'Hardcore?' The Chicken Wings guy cut him off, spraying bits of meat everywhere.

'TOTALLY!' the girl with the arm cast said, slamming down the hot sauce, and everyone joined in, in a hoarse chorus, 'Totally, totally!'

'Totally,' Mary Kate murmured in confusion. As she ate her fajita, she looked around at the athletes in bewilderment, trying to comprehend the type of humans who thought the Toothless Beast, national champion buster of bones, spiller of guts, could be more hardcore.

She met my eyes and shook her head. Then she took a small sip of iced tea to brace herself and said: 'So about this game that's coming up. I've actually just realized –'

'I am so pumped about it!' Football Michael interrupted her. 'We are gonna CRUSH it!'

Smiling adoringly at Mary Kate, he threw a casual arm around her shoulders. She looked down at the arm. She looked up into his bright blue eyes.

'I actually just realized . . .' she repeated, and plastered a brave smile across her face. 'We're gonna crush it!'

The athletes all cheered and whistled and pounded the table until the glasses of blue Powerade rattled and splashed over, and Mary Kate began shoveling steak fajitas into her mouth at double speed. *Protein*, she mouthed at me, and held up her weak little bicep in despair.

We had eight days to teach Mary Kate football.

'We' being me, a chick who spent eighth-grade sports day piercing her friend's nose with a staple remover and Mary Kate, who doesn't have the physical stamina to fit the little peg people in the cars while playing the Game of Life.

Saturday night and the *Rocky* theme song was blaring from my laptop, protein bars were stacked on the dressers, and Mary Kate was dangling from the top railing of our bunk bed with her legs curled up lamely behind her while I, in lime-green spandex and a sweatband I'd borrowed from a junior Olympic fencer down the hall, barked, 'Pull-ups! Come on, weakling! Let's build those biceps!'

'Help! I can't even do one!'

'Just one, Mary Kate!' I told her encouragingly. Maybe my tough-love approach had been too tough for a chick who owned a *Little House on the Prairie* coloring book. 'You can do one pull-up!'

'My arms are spaghetti!' she wailed.

'All right, all right, drop down,' I said, switching off the pump-up music.

She dropped down, then flung herself face down on my bed in despair. I leaned against the bunk-bed ladder.

'I don't even see why you're doing this in the first place,' I told her. 'If you don't want to play football, don't play football.'

Mary Kate rolled over and hugged my pillow. 'You saw him! Alex, those eyes!'

'They were pretty blue,' I admitted.

'The bluest eyes in the world! I got lost in them. I felt like his eyes were the ocean in *Life of Pi* and I was just floating in the middle of them with a tiger about to eat me. I can't say no.'

'Yeah, but, if you say yes, the tigers *will* eat you.'

'I know.' She sighed, got up and began pacing. 'But I'm completely torn about the whole thing. I couldn't even sleep last night. I was just tossing and turning all night . . .'

'I know.' I'd been rudely awakened at 3 a.m. when Sir Shackleton hit me in the face.

'And it's just insane. My body is at war with itself.' Mary Kate paced anxiously to the door. 'My fight-or-flight reflex is going crazy, like, *Mary Kate, don't go into that game, they'll kill you, they'll crush your little rib cage and make soup out of your bones!* But my ovaries are whispering to me, too – they won't stop hissing in that creepy little Voldemort snake voice: *But, Mary Kate, your babiessss could have those beautiful eyesssss. Those beautiful eyessss, Mary Kate . . .'*

Mary Kate's own eyes were kinda freaking me out at this point. They were all huge and possessed, as if she was under a spell or something. I took a nervous step back. I was beginning to think Football Michael had some kind of hypnotic power over her, like a young, hunky Rasputin.

'Why don't you just tell him you got hurt?' I suggested cautiously. 'We could still go stand on the sidelines and, like, ogle him, but then you have an excuse not to play.'

Mary Kate grabbed my collar and shook me. 'Alex, you met these people! They don't care if I have some mild injury. These kids were thrown into icy rivers as newborn babies and had to learn to swim and kill and eat raw fish, and then they survived and grew up and devoted their lives to flag football. These are blood-sacrifice people. These are Vikings. These are *Spartans.'*

Neither of us could think what to do. I hopped up on my desk and began picking the chocolate chips out of the protein bars and eating them. Mary Kate sat in my desk chair, spinning in slow, obsessive circles, frowning in deep thought. Then suddenly, out of nowhere, she spun around excitedly to face me.

'Pat!' she bubbled. 'Hockey Player Pat! He's sporty. He'll know all about football!'

I raised an eyebrow in confusion.

'Ask him to help us! He's always texting you – don't pretend he isn't. I feel your phone vibrating in your bed at three in the morning.'

'Uh sure,' I said awkwardly. 'That's definitely my . . . phone.'

'Text him!' she said, clapping her hands. '*Texthim-texthimtexthim!*'

'No way! He's already the stage manager on the *Monologues*. He's gonna think I'm asking him favors to flirt with him. You know hockey players and their big, dumb frosty egos.'

'*Text him*,' Mary Kate growled. She was gripping the armrests of my chair and her eyes were getting all big and possessed again.

Groaning, I slid down from the desk and grabbed my phone. 'Fine,' I grumbled. 'But he's a know-it-all and a pain in the ass, I'm warning you.'

Pat insisted on meeting us before classes Monday morning. It was freezing and the sun was just starting to rise as Mary Kate and I trudged against the wind out to the sports fields. He was already there, in his fleece and basketball shorts and cleats, with a shiny whistle dangling around his neck, all pumped up and energetic, jogging in place, tossing a football from hand to hand. Half of me wanted to tackle him to the ground and kick his stupid football away. The other half wanted to tackle him to the ground, make out with him for a good sweaty ten minutes, *then* kick his stupid football away.

'Good morning!' he boomed in greeting. 'Who's ready for some football? Don't you love an early-morning workout? Gets the heart pumping, gets the blood flowing, gets those feel-good endorphins movin' through you all day long! So let's –' He stopped jogging and frowned at me. 'Are those . . . leather pants?'

'They are faux-leather *jeggings*,' I corrected him. 'They're the only stretchy pants I have. My gym shorts are in the wash.' I was also wearing giant sunglasses. Clearly, I wasn't too into this whole 'athletic' thing.

'See, this is the problem with you sporty people,' I told him. 'You always wanna drag people out of bed at the butt crack of dawn. And then you annoy them with all your happy, perky bullshit until I just want to shove badminton shuttlecocks into all your faces and go back to sleep.'

'No need to thank me,' Pat said grandly. 'I'm happy to help you out. No, really, you *are* welcome, but I'm happy to. What's that? You want to buy me a thank-you gift? That's really too generous . . .'

I just grumbled and lit a clove cigarette.

'So, Mary Kate!' He turned to my room-mate. 'How much do you know about football?'

Mary Kate gave me an anxious look. She was holding a notebook and pen; she had written *How to Play Football* neatly across the first page.

'Scoring?' Pat suggested. 'Touchdowns? Passing plays? Running plays?'

We exchanged a look and shrugged.

Pat held out the ball with both hands. 'Um . . . you do know this is a football, right?'

Mary Kate scribbled that down in her notebook.

Pat took in my sunglasses, cigarette and leather jeggings; the cupcake-print pajama pants my room-mate was wearing over her gym shorts because of the cold.

'So I'm guessing you guys aren't the biggest sports fans in the world?'

We exchanged a brief dark look.

'We had a . . . bad experience once,' Mary Kate said, and then primly shut her mouth.

Frowning, Pat shook his shaggy hair out of his eyes. 'Um, so what exactly are we doing here?'

'Well . . .' Mary Kate began to launch into some bull-crap discourse about our wanting to learn football because the sport was 'part of the cultural quilt of American life and, indeed, the cultural and social life of St Mary's –'

I cut her off. 'Mary Kate wants to bone a dude who likes football.'

Pat shrugged. 'Fair enough.'

'Alex!' Mary Kate looked horrified. Bright red, she hastened to tell Pat, 'She's lying. I don't want to . . . Don't believe her! She's a huge liar, seriously.'

'How about we start off with a little jog?' Pat suggested.

'Okay,' I said. 'Just let me finish my cigarette first.'

The lazy-ass sun finally rose, turning the frost on the grass into mud, as we ran drills. Pat had us move around the field so we could understand what the quarterback did, where the offense and defense were, the different plays. Then we did some 'conditioning', running around the field until I really wished I was wearing a sports bra. Afterward, Mary Kate and I collapsed in the sun-warmed grass, winded and red in the face.

'All right!' Pat blew his whistle just to be an asshole, then recapped: 'Mary Kate, you've learned four important plays: the Hail Mary, the Counter, the Slant and the Hook. And Alex, you have made dirty jokes about the following terms: pocket, sack, and one I still don't completely understand about the quarterback sneak.'

'I'll send you a video that will clarify everything.' I winked.

'Now.' Pat squatted on his haunches and set the football down. 'You owe me. I wanna know why you guys hate sports.'

Mary Kate sat up. I sat up. We looked at each other, very serious.

'Is it time?' I asked her.

She nodded. 'It's time.'

And we told him the story of how we met.

We told him about that infamous day during freshman orientation. We told him how a fun, casual, get-to-know-you dodgeball game transformed into a dog-eat-dog fight to the death. How our friendly, freckly new dorm mates morphed into monstrous, bloodthirsty beasts, growling and spitting and exchanging viciously satisfied high fives when they struck an enemy and she crumpled to the ground.

How, in the horror of that Roman arena where whip-fast rubber balls bombarded us relentlessly and cries of pain echoed to the ceiling, we found each other hiding by the back wall. Normally, Mary Kate would have been terrified of my purple hair and piercings, but there was no time for that. We had to get out – and there was one glimmer of hope: the emergency exit.

'We knew it would set the alarm off,' Mary Kate explained. 'But it actually *was* an emergency because we thought we were going to die.'

'And, just as I grabbed Mary Kate's hand to make a run for it, we looked up,' I said. 'Everyone else on our team was gone.'

'It was just me and Alex . . . face to face with one of the Rowers.'

'Who?' Pat asked.

'These terrifying crew chicks in our dorm,' I said. 'They're insanely ginormous. Think offspring of Boudicca and that tree monster from *Guardians of the Galaxy*.'

'And she was holding a dodgeball,' Mary Kate continued.

'Which looked like a grapefruit in her hand,' I added. 'But I knew I had to protect Mary Kate. She was so tiny and scared!' I reached over and pinched her cheek.

'Yup, Alex stepped up to the line,' Mary Kate said. 'And, when the Rower threw the ball, she caught it!'

My room-mate looked at me proudly and reached over to pat my shoulder.

I nodded solemnly. 'Right between my boobs.'

Pat, who was lounging with his legs stretched out in the grass, whistled in admiration. 'Maybe your boobs should get in on this football game then.'

'Oh *hell*, no,' I said, lighting a clove. 'This hit my exercise quota for the month.' I looked at Mary Kate and said, 'I'll be on the sideline cheering you on – but you're on your own, Cupcake Pants.'

The Saturday of Mary Kate's flag football debut was rainy and cold. I was huddled on the sideline, shivering in my pleather jacket. But Mary Kate, thanks to three more football lessons from Pat, was in full game mode. Having decided that her cupcake-print pajamas might not be the most intimidating, she was dressed in a grey varsity sweatsuit she'd borrowed, and I had braided her two braids together into a single MegaBraid that was way more Khaleesi and way less Laura Ingalls Wilder. The red football flags dangling from her waist seemed to give her a bit of swagger.

The other Bonecrushers were out on the field doing a light warm-up – you know, stretching, sprinting, cracking people's skulls open. The usual. As my room-mate jogged in place, Pat, still in his fleece and basketball shorts despite the damp wind, gave me advice about how to support her.

'Winning is all about that killer drive,' he said. 'You need to get Mary Kate in the right frame of mind. We need her pumped up. We need her *angry*. You told me she threw a killer spiral that day on the quad; that was because she was pissed off. So let's piss her off again.'

'Look at this weather, Mary Kate,' I said. 'It *sucks*. It's cold and it's rainy and it *sucks*. Fuck Minnesota! And it's only gonna get worse. Snow is coming, and frostbite, and those icy-ass temperatures that freeze your nose hairs . . .'

Mary Kate was just nodding. I had to get more personal.

'Ooh, what about Caleb?' I said. 'He chose Jesus over you! And now Jesus is smugly hanging in every classroom on this campus, flaunting his abs and rubbing it in!'

Mary Kate started jogging faster.

'He was supposed to walk you around the lake, and he didn't,' I continued. 'Now you'll probably *never* walk around the lake with anyone.'

Her eyes narrowed. It was working.

'I bet the freshmen in our dorm will walk around the lake before you do.'

Her jaw clenched.

I glanced at the team warming up on the field and saw the girl with the sprained arm take down two huge guys at once. Time to deal the final blow.

Gripping Mary Kate by the shoulders, I looked into her eyes and said, '*I'm* gonna walk around the lake before you do. And *I think that shit is stupid*.'

That was all she needed. Her shoulders tensed into tight knots of rage under my hands, and she tore off her sweatshirt. There she stood in her T-shirt, damn the cold and rain. She slammed her fist into her open palm. This was Mary Kate's version of Hulking out.

'It's go time!' she shouted.

'Okay, so remember what you learned,' Pat told her. 'You are the quarterback. Your job is to throw the ball. Your worst enemies are the offensive linesmen. Their job is to tackle you before you can throw the ball. I mean, grab your flags.' He glanced out onto the field where that giant Chicken Wings man was squatting in the grass, spitting blood. 'No, probably tackle.'

'Let them try!' Mary Kate growled. 'Let those offensive linesmen *try* to tackle me! I am a brick wall! I am a skyscraper!'

Okay, so the girl was quoting Demi Lovato songs, but whatever gets you pumped up. And she was definitely pumped up. When Football Michael ran over to join us, slung an arm around her shoulders and asked, 'Hey, QB! You wanna run out there and toss me a few to warm up that killer arm of yours?' she shook her head emphatically.

'No need. I'm ready to kick butt!'

'That's the spirit!' Football Michael gave her an enthusiastic high five, which had to have hurt her hand like hell, but my room-mate didn't show it. She was too busy jogging in place, kicking her knees up and punching the air in front of her.

'Oh look!' Football Michael said. 'Here comes the other team. Now they're pretty tough. They're first in the league right now. But I think we can take 'em.'

'Hell, *yeah*, we can take 'em!' Mary Kate said. 'We're gonna take 'em *down*! We're gonna *murder* them! This is gonna be mass murder! This is gonna be like one of those serial-killer shows I'm too scared to watch by myself!'

'We may need to work on her trash talk,' Pat whispered to me.

'Now show me the offensive linesmen,' Mary Kate ordered Football Michael. 'Show me those pathetic, sneering *weaklings* on that other team who think they can get me. As if!'

Until now, girlfriend had been jumping, kicking and punching like she was in that tae-bo DVD my middle-school gym coach used to put on when she was too hungover to teach. My room-mate was pumped. She was fired up. She was hardcore. She was ready for action. Then Football Michael squinted across the grey, overcast field and pointed to the approaching team – specifically, to two members.

'There!' he said. 'Those are the offensive linesmen.'

Mary Kate stopped jogging. She stopped mid-punch, and her arms dropped to her sides. Her mouth fell open. Her shoulders slumped and all the color drained from her face. I can only describe it as de-Hulkifying. A second ago, she'd been a killer, a champion, a Bonecrusher. Now she was terrified, trembling all over, and squeaking like a mouse in a Pixar movie.

'*Them?*' she squeaked.

I looked. My stomach sank. 'Oh shit.'

Coming towards us, towering over our heads like massive redwood trees in the XXL blood-red shirts of the opposing team, making the field tremble beneath our feet with every step their size-13 cleats took, were a pair of six-foot-two, incredibly muscular, ruthless athletes with matching scowls on their faces.

Pat pushed his shaggy hair back for a better look. 'Are those . . . ?'

'The Rowers,' Mary Kate breathed.

'What are the friggin' chances?' I said in awe.

For years, we had lived in terror of these enormous women. For years, we had tiptoed down the hallway, hushing each other as we passed their door, not daring to take the last Kit-Kat in the vending machine for fear of retribution, never removing laundry from the dryer in case it was one of the dreaded XXL grey Varsity Crew sweatshirts, never completely relaxed in our own home.

Now this fearsome two-headed monster was looming above us, ready to swallow Mary Kate whole.

A shrill whistle blew. The referee called out, 'GAME TIME! QUARTERBACKS ON THE FIELD FOR THE COIN TOSS!'

Football Michael clapped Mary Kate on the back. 'Let's go, QB!'

I have to hand it to the girl: as she walked out to face the firing squad, her plastic flags were flapping in the wind, but her Khaleesi braids did not budge an inch, and she held her head high.

'You can do it, Mary Kate!' Pat called after her, but his words were carried away by the wind.

14

'You know, it could have been worse.'

Those were the half-assed words of reassurance I offered as, two hours after the football game, I stood next to Mary Kate's hospital bed in the school infirmary.

'I mean, look at *that* girl,' I continued, gesturing to the next bed, where the previous Bonecrushers quarterback, Lauren, lay in a drugged, painkiller-induced sleep with her broken leg elevated with so many swings and pulleys it looked like she was in the sex dungeon from *Fifty Shades of Grey*.

'She's been here for, like, two weeks. The school nurse even bought her a Kindle Fire. And you only have to stay here overnight!'

Mary Kate didn't answer. She was conscious – now – but she refused to look at me. She was just staring up at the ceiling in despair in her mud-splattered shirt and sweatpants. The bedraggled red flags still hung from her waist. I kept up a cheery stream of conversation – at least what I *thought* was a cheery stream of conversation. I may have gauged incorrectly the amount of humor that Mary Kate found in her situation when she was lying in an infirmary bed and missing out on the possibility of seeing victory Gatorade droplets running down Football Michael's beautiful abs. And actually it *was* possible it had been a victory; Pat had stepped in as quarterback after carrying Mary Kate off the field and putting her on a stretcher.

'You know, as an advanced lit student, you should really appreciate the irony of all this!' I said. 'I mean, just last week, in the very conversation that set this whole situation in motion, you said you wouldn't mind breaking your nose! Because your nose isn't what's important, your brain is! And now your brain is perfectly fine – which we know because the doctor did all those tests – and your nose . . .'

I trailed off. Even though Mary Kate's face wasn't at its most expressive or mobile right now, somehow she was still managing to shoot me her trademark Demon Anne of Green Gables Death Glare . . . over the plaster mask of bandages that would be covering her fractured nose for the next few weeks.

I stood with my motorcycle boots planted on the old floorboards of the McLaughlin stage, facing Katie Casey while gripping a long wood-and-metal object and trembling with rage.

'You are not taking this away from me,' I warned her. 'You've already taken away my vagina. You are not taking away *this*. *This* is a symbol!'

And I thrust it over my head defiantly.

The symbol was, technically, one of Tiny Tim's crutches from an old production of *A Christmas Carol*. Pat had found it backstage when I asked him to help me build something for the *Monologues*. It was an essential element of my directorial vision: Claudia was going to perform her monologue spread-eagled, with her legs up in a set of gynecologist's stirrups. And Tiny Tim's crutches were going to become the stirrups.

'I'm just not sure it's appropriate onstage,' Katie explained again.

I rolled my eyes, lowering the crutch and leaning it against my leg. 'She's going to be wearing pants!' Then I looked over at Claudia, who was trying to selfie-video herself doing a yoga sun salute in a sports bra, and added, 'Probably.'

For two weeks before the fateful football game, we had been putting together *The Non-Vagina Monologues*. Claudia and I had recruited her Drama Club friends to perform alongside our own Feminist Club members. Robbie Schmidt and I had negotiated his role moving props back-stage in a black turtleneck after he almost passed out in the first read-through and refused to perform. Mary Kate and I had – according to the heavy compromise Father Vincent had coughed out of her – painfully cut every vagina out of *The Vagina Monologues*, and all the best curse words, too. And, for the past week, we had spent every afternoon after classes in McLaughlin Hall with the Save Your Heart army, figuring out the logistics of the event and making decisions about timing, lighting and props.

There was friction, to say the least. But Mary Kate had been there every step of the way – not only entirely rewriting the play with me and coming up with vaginal euphemisms ranging from 'body' and 'private parts' to 'down below' – which made it sound like you could find the clitoris on a globe somewhere around New Zealand – but playing peacemaker between me and Katie Casey, too.

But Mary Kate wasn't here anymore; she was hiding her plastered nose back at the dorm, only leaving (with a scarf wrapped around her face) when she had to go to class. She wasn't even coming to rehearsals. And now, at a rehearsal that had run so late we had all missed dinner, the friction was about to spark into a fire.

'I just don't know about Claudia being in that position onstage,' Katie said.

'That *position*,' I informed her, 'is for medical reasons. This isn't Claudia doing a striptease.' Again I looked over at Claudia doubtfully. 'Probably. This is a medical procedure. People should know about pap smears and personal health.'

'You're totally right, Alex; I totally agree with you that health is important. I just don't think this needs to be right out here onstage. The whole idea of Save Your Heart is saving some things – some special, personal things – just for ourselves.'

'You mean hiding things and being ashamed of them,' I shot back.

Claudia looked up from filming herself. 'You know,' she informed us, 'I don't even *need* the stirrups. I'm perfectly capable of spreading my legs for extended periods of time.'

That deserved some kind of joke, but I was not in the mood. Instead, I picked up the crutch again and told Katie Casey, 'Either I get my stirrups, or this thing gets shoved up –'

'Good evening, ladies and gentleman!'

I whirled around, crutch in hand, to see Father Hughes coming down the aisle, smiling calmly. *Fantastic*. What? Had Katie Casey secretly sent up the virgin signal? No, she didn't need to. Father Hughes was our faculty advisor now. He could come waltzing in, in those doomsday priest shoes, anytime he wanted and take control.

No way in hell was I getting my stirrups now.

Calmly surveying the terrified cluster of Save Your Heart girls in the wings, Claudia in her sports bra, Katie Cascy and I facing off center stage and the crutch raised menacingly in my hand, Father Hughes asked, 'Is there some kind of problem here?'

'Only the continued destruction of my creative vision,' I fumed. 'Apparently, *Ms* Casey doesn't appreciate my "original thinking", which you're always talking about when I get dragged up to your office.'

Katie Casey explained the stirrups in her own annoyingly sweet way, concluding, 'But I'm sure together we can find a more appropriate way to stage it.'

Father Hughes began, 'I'm afraid I'll have to agree with –'

But, before he could continue, Pat interrupted him, coming forward from the back of the stage where he'd started building the chair part of the stirrups. He was in his after-hours clothes, baggy jeans and a navy crew neck with the sleeves pushed up above his elbows. He set down his power drill carefully – and, pointedly, out of my reach.

'I had an idea,' he volunteered. 'Kind of a . . . compromise.'

'By all means, Mr Clarke-McCann,' Father Hughes said. 'Let's hear it.'

'Oh yes, by all means,' I echoed mockingly. 'Katie and I are discussing important and sensitive issues involving women's health and self-expression so, by all means, let's step aside so the men can have the floor. What is this, Congress?'

Pat ignored that. 'Have you guys heard of Thornton Wilder?'

'No,' I said irritably, putting one hand on my hip. 'But if he's a freakin' priest I don't want to hear about him.'

'He was the playwright who wrote *Our Town*,' Pat continued. 'And, when they performed *Our Town* for the first time, all they had onstage was, like, a ladder. It was totally minimalist. Basically *no props*.'

He looked between me and Katie Casey meaningfully. After a second, it sank in.

'WHAT?' I burst out. 'No stirrups? You're on her side, too? I knew *he* would be –' I pointed accusingly at Father Hughes – 'but *you*? What, are you hooking up with her, too? Or, like, spooning her and watching *Frozen*, or whatever her G-rated version of hooking up is?'

Katie Casey looked totally confused, and her little Save Your Hearts were creeping forward from the wings, watching in fascination.

'Hold on,' Pat cautioned me. 'I'm talking about seriously minimalist here. So we get rid of the stirrups . . .'

I balked, but he held up his hand to stop me and continued: 'And we also get rid of THAT.'

All our heads turned to the back of the stage, behind the parted red velvet curtains, where there stood, at least seven feet tall, casting its inescapable shadow over the whole stage, a massive wooden cross.

'No stirrups,' Pat concluded. 'And no cross.'

Father Hughes spoke up immediately. 'That sounds fair enough to me. What do you think, Ms Casey?'

'Well, I guess no props at all would be easier,' she admitted hesitantly. 'I was worried about getting everything done in time.'

Father Hughes looked to me. 'Ms Heck?'

'Fine,' I said. 'Whatever. I don't even care anymore.'

But I did care.

Backstage there was a lofted storage room where the theater kids kept all the props and costumes from school shows, and I sat there for a long time on King Arthur's Round Table, brooding over the event schedule for the Save Your Heart Festival.

Welcome Blessing by Sister Winnifred. That was Katie Casey's.

Saturday afternoon, group workshop – *What Does Purity Mean to You?* That was Katie Casey's.

Sunday morning – *Post-Mass Doughnut Decorating.* That was Katie Casey's – although I was definitely gonna eat a doughnut.

I had ONE thing on the whole schedule, ONE thing: *Performance by the St Mary's Feminist Club: An Extract from the Works of Eve Ensler.* The one thing on there that was mine, and I didn't even get to do it the way I wanted.

When rehearsal was done and everyone else had left, Pat came backstage to join me.

'I'm sorry about your stirrups,' he said, hopping up on the Round Table next to me. 'I felt like I had to step in. I mean, I'm stage manager here. It would be my job to scrub Katie Casey's blood out of the floorboards, so I wanted to prevent violence if possible.'

'Yeah, whatever.'

His voice softened. 'But I *am* sorry about the stirrups. I know they were important to you.'

'Yeah, they ARE important to me,' I said. 'Do you know how scary and weird it is the first time you go to the gynecologist? Especially when you're totally clueless going into it and the whole place looks like a torture chamber from a Japanese horror movie and your DAD is out in the waiting room, reading an article in *Shape* magazine about how to Get Your Best Butt Ever.'

Pat raised his eyebrows under his messy hair. 'Your dad took you to the gynecologist?'

'Yeah. I was living with him at the time. My parents had just gotten divorced, so –'

'How old were you?'

'Thirteen.'

He whistled softly. 'Not a fun age to start with. Why did your parents get divorced?'

'My dad made all this money on some tech stock thing, and he was really amped about it and wanted to buy this big new house and this mid-life-crisis car . . . at the exact same time my mom decided we should embrace "anti-materialism". In fact, she was so anti-materialistic that she dematerialized completely in a puff of patchouli-scented air and a postcard three times a year from a Buddhist meditation retreat.'

Pat had found one of the leftover beards from *Fiddler on the Roof* and he put it on, hooking the elastic over his ears. He stroked it wisely and said, 'Ah, so that explains it.'

'Explains what?'

'Why you care about this play. Why you ditch school to take freshmen to Planned Parenthood.' He stroked the beard again, putting on a terrible Austrian accent: 'It all stems from zee traumatic experience of your *fah-zer* and zee stirrups and zee *Shape* magazine, *ja?*'

'Thank you, Dr Freud.' I rolled my eyes. Then, after a minute, I said, 'You know, the weird thing is, my dad and I actually got along pretty well when I was living with him. I mean, he had a pool so that helped. But then, as soon as the divorce was final, he shipped me off to St Mary's.'

Pat still had the silly grey beard on, but his face was serious. His eyes were so soft and brown – no hint of that teasing glint in them now.

'Actually, *that's* kind of why I started this whole *Vagina Monologues* thing,' I confessed. 'I told everyone that I care about St Mary's, and want to change things, and help all the clueless freshmen who think a pap smear is someone insulting the pope. But really I just wanted to piss off Father Hughes and get sent home . . . to live with my dad in California. But I should've known it wouldn't work. At the beginning of the semester, I was in big trouble – my dad even flew in to talk to Father Hughes. I thought he was definitely gonna take me home then, but he didn't.'

I picked up a ruby slipper from *The Wizard of Oz* and threw it over the cardboard hillside from *The Sound of Music*.

'He'd rather have me die here of torture-inflicted Catholic frostbite at the hands of a sadistic priest than actually be a dad,' I finished bitterly. 'He wants me to be miserable.'

Silence. Pat had picked up a cowboy hat from *Oklahoma!* and was turning it around in his hands. 'Maybe he doesn't want you to be miserable.'

'Well, he's not doing a great job at it.'

'The middle-aged are not always on point when it comes to dealing with their kids,' Pat said. 'I mean, does my mom commenting "hot stuff" every time I change my profile picture boost my self-confidence, like she's hoping? No.

It gets my head shoved in a duffel bag full of jockstraps. But she has good intentions. Didn't you say your dad went to St Mary's? And played hockey, and won the championship, and all that stuff, right? And those were, like, the best years of his life?'

He placed the cowboy hat softly on my head.

'Maybe he thinks it'll be the same for you,' he said. 'Maybe he thinks St Mary's will kinda be like a family for you, since yours split up.'

I sighed. 'Well, my dad is delusional, especially when it comes to St Mary's. He thinks there's some, like, secret spy tunnels under the campus. He's seriously clueless.' I shook my head.

Then I saw that Pat was looking at me strangely – narrowing his eyes as if he was trying to make a decision about something. I guess suddenly he decided because he hopped off the Round Table and held out his hand.

'I wanna show you something,' he said.

'If it's a duffel bag full of jockstraps, I think I'll stay here, thanks.'

'Get your coat,' he whispered. 'We're going for a walk.'

Running around campus at night always gives me a rush. Two beams of light – our phones on flashlight mode – led the way as we hurried into the October wind, the old stone dorms sleeping in the dark around us, eerie dark clouds shifting in the deep purple sky above the lake. It was close to curfew, and everyone was already in their dorms. Everyone except us. We were in disguise – Pat still in the fake beard, me in the cowboy hat – and it was easy to imagine we were spies on a secret mission.

'Here,' Pat said suddenly. He tugged down the fake beard so it hung down the front of his fleece like a scarf.

'Wait . . .' I frowned and looked around suspiciously.

Before, when I'd noticed those spooky clouds gathering over the lake, I hadn't totally realized that we were heading *towards* the lake – and now we stood mere feet from the stone steps that led down to that infamous pathway . . .

'Oh HELL, no!' I spluttered, my voice ringing out in the cold air. 'You want to walk around the LAKE with me? If you think I'm the kind of girl who wants to walk around the LAKE, then clearly you've taken one too many hockey pucks to the face . . .'

'Not *there*,' Pat corrected me impatiently, waving his hand towards the lake. '*Here*. Right here.'

He shone his phone light down at his Chuck Taylors. He was standing on a metal grate.

'The sewer?' I said.

'Trust me.' He squatted and started turning the criss-cross metal grate.

I sighed. 'Well, we've been flirty-texting for a few weeks now, so I guess it was inevitable – this was the time in the relationship when you'd show me your underground lair.'

I squatted to help Pat lift the heavy grate and push it over into the grass. Kneeling on either side, we shone our lights down into the void.

'I'm going in,' Pat declared cheerfully.

'WHAT?' I couldn't believe what I was hearing. 'Are you serious?'

But already he was lowering himself into the hole, gripping the grass on either side, and then he disappeared completely into the darkness.

'Come down!' his echoey voice called up to me. 'There's steps!'

It turned out to be true. Of course, by the time I confirmed that, I had already stuffed my iPhone in my jacket pocket, tightened the laces on my motorcycle boots, gritted my teeth and accepted my impending death. Then I lowered myself down into the hole, my arms trembling (*friggin' fake fitness-test pull-ups AGAIN!*), flailed my legs in hopeless panic for several adrenaline-fueled seconds, and finally, with relief, found somewhere solid to rest my feet – a wooden platform cut into the side of the tightly packed earth wall.

There *were* steps.

It wasn't long before, using the wooden steps as a ladder, I touched down on the soft dirt bottom of the – Where the hell was I?

Turning around, I saw by the light of Pat's phone a long, long pathway stretching ahead of me, as far as I could squint into the darkness. It went on, and on, and on . . .

'Oh my God,' I breathed in disbelief.

The tunnels – the mythical tunnels under St Mary's – were real.

'Right this way, ma'am,' Pat said in his chipper fake-tour-guide voice, waving me forward with his light. 'Our next St Mary's underground tour will be departing in approximately eight seconds. Please fasten your seat belts and keep all arms and legs inside the trolley. No gum-chewing, profanity or flash photography.'

He flipped the phone back towards me and shone the light in my face. 'I meant that one about the damn profanity, Heck.' Then he snapped his fingers. 'Gosh darnit, Heck, I've broken my own profanity rule! Well, fuck it. Let's explore these motherfuckin' tunnels.'

There we were, twenty feet under St Mary's. The tunnels were pretty friggin' legit: ten feet wide, and so tall that even the seven-foot center on the basketball team (who I'm pretty sure has the coach mixing human growth hormone into his Powerade) could stand up straight in them. And they weren't some kind of accidental geological formation either: someone had built them on purpose, and they'd done a good job, too. Shining my phone light upward, I saw there were wrought-iron archways every ten feet or so, and even old-school metal lanterns hanging from them, although they weren't lit.

'How long has this been here?' I marveled.

'Forever,' Pat told me over his shoulder. 'Some people think the school was part of the Underground Railroad. Other people said moonshine smuggling during Prohibition or something.'

'Moonshine smuggling at St Mary's?' I scoffed. 'Yeah, right. More likely the school dug them so priests and nuns could scurry around spying on everyone, and make sure no one was dry-humping during vespers.'

'Here.' Pat suddenly stopped short. 'So, right now, we're standing directly under the main building.' He shone his flashlight and I saw that the tunnel curved sharply to the right. 'And in that direction is Girls' Quad.'

'How the hell long is this thing?'

'Oh, you ain't seen nothin' yet. It goes on forever, dude. There's another exit in Girls' Quad – the grate behind St Anne Hall – but the tunnels keep going. They circle around behind the main building, then Boys' Quad, then straight back down the whole avenue. The only place under St Mary's that isn't tunneled is the lake – that's why we started by the staircase down to the lake path. C'mon.'

He set off at a little jog, his light flashing in the dark. Usually, Pat sauntered. But, in the tunnels, he was excited. He wanted to impress me.

And I was impressed. But, as we curved along in the dark, me running my hands along the packed-dirt walls and the rusted iron of the archways, I began to get a little annoyed, too.

'So these tunnels have been here all along,' I said. 'And we still have to walk to class when it's negative-forty wind chill with snowdrifts up to my tits? We could be strolling along down here all warm and cozy, sipping hot cocoa. Total bullshit!'

'They're *secret* tunnels. That's the whole fun of it! No one's supposed to know about them.'

'So how do *you* know about them?'

'All the hockey guys do. Every year we do this ritual with the freshmen hockey players. We wake them up at midnight, pull them out of their beds, drop them down in the tunnels and shut the sewer grates. No phones, no flashlights, nothing. Just them in the dark. If they find their way out, they make the team. If they don't . . . well . . . watch out for that skull right there . . .'

I tripped over a rock and screamed. Pat burst out laughing.

'You jerk,' I said. 'You know, it's really unfair that you guys get to sneak around down here and no one else does.'

'Not only that,' he added. 'We carve our names down here, too. Major conquistador complex going on. Look.'

He shone his light on the next iron archway. It began with 1932. The year was carved high up on the iron archway, a foot above my head, and below it were the initials, all down the rusty metal surface: J. D., T. S., M. O. D. . . .

'I think it's pretty rad,' Pat said. 'Look at how long this has been going on. World War Two, Kennedy, the sixties! The summer of love . . .'

'All hockey players?' I shook my head. 'Just another example of the patriarchy at work. Yet another reason the only people who ever have any fun at this school are you Gatorade-guzzling cavemen . . .'

But my rant drifted off because we were in the eighties now. I was curious. I slowly approached the next archway and shone my flashlight up at it: 1989.

That year was special. Carved under 1989 was a sentence: *We Brought It Home: NATIONAL CHAMPIONS!*

And under that were the initials . . . I slid my finger down the letters until I found it: T. I. H.

Thomas Ian Heck.

'My dad,' I said softly. 'I can't believe he was actually right about the tunnels.'

Even in the dark, I could hear the soft rustle of Pat's hair as he shook his head. 'O ye of little faith.'

Little faith, sure. But as we switched off our phone lights and walked side by side, bumping shoulders in the velvety dark deep under the school, feeling our way along the walls, inhaling the sweet, rich smell of the earth, I did feel *something*. Amazement. Wonder. Shock maybe that there was anything cool on the St Mary's campus, even if it was something we had to shimmy down a sewer drain to access. Shock that my dad hadn't been bullshitting me. I mean, how are you ever supposed to trust parents after all those lies they feed you about the Tooth Fairy and watermelons growing in your stomach? But he had been telling the truth . . .

And there was some part of him down here, carved here, permanently, part of St Mary's forever. Some part of him and – kind of, by extension, if you thought about all that Mendelian genetics crap I slept through in freshman biology – some part of me. That had been here before I was even born. That would be here long after I graduated.

We Brought It Home.

'You know,' Pat said, 'I have my own theory about where these tunnels came from.'

'Oh yeah? Underground nuclear-missile silo from the Cold War? Secret superhero lab for the biology department to breed a she-hulk for the impending apocalypse? Wait, that would explain the Rowers!'

Pat ignored me. 'I think,' he continued, 'back in the 1930s, a St Mary's student fell in love with one of the novices in the convent by the lake – they were the only girls on campus then. So he started digging a tunnel, and every night he would sneak out and dig a few feet. And eventually he got all the way down to the lake. And they would meet in secret, here –'

Before he could finish, I reached out for him in the dark, steered him into the soft earth wall and began to kiss him.

November

15

It was friggin' cold. Outside, wind howled in the quad. Bare branches clawed at the frost on our windowpanes. We sprinted from class to class with our hoods up, and athletes rode their bikes with their hands jammed in their coat pockets, racing dangerously into the wind without touching the icy handlebars. Inside, Uggs smelling like damp dog lined the dorm hallways. Radiators clanked and hissed and steamed.

I barely noticed. I was too busy running around, doing a million things for *The Non-Vagina Monologues*. There were rehearsals to direct, playbills to write, flyers to print, Katie Casey to annoy as much as possible without Pat dropping a spotlight on my head. So I dug my fleece-lined tights out of my army duffel bag, pulled a beanie on my head, even though it crushed my lady-fauxhawk, and got on with things. And, as much as I hate to admit this about a school-approved event – especially one involving a whole club of doe-eyed Bible thumpers, Sister Winnifred and four dozen virginal doughnuts – I was actually getting excited about it. I even thought about making a Vagina

Advent Calendar counting down the days to the show, with a different happy, dancing vagina hiding behind each little cardboard door, but I was way too busy.

Mary Kate was busy, too. But, while I was running around campus with three sweatshirts on, she was shut up inside our room, deeply and obsessively focused. My roommate was transforming.

You know that part in every superhero movie where the young pre-hero, reeling from the tragedy of witnessing their parents murdered in cold blood, must travel to the remote mountains to find a wise and ancient Zen master? And then there's a whole training montage with the young hero blindfolded, sword-fighting with sticks, hiking mountains and all that crap? And, at the end, they emerge a powerful warrior with ripped biceps and cheetah-like reflexes and usually a bandana, finally ready to seek bloody revenge on their enemies?

That was sort of what Mary Kate was doing right now, except her end goal wasn't bloody revenge. Which is kind of a shame – bloody revenge would have been way more interesting and I definitely would have lent her my duvet to drag a body down to the lake. But no, Mary Kate's goal was a boyfriend, and she was transforming herself into a master seductress.

How exactly was she doing this? Well, the girl was a friggin' nerd, so mostly she was reading. I mean, she was always reading, but now, instead of the historical novels she loved where a feisty heroine overcame a deadly cholera outbreak armed only with her underrated female brain and her trusty embroidery needle, her desperation had driven her to self-help and dating books. *Men Are from Mars, Women Are from Venus* to understand the oh-so-complex male mind (barf); *The Rules* for archaic 1940s dating tips and *Taylor Swift's Guide to Mass Mind Control.* (Okay, I may have made that one up.) Beyond that, she was watching TED Talks on body language and make-up tutorials on YouTube. Also, she had learned the entire fan dance from *Memoirs of a Geisha* and ordered pheromone attraction perfume from a sketchy online herbalist named Madame Moon.

The transformation was in process: Mary Kate was on her way to becoming an eyelash-curling, pheromone-emitting, conversation-manipulating virtuoso of flirting and seduction. More importantly, she had cultivated the obsessive and nearly psychotic mindset of ruthless determination that teenage boys find so attractive in a girl.

Oh wait. Well, anyway.

I was worried about her. I mean, I also thought she was an idiot, but I was worried about her nonetheless. She barely left the dorm. She just sat on our futon, wrapped in a furry blanket with her bandaged face buried in book after book. Even for Halloween last month, she refused to go out to either the lame school-sponsored dance where freshmen guys threw candy corn at everyone or the after-party in Pat's dorm that got busted by the dorm priest.

'Come on!' I'd urged her. 'This is the perfect chance to go out! It doesn't matter that you look freaky! Everyone looks freaky tonight!'

Somehow that didn't convince her, although she didn't even remark on my freaky comment. Instead, gravely serious, she quoted poetry:

'*At my back I always hear, Time's wingèd chariot hurrying near.*'

I rolled my eyes. Leave it to my room-mate to take life advice from a poem where a creep in linen breeches tries to convince a virgin to bone him before they both die of plague.

And, while I had barely noticed the cold, Mary Kate was all too aware of it and what it meant: the first snow was coming. With a full week left of her masked face, and the temperature dropping and ominous grey clouds gathering over the lake, a sense of desperate urgency fueled her to the brink of hysteria. One night, when we heard a rapping sound at our window, she jumped off the futon as if someone had shoved an icicle down her pants.

'Is that hail?' she asked frantically. 'Hail doesn't count! Hail is NOT snow! I still have time!'

'Relax,' I told her, leaning across my desk to open the window. 'It's just Pat. He's bringing me his old physics report to copy. And a Snickers, if he knows what's good for him.'

Relieved, Mary Kate sat back down and returned to her latest creepy task: identifying potential targets. With our school yearbook open in her lap and a red Sharpie in her hand, she was combing painstakingly through the male population of St Mary's, labeling them 'Girlfriend', 'Too Young' or 'Too Mean' based on information she'd gathered via gossip in our dorm laundry room, online and from her own female intuition.

'You know,' I told her, after I'd shut the window and Pat had jogged away across the howling quad, 'you should really put these skills to better use. You could go into Central Intelligence. You could negotiate peace talks with Putin. Of course, you'd have to ride a horse topless with him, but you're a My Little Pony fan. I'm sure you've fantasized about that at some point.'

Completely ignoring my suggestion, she looked up from the yearbook. 'What about Chase Rajatowski? You've never seen him with a girl, have you?'

'No . . .' I said, tossing her one of the candy bars Pat had smartly brought. 'But I do see him with Father O'Hanlon a lot . . .'

She frowned for a moment, then drew a decisive red X through Chase Rajatowski.

And then, one day, she was ready.

It was Friday afternoon, exactly one week before the show. I was on my way out of the door with a stack of flyers in my hand, heading to Boys' Quad to invite some guys to *The Non-Vagina Monologues*.

Save Your Heart and the Feminist Club were both technically co-ed, but, in reality, they were mostly female – and the festival probably would be, too. Not just all girls, but all girls like Katie Casey: bubble-headed, pink-sprinkled purity doughnuts in human form.

So I was going after a new demographic. And I had designed a very different handout: something eye-catching, tantalizing, with edge and sex appeal. The flyer announced a FREE can't-miss performance of *'An Extract from the Works of Eve Ensler ... author of The VAGINA Monologues!!!'* All that was printed in bold against a background of a Georgia O'Keefe painting to inspire subconscious erotic thoughts. Clearly, Mary Kate's reading about subliminal mind control had subliminally seeped into my subconscious and was controlling my mind, but it was all for the better.

Then, just as I headed out, making sure my stack of flyers were *VAGINA* side up in case I ran into Sister Hellda, Mary Kate stopped me and said very dramatically: 'WAIT!'

She rose from our futon. She shed her blanket cocoon. 'I'm coming with you.'

Then, standing in the center of our room, she took a deep breath, gripped the edge of the bandage covering her nose and ripped it right off her face.

I gasped. 'Mary Kate!'

She panicked and faltered suddenly, bringing both hands up to her nose. 'Wait, does it look okay? Technically, I wasn't supposed to take it off for three more days.'

'No, it looks good!' I took a step closer and squinted. 'And your skin looks really clear, too. I think the bandage acted like one of those blackhead pore-strip thingies.'

'All right.' She rubbed away the red marks on her cheeks where the bandage had been. 'Let's go talk to some boys.'

'Hi! I'm Alex, and this is Mary Kate. There's an amazing event going on next Friday night, and we wanted to invite you. The St Mary's Feminist Club is putting on a play called *An Extract from the Works of Eve Ensler*, who's the author of *The Vagina –*'

The word *vagina* was – as it had been for so many months now – the end of the conversation. The latest in a long string of preppy, freckle-faced boys who had opened his dorm door to us blushed bright red at the sound of the word, stuck his head anxiously out into the hall to check if his dorm priest was around and snatched the flyer quickly from my hand.

'Thanks,' he said anxiously, 'I'll think about it,' and slammed the door on us like we were a pair of pornographic Jehovah's Witnesses.

This was the eighteenth door we had knocked on, and our eighteenth rejection.

Mary Kate didn't care too much about that – she had her own goods to sell. And, this time around, we weren't talking Girl Scout cookies.

'You can bring your girlfriend!' she would say brightly, making intense eye contact, blinking her eyelashes, and trying to brush her hand subtly against his as she handed him the flyer. 'That is if you HAVE a girlfriend. DO you have a girlfriend . . . ?'

But, by then, the bright, suggestive shapes of the flyer, my purple hair and the word *vagina* throbbing like a neon sign in Mary Kate's hot, desperate hand had usually frightened the guy so much that the door was already slamming in our faces.

As we continued, though, some dudes *were* pretty inter-ested in a throbbing neon vagina. At St Ambrose Hall, a guy in a sweatshirt with the sleeves ripped off grabbed the flyer, flexing his biceps noticeably. When he saw the word *vagina*, his eyebrows rose in interest.

'There gonna be nudity at this thing?' he asked, looking from me to Mary Kate.

'No!' Mary Kate said immediately.

'Sure!' I said at the exact same time.

When my room-mate frowned at me, I amended my answer, 'Well . . . some. PG-thirteen at least. And it's free! See ya Friday!'

On the top floor of St James Hall, a senior opened the door to a messy four-guy suite with a bay window obscured by two sets of unmade bunk beds and greeted us with a Twizzler hanging out of his mouth. He snatched the flyer from Mary Kate's hand and studied it. Seeing the word *vagina*, he nodded, intrigued. Then he noticed the venue at the bottom.

'McLaughlin?' he said. 'Isn't that the place with the ghost?'

He snapped off the end of his Twizzler, turned around and called to his room-mate, who was sunk into a giant beanbag chair, frowning at his math textbook, 'Yo, Paulie, you wanna go to some haunted vagina thing?'

Paulie threw his textbook down and hopped up from the giant beanbag in enthusiasm. 'Hell, yeah!'

So that made at least three boys for our audience. We weren't exactly on a roll, but we were still going and Mary Kate was still by my side. When we came across rowdy jerkoffs playing catch in the hallway, she raised her hand to her nose protectively, but still braved her way to the next door. And, on the third floor of St Francis Hall, she was rewarded for it.

To me, the ordinary preppy dude who opened this door – our eighty-first – was nothing special. But, to be fair, sometimes looking at too many homogeneous, wholesome doofuses on this campus gives me face blindness. To Mary Kate, his telltale tasseled loafers and dopey face were a godsend.

'Theology John!' Mary Kate blurted out in surprise. Immediately, she turned bright red.

'Theology Mary Kate!' Theology John blurted out at almost the same moment. Immediately, he turned brighter red. Even his ears were crimson.

As much as my shriveled black heart hates to admit it, it was kinda cute. These two sexually clueless dorks were so clearly meant for each other.

'How are you?' Mary Kate asked.

'Good, how are you?' Theology John replied automatically.

'Good!' she answered, all blinky and alert. Then, after a second, panicking as if she'd forgotten her manners, 'How are you?'

This friggin' thing went on for nine whole minutes. I know because I finally had to look down at my phone when it became too cringeworthy to watch. There was Mary Kate, jumping from startled mode to Super Seductress, desperately flashing her oh-so-subtle signs of allure: blinking to show off her long, silky eyelashes, putting one hand on her hip to emphasize the ideal cavewoman breeding ratio of waist to hips, leaning forward to waft her pheromones towards Theology John and bursting out in hysterical strained laughter when he made the slightest attempt at a joke (and, trust me, this kid was about as funny as Paul's last letter to the Corinthians).

And there was poor terrified Theology John, shifting awkwardly from boat shoe to sweaty boat shoe, probably trying to conceal his theological boner in his basketball shorts, blushing and stuttering and smiling hopefully at Mary Kate as she smiled hopefully at him during one of the long silences that I wondered if I should interrupt with a dirty joke. It was like a Wild West shoot-out between two scared virgins armed only with their social awkwardness and fear of rejection, each daring the other to shoot first.

Finally, one of the silences lasted so long that Theology John wussed out and put down his weapon. 'Well,' he said reluctantly, 'I guess I should . . .' and glanced back into his room as if to indicate he had important code-cracking, top-level FBI shit to get back to, when in fact all that was waiting for him was an open bag of pretzels and the fifth level of *Mario Kart* on pause.

Mary Kate's face fell. 'Yeah,' she agreed reluctantly. 'Sure . . .'

But then, as he slowly began to close his door, courage seized her. The flush of her face from her bravely beating heart, the determined set of her jaw told me what she was thinking – *Fortune favors the bold! Faint heart never won fair lady!* (Or, you know, fair dude.)

She reached out and grabbed the door, startling him. Then, trembling with adrenaline, she blurted: 'Let's go out!'

He panicked. He blushed. He spluttered. But she didn't give him time to say no.

'Tomorrow night!' she rushed on, steamroller style, her voice breathless but loud and clear and decisive. 'Let's walk around the lake. Come to my dorm – St Theresa Hall – to the front door at seven. Okay?'

A tense moment of silence. Even I was anxious. My hand gripped the vagina flyers. All that hope and determination and desperation in Mary Kate's big Bambi eyes! If he said no, I would rip the dumb sweaty boat shoe off his dumb sweaty foot and beat him with it. Then I would eat his pretzels.

But instead he smiled. His face lit up, and I could kind of see why she thought he was cute.

'Okay.' He nodded and said again, more confidently, 'Okay. See you then.'

As soon as he closed the door, I lifted my hand for a high five.

'Proximity!' I said.

'Proximity!' Mary Kate cheered, and slapped my hand with a decisive, triumphant smack.

'This is it. I know it. I *feel* it. First there was "Father" Caleb. Then there was Football Michael. But this is my third guy of the semester, and the third time's a charm. I mean, look at the MOON! It's a sign!'

Mary Kate stood in raptures by the window. A full moon had risen in the lavender twilight. It was Saturday night, the night of her walk around the lake with Theology John, and the night was, as she would say, perfect. It was still chilly enough that she looked cute and bundly in her pompon hat with her rippled, unbraided hair streaming down her pea coat, but not so cold that she had to wear mittens – which, as she had informed me very scientifically back in August, would block the hand-holding love magic the lake uses to create lasting relationships.

Before she left, she took one last dramatic glance around our room.

'By the time I come back here,' she said with certainty, 'I will have a boyfriend.'

Then, as she skipped out the door, she called, 'Don't wait up!' But, just before it closed, she stuck her nose back in and said, 'Actually, do wait up because I want to tell you everything.'

Then the door shut and opened a final time, and she added, 'Not that you'd be asleep before eleven p.m. anyway.'

'Go, go!' I told her, waving her away.

It was Saturday night, I had the room to myself and I was doing homework. I know, I know. Who the hell am I these days? But all week I'd been in rehearsals for *The Non-Vagina Monologues*. The haunted theater had been bustling with live people for once, and I had been running around, yelling at Claudia when she 'improvised' new lines for her monologue, comforting freshmen with stage fright, and corralling everyone backstage and pushing them out into the bright stage spotlights. It had been chaos.

For weeks now, I had been handling my homework with a combination of feigned migraines and plagiarism, and it had caught up with me. I had forty-two geometry problems to do.

Luckily, I also had a Le Tigre album and a bag of Flamin' Hot Cheetos. But I had only finished twenty geometry problems – okay, and the entire bag of Cheetos – when my phone buzzed on my desk and I saw a text from Mary Kate that made me grab a hoodie and dash through the hallway without even bothering to close the door behind me.

Outside. Now.

Out on the quad, I squinted into the darkness for any sign of her. The campus was quiet and still under the full moon. Then I saw a lone figure hurrying along towards the Memorial Fountain.

The Memorial Fountain was built to honor St Mary's students who'd died in the Korean War. After we won the 1989 National Hockey Championship, all the students streaked Academic Quad and jumped, hooting and hollering, into the fountain. A picture of the ecstatic crowd in streaky green body paint splashing each other hangs in the student center. And my dad is in it, too (thankfully in his hockey jersey).

Jumping into the fountain became tradition. Every hockey win is followed by a wild orgy of water, green body paint and probably cum and who knows what else. Thanks for your service, Korean War vets.

Tonight, though, the fountain was quiet. Mary Kate crossed the quad towards it, stepped up onto the edge and then – without removing a single item of clothing – stepped into it and submerged herself fully.

'Mary Kate!' I shrieked, and raced over at lightning speed.

At the fountain, breathless, I clambered up the marble side, grabbed my room-mate under the arms and hauled her out. Shocked at being grabbed suddenly, she struggled, swatting at me as I sat her on the side of the fountain.

'Mary Kate!' I shouted. 'Don't DROWN yourself!'

'What are you talking about?' Mary Kate looked glum, but not suicidal. She tugged off her wet pompon hat and tilted her head to shake the water out of her ears, then pulled her loose wet hair out of her coat collar and twisted it back into a bun. 'I wasn't DROWNING myself.'

Immediately, I was unbuttoning her sopping wool pea coat and tearing it off, unlacing her sodden heavy boots and talking furiously. 'What did Theology John do to you? Did he try something weird? I'm telling you, it's always the shy guys who have secret, twisted fetishes. They're the ones who put on a Kermit the Frog mask, force you to recite the multiplication tables and pinch your nipples when you get the eights wrong. I KNEW there was something wrong with him! I mean, who wears boat shoes without socks in NOVEMBER? I am gonna KILL that kid. I am gonna make him so miserable –'

'You don't need to.' Mary Kate sighed, pulling her legs up to her chest. She finished unlacing her other boot and let it drop to the grass with a sad squish. 'I'm pretty sure he's miserable already.'

And then she told me what had happened. Because she refused to go inside – sticking to the fountain's marble ledge like a stubborn piece of pigeon crap – she told it to me right there, sitting on the Memorial Fountain, soaking wet, her bun drip-drip-dripping into the grass.

'I should have known something was wrong right away,' she began. 'When we met up, we hugged. And I *did* actually notice that he smelled like alcohol. But I remembered that Pat said John is super shy around girls, so I just thought maybe his friends gave him a beer because he was nervous about meeting me. Which I thought was cute!'

I was rubbing Mary Kate's shoulder, trying to keep the blood flowing from her broken heart around her frozen little body, but she was barely aware of how cold it was getting. And that it was almost curfew. Her sad-panda, mascara-smeared eyes were shining in the moonlight now as she remembered the most romantic part.

'You could see the full moon in the water, and "Moon River" from *Breakfast at Tiffany's* was playing in my head when he reached for my hand. We were holding hands! *This is it*, I told myself. *This isn't like Caleb. This time, we're making it all the way around the lake.*

'So we started walking. I got nervous when we got to the seminary, but John didn't say anything about being a priest or anything. He didn't even notice it. We were still walking. I got so excited that I actually got a chill up my spine. John thought I was cold, so he asked, "Do you want my coat?" because he had this big comfy parka that was warmer than my pea coat. But I was trying to be super polite so automatically I was like, "No, it's okay!" Then, of course, I spent the next hundred steps thinking, *You are so dumb – you could be wearing his coat right now! That would be so cute!*

'But it didn't matter. We were still walking, still holding hands. We were halfway around the lake. Three-quarters of the way. Everything was *perfect*. My heart was soaring. I was thinking, *This is my boyfriend! This is my soulmate! Screw ginger Rupert and his sonnets!*' Mary Kate took a deep breath. 'There was only one teeny-tiny problem: his palm was starting to get pretty sweaty.'

'Uh-oh.'

'But I didn't even think it was a bad thing! I thought it was a *good* thing. I was on such a high, I thought, *Great! His palm is sweating because his pulse is speeding up, because he's having some kind of biochemical love reaction!*'

It took a lot of focus to keep my mind on Mary Kate's story and not on what a great EDM band name Biochemical Love Reaction would be.

'And then he started stumbling,' she went on. She seemed to sag, like a sodden rag doll. 'And I've never heard of stumbling as a biochemical sign of love. But I tried to stay positive. I said to myself, *I haven't taken advanced bio yet so what do I know?*

'The end is in sight. We've made it ninety percent of the way around the lake, and we've been holding hands the whole time. Now his palm is really sweaty, but I don't even care. That sweat is the glue that's holding us together. I am GRATEFUL for that sweat. That sweat means we are going to make it. This guy is going to be my boyfriend, I'm finally going to have the St Mary's love story I've been waiting for.

'Then, suddenly, he starts to pull away,' she continued slowly. 'He says, "I think I just need a second . . ."'

I reached out and put a comforting hand on her leg.

'But my panic kicks in. I clamp onto his sweaty hand tighter. We're so close! I'm saying, "The stairs are right there!" but he's mumbling, "I need some air," and pulling away towards this bush. But I can't let go. I won't let go. I've waited sixteen years to hold a boy's hand and I've finally got one, a cute, preppy one who's getting an A in advanced theology, and I'm going to hold onto him, dammit!'

Her knuckles were white now as she gripped the side of the marble fountain.

'John was pulling away, but I refused to let go. Do you remember during the European history final when I really, really, really had to pee, but I had one last essay to write and I managed to scribble the whole thing like a crazy person, with an introduction and a thoughtful conclusion and everything, before I ran out of the room?'

I did remember. 'You got a perfect score.'

'I kept telling myself the same thing I said during that test: *Mind over matter, Mary Kate, mind over matter*, and with this great big adrenaline rush I yanked this six-foot-two kid away from the bush he was pulling towards and back to me.'

For a moment, there was a look of grim satisfaction on her mascara-streaked face, her little jaw firmly set, her hair slicked back like a battle helmet. Then, slowly, she turned to look at me at last.

'And that's when he puked all over me.'

I pulled my hand back from her leg. 'Ew, seriously?'

Then I looked back at the fountain. 'Oh! So that explains the drowning.'

'That explains the drowning,' Mary Kate said. 'I mean, I couldn't walk into our dorm and face Sister Hellda looking like the Creature from the Barf Lagoon.'

We got up and walked slowly across the quad, Mary Kate's eyes downcast, as if in mourning for the more innocent time before she knew what it was like to be puked on. We should have paid more attention when Pat told us that just one drink makes Theology John puke or pass out.

'Don't worry,' I told her. 'We'll go straight down to the laundry room and, if anyone else has stuff in the machine, I'll throw it right on the floor for you. Even the Rowers! We'll get your clothes totally clean and brand-new. All we need is a bottle of Febreze.'

A gust of wind across the quad blew another whiff of my room-mate's stink towards me and I amended my comment, 'Or an exorcism.'

'You know,' Mary Kate said sadly, 'I really wish I'd taken his coat.'

16

In McLaughlin Hall, my Feminist Club girls Sarah and Sophia sat on the edge of the stage in their uniforms, their legs chastely crossed at the ankles, their faces bathed in a beatific yellow glow.

First S1 spoke a line of their monologue, then S2 said the next. They took turns until the end, which they recited together in sweet unison:

'The heart is able to forgive and repair. It can change its shape to let us in.'

Claudia, Katie Casey, Robbie Schmidt and the Save Your Heart girls in the first row burst into applause. Smiling, S&S stood up and gave a modest little bow. The velvet curtains closed. The first full dress rehearsal of *An Extract from the Works of Eve Ensler* was complete.

And there was no way in hell it was getting me kicked out of St Mary's.

Up in the lighting booth suspended above the audience seats, I stood next to Pat at the sound and lighting boards.

'You're the stage manager,' I told him. 'Can't you do something to make that ending a little more . . . edgy? Project some satanic imagery behind them? Blast out Metallica's "Enter Sandman" when they walk onstage? That warm yellow light is so friggin' wholesome and heart-warming, it gives me stomach cramps.'

Pat switched the spotlight off and tugged his headphones down so they hung around his neck. 'Cheer up!' he said, clapping me on the back. 'Claudia's so intense, even without the stirrups, that after her everyone will need something a little softer.' Leaning closer to me, he whispered, 'But if people start to fall asleep I've got the *Grand Theft Auto* sound effects ready to go.'

It was Wednesday night. The dress rehearsal was over. It had run smoothly: everyone had been well behaved, smiling and enthusiastic. Father Hughes had watched the whole play from a third-row corner seat and, at the end, he stood up, did the sign of the cross to bless everyone and strolled out in contentment. Everything had gone well.

Now all the little Save Your Heart girls were hugging each other and saying, 'Should we go get hot cocoa? Oh my gosh, we should TOTALLY get hot cocoa!' I sat down at the edge of the lighting platform with my legs through the railings and my motorcycle boots dangling over the audience of empty seats and watched them.

Pat came over and sat next to me, dangling his Chuck Taylors.

'You know what I think?' he said. 'I think you were lying.'

'What? When?'

Pat looked at me in this way he has of looking at me . . . Priests and nuns might not have X-ray vision to see my leopard-print thong or my regrettable tattoo or my dark, twisted sinner's soul and black heart, but Pat had already seen the thong and the tattoo – and sometimes I felt like he could read my mind, too.

'I think you were lying to yourself,' he said. 'You told everyone else you wanted to put on *The Vagina Monologues* because you cared about sex and gender and all that stuff. And you do care about that stuff. But I also think you care about St Mary's. More than you realize.'

I sighed. 'Whatever I wanted to do, I don't think I did it. This play was supposed to force people here to talk about things they don't want to talk about. I didn't want Jesus in it; I didn't want his little minion Katie Casey in it. But I compromised and compromised and cut out F-bombs and compromised some more. And now, what was supposed to be *The Vagina Monologues* is, instead, a very special episode of *Peppa Pig* where Peppa gets her period.'

'Okay,' Pat acknowledged. 'It might be a baby step towards what you actually wanna do, but it's something. One small step for a vagina, one giant leap for vaginakind!'

I burst out laughing.

'And you had to compromise,' he added, 'or the show wouldn't exist at all.'

'Compromise.' I shook my head. 'Ugh. I hate that word.'

'Well, I have four sisters,' Pat said. 'I've spent my whole life compromising. I had to train myself to wake up at three a.m. to take a crap because that's the only time the bathroom was free. I used Lady Speed Stick deodorant for three years after puberty because my mom bought bargain packs from Costco and didn't want to waste it. Take it from me: compromise is sometimes necessary for survival.'

Our legs swung side by side, falling into the same rhythm. When I looked up, he was watching me, his eyes narrowed again in that reading-my-mind way.

'You're proud of it,' he said.

I rolled my eyes.

'C'mon! Admit it!' He nudged me with his shoulder. 'You're proud of *The Non-Vagina Monologues*.'

He kept nudging me, and I kept shaking my head, but I was changing my mind a little, too. It was true that I was excited about the show. Yes, I'd be sharing ideas I was passionate about in a tame, school-approved way – but we'd be onstage, in the spotlight, speaking them out loud, talking to people who disagreed with me or had never thought about it either way. Maybe Mary Kate had been right and I was just an attention-obsessed only child at heart, always seeking an audience. Or maybe I truly did believe these ideas mattered – and it was possible, like Pat said, that the people who'd be listening mattered to me, too . . .

He was still nudging me, almost knocking me over now, and finally I admitted it. 'Okay, fine!' I cupped my hands and called out from the lighting booth: 'I MADE *THE NON-VAGINA MONOLOGUES* AND I'M FUCKING PROUD OF IT!'

My voice echoed.

The theater was empty now, silent except for the hum of the still-hot spotlights under us. Darkness had fallen outside, and the gold fixtures gleamed in the low light. Pat was looking at me under the hair falling in his dark eyes. My first instinct was to sass him for trying to mansplain compromise and vaginakind to me. But my stronger instinct was: *Hey, I've never gotten to second base in a lighting booth before.* I leaned in very close to Pat, took a deep breath and whispered: 'You're still using the Lady Speed Stick, aren't you?'

'Hey, they know their stuff,' he whispered back. 'Ladies can't resist the spring blossom scent.'

His mouth curled up in that one-sided smirk and his bright white teeth flashed. I grabbed his sweater and pulled him towards me.

But, before I could kiss him, the heavy door opened downstairs. We heard footsteps, then a familiar voice. 'Hello? Is anyone still here?' Katie Casey called out.

'*Get down!*' I hissed to Pat, and we pulled up our legs and crouched at the railing, watching her strawberry-blonde ponytail bob perkily down the aisle.

'Hello?' she called out again, and Pat nudged me with a mischievous grin and signaled something. I grinned back.

Cupping our hands around our mouths, we began an ominous hiss, just barely audible:

'*Ice . . .*'

By the time I got back to our room after the dress rehearsal, it was only a few minutes before curfew. Pat and I had stayed so late in the lighting booth that he'd even missed hockey practice. I ran from the McLaughlin back to Girls' Quad and burst into our room.

'*The Non-Vagina Monologues* is ready!' I announced to Mary Kate, kicking off my motorcycle boots and shoving my feet into my panda slippers. 'I mean, it's vanilla as hell and some of those vagina synonyms still make me want to sit on a curling iron, but everyone remembered their lines and no one was murdered, so I think we'll call it a win. You're coming on Friday, right?'

Mary Kate was cocooned in six layers of blankets and a sweatshirt on the futon. 'Yeah,' she answered half-heartedly.

Then she gave a weak cough and turned back to the bleak British mini-series she was watching about Victorian people suppressing their emotions on a windy hilltop.

My room-mate was in a really sad place. Even Netflix knew it. It had started suggesting categories like 'Suicidal Scandinavian Films, Black and White' or 'Female-Centered Gothic Stories with a Tragic Twist'. Her post-vomit plunge into the fountain on a November night had given her a bad cold, and she had missed two days of classes to curl up on our futon, spooning a box of Kleenex.

But she wasn't just sick; she had given up hope.

That's why I didn't push her to be more pumped about the *Monologues*. I mean, her lack of enthusiasm was partially my fault anyway, for not creating that Vagina Advent Calendar. Instead, I went over to the futon and tried to cheer her up.

'Hey, you know what I was thinking?' I said. 'This happens in every single Jane Austen book, doesn't it? Halfway through the story the main chick comes down with a dreaded case of Corset Lung, and is down for the count in bed. And THAT'S when the Colin Firth-type whose ass looks great in riding pants realizes he's loved her all along! And then they live happily ever after! Well, for like ten months, until she dies in childbirth . . . But, what I'm saying is, maybe this is your moment for romance!'

But even the thought of a British dude in riding pants couldn't cheer her up. Things were dire.

'No,' she rasped through her phlegmy vocal cords. 'I'm done looking for love. I'm done trying. It's impossible. I'm unlovable.'

'Aw, c'mon! You're lovable! You're so lovable! You're the most lovable person in this room – besides Sir Shackleton obviously.'

'I'm repulsive. I'm gonna die alone.'

'Mary Kate, you're sixteen. You're not gonna die anytime soon unless you get involved in a nude Snapchat scandal with a senator.'

A frantic knock on our door interrupted me and I shuffled over in my panda slippers to answer it.

'Bedchecks from Sister Hellda,' I said over my shoulder to Mary Kate.

But no. It was a girl from the fourth floor, flushed with excitement, panting heavily and waving a green flyer. As soon as I opened the door, she burst out: 'The TOOTHLESS BEAST is coming!'

The Toothless Beast. Dominic LeClair. I had almost forgotten about him during the *Monologues*, but Dominic LeClair was still a thing. The latest I'd heard, he'd taken a leave of absence from St Luke's, which meant he could *potentially* enroll in another school and *potentially* start classes this semester, just in time to *potentially* secure our hockey team a spot in the play-offs and carry us through to the championship. But that had all been hypothetical, and we hadn't heard anything else . . . until now.

'He's coming to visit,' Fourth-Floor gushed. 'If he likes it, he'll officially announce he's coming to St Mary's. So the guys are throwing a recruit party, and they need lots and lots of girls.'

'Ugh,' I groaned. 'That is so gross, honestly. Those recruit parties are the WORST.'

Fourth-Floor handed me a flyer. 'Will you come?'

I slammed the door in her face.

'Can you believe her?' I asked Mary Kate, balling up the flyer and throwing it on the floor. 'Does she really see me spending an entire night of my life trying to make conversation with a bunch of Gatorade-soaked jockstraps?'

While I was raging, Mary Kate had put the lid back on her little tub of Vicks VapoRub, picked up the green flyer off the floor and slowly uncrumpled it.

'Has it snowed yet?' she asked me.

Pacing the room in annoyance, I glanced at the window vaguely. 'No, not yet. It was friggin' freezing this morning, though. I forgot my bra and my nipples almost sliced through my sweatshirt. Why?'

Then I turned around and saw my room-mate smoothing out the green flyer on the blanket in her lap.

'Mary Kate, no!' I protested.

'*Recruit Party, St Ambrose Hall Common Room, Friday night*,' she read aloud.

'HAH!' I ran over and shoved a triumphant finger in her face. 'You can't go even if you wanted to! You just said you're coming to *The Non-Vagina Monologues*, and *The Non-Vagina Monologues* are Friday night.'

She shook her head. 'Nope. Everything is canceled this weekend.'

'What are you talking about?'

She handed me the flyer. At the bottom it said: *All school events are canceled for this weekend's special pep rally and speech by Father Hughes.*

'No way they're canceling the *Monologues*,' I said. 'We've been working on this for months! No way would the school just . . .'

Cancel an event they were completely morally opposed to and had tried to stop, sanitize or virginize at every turn? Choose sports over a sensitive, nuanced expression of the female experience?

OF COURSE THEY WOULD.

'This is BULLSHIT!' I raged, tearing the green flyer to shreds. 'Do you remember how much actual effort I've put into this thing? Do you remember how many teachers I've had to negotiate with? Do you remember how many nuns I've had to say *vagina* in front of?'

'Too many.'

'And all the anal-retentive bullshit I had to put up with! All the dumb hoops I had to jump through, all the stupid patriarchal red tape! Not to mention everything I had to give up. Forget about the stirrups – there is not ONE F-bomb in this show. And now they're CANCELING it because some French-Canadian human bumper-car deigns to set one of his size-fourteen sweatshop sneakers on this campus? Oh HELL, no! St Mary's, I am so done with you!'

Storming over to my desk, I slammed my hand against the windowpane so it rattled. 'I am going to burn this place to the ground!'

I was still fuming, smoke practically hissing out of my ears, when Mary Kate stood up, casting off her blankets and sending a thousand used tissues cascading to the ground. 'I'm gonna go,' she announced.

I whirled around. 'WHAT did you say?'

'I'm gonna go to the party,' she said.

'Hell, no, you aren't!' I told her.

'Yes, I am,' said Mary Kate simply. 'I made a vow to get a boyfriend before it snows, and this recruit party will have lots of guys. This is my last chance.'

I groaned. 'Seriously? I thought you were done with that whole thing.'

'I thought I should give up because I'd never find love,' she clarified. 'But maybe my destiny was to meet the love of my life at the recruit party. That's why my boyfriend search didn't work until now.'

'You know why your boyfriend search ACTUALLY isn't working, Mary Kate?' I said. 'Because it's STUPID!'

A bright red flush colored her face, like I'd slapped her.

But I didn't care. Never – not even when she said she was anti-*The Vagina Monologues*, not even when she refused to say *vagina* – had I doubted that Mary Kate was on my side. We were on the same team, and we had been since the terrifying dodgeball game where we'd met: me ballsy and defiant, Mary Kate proper and reticent and timid sometimes, but the two of us unquestionably united. Her and me facing down everyone else at St Mary's; Mary Kate and me against the world.

Never had I doubted that – until now.

'That's right,' I repeated. 'It's STUPID. I should have said it before now. Maybe, if I had, I could have kept you from getting your nose broken and getting puked on. But you know what? I'm GLAD your nose got broken. I'm GLAD you got puked on. That's what you get for wasting all your time and all your creepy little master-mind brainpower on nothing but wanting a boyfriend. You know, I am so sick of all this! Ever since the first pea-brained caveman whacked a deer on the head and a bunch of women in badger-skin bikinis clapped for him, women have been obsessing over men and catering to men and bending over backwards for men. For years, we've been imprisoned by corsets and property laws and really terrible home-made tampons, and, now that we're FINALLY starting to break free of all that, we go and imprison ourselves! So you feel bad about yourself because you don't have some hipster douchebag dedicating his terrible YouTube Ed Sheeran covers to you? You should feel bad that your boy-crazy brain is shriveling away because you're wasting your intellect!'

'Oh, *I'm* wasting my intellect?' Mary Kate crossed her arms. 'That's interesting because I have a 4.0 and YOU are failing physics for the third time!'

I gasped in righteous outrage. 'I am failing physics for the SECOND time!'

(Okay, that didn't sound much better.)

'And at least I aspire to stuff! At least I'm trying to change things around here!'

Mary Kate rolled her eyes. 'Oh yeah. You're a real rebel. Watch out, Che Guevara! Here comes Alex, who shaves her legs above the knee and makes merkin jokes in front of a deaf priest. What a revolutionary! What a badass! She really lives life on the edge!'

'At least my goals mean something. All you want is a boyfriend!'

'All I want?' she spat in disbelief. 'ALL I WANT?'

Her uncombed hair was a wild mane, and she came at me like a jungle cat, backing me into my desk.

'Are you kidding? Clearly, I haven't shown you my Excel document called LIFE GOALS, because I want way more than that. I want to be valedictorian. I want to get a master's degree and a PhD, and figure out if Shakespeare was actually a woman. I want to travel. I want to see the Seven Wonders of the World and that castle where they filmed *Downton Abbey*. But you know what, Alex?'

She took a deep breath and stood up straighter, and suddenly she seemed as tall as the Rowers.

'It doesn't matter if I want all those things, or none of those things, because who are you to judge what I want? You go on and on about being a feminist and how you're not supposed to judge people's bodies or choices or sex lives. And, if someone is, like, a polyamorous unicorn with a butthole ring, that's just *fine* by you. But you judge Katie Casey and the Save Your Heart girls for THEIR choices and you judge me for mine, because the things I want are different from the things you want. You –'

Now she narrowed her eyes, those Bambi eyes, into predator's eyes, savage, her face still flushed with fever.

'You are a bad feminist.'

Her words rang in the silent dorm room. I was speechless. For once in my life, I couldn't think of anything sassy to say to defend myself.

'So go ahead, judge me,' Mary Kate continued. 'But I won't sit around being judged. I have a life to live, and cough drops to buy from the vending machine!'

Then we heard it, of course – inevitably – because we'd been yelling for several minutes: that anal-retentive *rat-tat-tat* knock on the door.

But Mary Kate just whirled around and yelled at the door, 'We're *fine*, Sister Hilda!'

And, amazingly, Sister Hellda went away.

Then Mary Kate, her face flushed, her wild mane still uncombed, grabbed her ID keychain and stormed out of our room in a huff, leaving me with a weird, hot, tangled ball of rage in my stomach.

*

That hot, tangled ball of rage didn't go away overnight. And when I woke up early and saw that Mary Kate had already left for the day – her empty bed was neatly made, her backpack and pea coat gone – it spurred me into action. I threw my parka on over my pajamas, tugged my Amelia Earhart leather aviator hat on my head and stormed out into the freezing-ass wind to find Pat.

A group of hockey players were coming back from early-morning practice, all with duffels slung over their shoulders and carrying huge bottles of Powerade. When I caught up with them by the Memorial Fountain, they were annoyingly pumped up, laughing and occasionally giving a whoop or a cheer of 'Toothless BEAST!'

I walked right up and shoved Pat in the chest. He was in the middle of the pack, and at first he grinned.

'Hey! Why are you awake right now?' he asked me. 'Don't tell me you're working out.'

All the hockey guys were whistling at us and punching Pat in the shoulder. I ignored them.

'Did you hear?' I demanded.

'What?'

'They canceled the *Monologues*. Did you hear?'

Pat's face changed. He stepped away from the group, closer to the fountain, and I followed him. Finally, he looked up from under his sweaty bangs and met my eyes. 'Yes.'

'Were you going to tell me?'

'What?' He frowned. 'You probably heard before I did. I missed practice last night, remember? I was with *you*.'

'Yeah, at rehearsal for a show your hockey douche overlords canceled.'

Pat put his duffel bag down on the ground. 'Look, I didn't know until last night. I'm sure they're just postponing everything.'

'Well, I'm sure they're not.' I shoved my cold fists in my jacket pockets. 'And I'm pretty sure you couldn't give a shit either way.'

'I think it sucks!' he said. 'It totally sucks, but why are you mad at me? I'm not part of the problem. I *helped* you with the *Monologues*. The venue, the lighting –'

I scoffed. 'You did that so you could hook up with me.'

'*You* wanted to hook up with *me*!'

'I can't believe I ever thought you could help with this – *you* of all people. Look at you!' I eyed him up and down – his grey varsity sweats, his new white high-tops. 'You're like walking male privilege.'

Until this point, Pat had been pretty calm. But the hockey guys were still watching, and a bunch of other people were around, too – those type-A assholes who get up at the crack of dawn to exercise or go to church or whatever early-bird bullshit. We had an audience. And there's nothing guys – even guys who act all chill and claim to be feminists – hate more than when a woman 'makes a scene'.

So I raised my voice. 'Walking, talking male privilege!'

And Pat lost it.

'Privilege? You're seriously talking to me about privilege? You literally said to me you would've gotten expelled if your dad hadn't gone to school with Father Hughes. Your super-rich alum dad talked him into letting you stay, so you get to hang around here being an asshole.'

I gasped, ready to defend my assholery, but Pat plowed over my words. He was up on the marble edge of the fountain, pacing, ranting.

'You know why I'm here? I'm on a hockey scholarship because my parents have five kids and no money. Which means I have to get up at five a.m., when it's negative thirty-five-degree wind chill, and jog until I throw up. Which means I spend hours every week in a locker room that smells like a rat burrowed into a ballsack and died there.'

'Oh, poor Pat,' I began. 'Poor popular jock. Let's whip out the tiny violin –'

But he had anticipated me.

'And I don't complain about it! Have you ever heard me complain about it before now? Because I'm still luckier than ninety-nine point nine percent of people in the world. And you're even luckier than me, because you've got *me* helping you, you've got Mary Kate running around campus at your beck and frickin' call . . . you've got *Katie Casey* helping you, even though you're a total asshole to her, too. So you know what you should do, Alex? I'm gonna mansplain for a second here and *tell* you what you should do: get down on your knees, pray to whatever vegan tree god you believe in and for once – ONCE in your shitty, spoiled life – say thank you!'

He was panting, flushed and furious under his sweaty hair. That hot, tangled ball was in my throat now, choking me so I couldn't speak. But I realized that he was off balance – easy, graceful, athletic Pat off balance – so I saw my chance. I reached up with both hands and pushed him into the fountain.

A huge cry rose from the crowd with the splash. 'Oh my God!' People were gasping, and laughing, and whistling, and taking pictures. A few of the nicer hockey guys ran over to help him, but, when he came up, gasping in the cold, he waved them away. Instead, he pulled himself up easily onto the marble ledge and shook his wet hair like a dog, his grey sweats dark and waterlogged, dripping.

I looked back one last time before I walked away. 'You *are* privileged,' I told him. 'Because, if you were Mary Kate, you would've gotten barfed on first.'

17

That Thursday was my weirdest, loneliest day ever at St Mary's.

When I first came to Minnesota, I divided my life into two parts: there was my St Mary's life, then there was my real life when I went home. I had Mary Kate, who was my St Mary's best friend, but my 'real' best friends were in San Francisco. But every school break I went back, things changed a little, and over time they changed a lot. Three years into boarding school, I barely spoke to anyone from California.

And now I realized, maybe too late, that Mary Kate was my 'real' – my only – best friend.

That Thursday, instead of racing Mary Kate to classes through the cold wind, I clomped alone in my motorcycle boots. Instead of gossiping with her over French fries and barbecue sauce in the dining hall at lunch, I sat by myself. And, instead of whispering and writing notes to each other in history class, we sat side by side in stony silence. When I needed a pen, I asked someone else – even though

I knew Mary Kate had an adorable pencil case full of them.

Of all the days to be bummed out and lonely, this was the worst one of all. When the Toothless Beast comes to your school, let me tell you, it is a lot of hoopla. It was nuts. Seriously. Overnight, these huge green tents sprang up all around campus, there were St Mary's banners and green balloons everywhere and the school fight song was blaring non-stop. There were big, ugly green centerpieces in the dining hall and our favorite chocolate-brownie sundaes for dessert.

Okay, I didn't exactly hate that. But the rest of it was irritating – the buzzing hum of excitement and everyone rushing everywhere and all the bright camera flashes from the local Minnesota news channel that usually only covers stories about black bears spotted rifling through dumpsters. From the ecstatic way they were chattering into their microphones, you'd think another royal baby had been born.

Everywhere I went by myself, everyone else was clustered together, chattering in excitement, debating anxiously:

'Do you think he'll like St Mary's? What if he doesn't like it? He HAS to like it, right?'

Bitter and alone, I rolled my eyes and made snorting sounds. On one hand, who would like the homework, the rules and the iced-over owl pellet of ass-aching boredom that was St Mary's? On the other hand, *obviously*, the Toothless Beast was going to like it. The chocolate brownies were practically in the shape of his face. He was taking a magical train to a magical land where everyone worshiped him. He would love it for the same reason Harry Potter was voted 'Biggest Full-of-Himself Twat' in the Hogwarts Yearbook: the whole world revolved around him.

But did I care? Did I give a single green-ribboned Dominic LeClair-shaped chocolate-coated shit if the Toothless Beast decided to come to St Mary's? Hell, no!

Because I'd be gone before he got here. I officially decided on Thursday night, after Mary Kate came back from the library and went straight to bed without speaking a word to me. As I lay there in my silent bunk in the dark, I made up my mind. I was going to get kicked out, with one last, big, fiery gesture of defiance: I was going to burn my bra.

Bra-burning has a long history in feminism. Back in the sixties, all the most badass hippies got together and set their bras on fire in trash cans. Bras were basically metal cages constructed by sadistic male engineers to trap our boobs and make our lives sweaty and miserable. Also, they thought that the slightest glimpse of an erect nipple through a cotton T-shirt would send Very Important Men into distracted paroxysms and inadvertently cause nuclear war. Lock those boobs away, they declared! But the hippies weren't having it. They wanted freedom and, if it took destruction to get freedom, they were gonna destroy some shit.

And so was I. Friday night, when the Toothless Beast came to visit, I was going to burn my bra on Academic Quad. That would give the school a big wake-up call that SOMEONE existed on this campus – in fact, a whole

GENDER of people – outside their hockey and jockstraps and spitty mouthguards. WOMEN were here, and we had a voice!

Obviously, the patriarchy would not take it well, and the school administration would not take it at all. If I set a fire in the center of campus, I would definitely be violating at least thirty-five different rules in the student handbook and endangering the safety of pretty much everyone at St Mary's. There was no way my dad was talking Father Hughes into keeping me here after that, even if he gave the Church his Tesla. But I'd been here way too long anyway.

It was time for me to go.

On Friday night, after sunset, I marched out to the center of Academic Quad. I was wearing my aviator hat with the earflaps pulled down low and I was armed with my cigarette lighter, three bras – two of my own, plus a random one I found behind the dorm dryer – and some old failed physics pop quizzes for kindling.

All day long, steel-grey clouds had hung ominously overhead. Black trees with bare branches clawed at the sky above the dorms whose windows rattled with the terrible gusts howling across the wind-tunnel vortex that is Academic Quad, and there was a bitter chill in the air. But I didn't care. I threw my quizzes dramatically down on the quad, cast my bras on top of them and squatted in the grass to set the whole thing on fire.

I could already picture it – my big showdown with Father Hughes. I would stand my ground before a blazing wall of flame, looking like I'd strode straight out of the hell where he always thought I'd end up, look him straight in his disapproving eyes and shout:

'FUCK THE PATRIARCHY!'

That was my plan. Unfortunately, there was a problem. It turned out it wasn't so easy to match the raging flame of righteous rage in me with an actual physical flame. After ten minutes, I was still struggling, squatting in the grass, fumbling with the cigarette lighter. I was wearing my grey fingerless cat-burglar gloves with the rough wool unraveling at the knuckles, and my fingertips were blue with cold. Who would have guessed I was so terrible at burning things? Definitely not the girl who lost an eyebrow due to my recklessness with a Fourth of July sparkler at summer camp, I'll tell ya that. Every time I managed to get the lighter lit and the corner of the quiz paper to catch the flame, wind swept across the quad and blew it out. I would flick, flick, flick the cigarette lighter – the paper corner would catch light – the wind would blow, the flame would waver and die out. The whole thing was a damp mess – like a soggy birthday cake after that gross spitty kid in class tries to blow out the candles.

Finally, I had a decent little flame going – an entire quiz paper had caught fire. I was admiring my work proudly when I heard a perky voice behind me: 'Oh my gosh! Is this a bonfire?'

Three freshman girls were standing behind me, all rosy-cheeked and looking like cupcakes in their pastel hats with pompons on top.

'A bonfire!' Cupcake Number One squealed, clapping her mittened hands together. 'I think I have marshmallows in my room – we can make s'mores!'

'I'll bring my *Frozen* sleeping bag!' Cupcake Number Two offered.

'I'll bring my guitar!'

'Oh my gosh – Christmas carols!'

'I didn't even know they were doing a bonfire for the Toothless Beast. Beast Brownies *and* a Beast Bonfire! This is seriously the best Friday ever.'

That was it. Too far! I'd been trying to ignore the cheerful little chinchillas chattering behind me and focus on my pyromania, but that was too much. I turned around.

'Hey!' I barked. 'This is *not* a Beast Bonfire! In fact, it's not even a bonfire at all! This is a "Fuck the Patriarchy" bra-burning. It's a political protest. So, if you're burning with a passionate desire to destroy the inherently unequal and fucked-up structures of our society with a cigarette lighter and your underwear, you can join me. But, if all you want in life is just, like, hot chocolate with little marshmallows in it, you can move the hell on!'

The Cupcakes gave each other a look . . . and moved the hell on. As they scurried away in their snowboots, Cupcake Number Three looked back apologetically and told me, 'I have low blood sugar, so I really need the little marshmallows.'

Then another frigid blast of wind blew across the quad, and the Cupcakes were practically swept away, shrieking and giggling.

I turned around just in time to see the gust blow my fire sideways. My charred pop quiz sailed away on the strong wind. The flame was out.

Time to start over. I crouched in the frosty grass and flicked the cigarette lighter again and again with numb fingers. Howling wind slapped my leather earflaps against my cheeks. After ten minutes of struggling, and failing, and cursing, I heard another perky greeting behind me: 'Hey there!'

Thinking the Cupcakes were back, I whirled around in irritation. But it was Katie Casey, looking predictably precious and snow-bunny-like in a pink beanie and white ski jacket.

'I went to your room, and Mary Kate said you might be out here,' she explained.

'What? I didn't tell her that. I'm not even speaking to her.'

'She said she saw you leaving with a lighter and some bras, and that you'd probably be setting them on fire in the middle of campus.'

Dammit! The dimpled witch knew me too well.

'So you're really gonna start a fire?'

'Yup.'

'Aren't you gonna get in trouble?'

'Yup.'

'So you're not worried that a dorm nun is gonna come by, or a teacher, or Father Hughes?'

'Oh, Father Hughes is definitely gonna come by,' I told her. 'So, if you're scared of getting in trouble, you'd better hit the road.'

Unexpectedly, Katie Casey said, 'I'm not.' Then, surprisingly, she sat down, cross-legged in her ski pants, right there in the cold grass.

'You know,' she said, 'it's been so crazy these past two days, I haven't had the chance to tell you how sorry I am about the *Monologues*. I know all of us are, like, totally heartbroken about the festival. We've been working this whole semester, and –'

'Look,' I told her, hopping from motorcycle boot to motorcycle boot to keep warm, 'I get that you're trying to be nice. And that your thing got canceled, too. And that your thing was actually bigger than my thing, with way more people involved, and you had to recruit all those nuns, and you had to bake all those doughnuts, and then have that weird debate about whether the Boston cream ones were too "suggestive" . . .'

Boston cream doughnuts actually sounded really amazing right now. I shook my head. *Focus, Alex.*

'But this is about way more than just, like, them canceling my thing,' I continued. 'This is about the fact that I never got a chance to do what I *really* wanted in the first place. I should have realized that, no matter how much I compromised and changed and took the friggin' vagina out of *The Vagina Monologues*, this school would never let it happen. Because this school – and everyone who goes here, including my own room-mate – is fundamentally against everything I stand for, and I'm the one who needs to take action here. So you should just go, like, pull out your hockey pompons and go to the recruit party for the Toothless Beast. I'm sure you don't want to miss it.'

But, instead of scurrying off like the little Cupcakes, Katie Casey stood up again and took a step closer to me.

'Actually, I'm not the biggest fan of recruit parties,' she said. 'I mean, I love St Mary's, of course, and school spirit is amazing! But I had kind of a bad experience at a recruit party freshman year . . .'

She trailed off, looking uncomfortable, and avoided my eyes by looking behind me.

'Um . . .' she ventured. 'I think your fire might be dying.'

I turned around and saw she was right. In fact, my fire was dead. All that was left was a black patch of grass with a few scraps of burnt paper and a couple of bras. It looked less like a fiery political statement, and more like the remains of an Alaskan Poetry Retreat-turned-orgy.

'You probably already know this,' Katie said, 'but if you make a teepee shape with the paper, the fire will withstand the wind better.'

'A teepee?'

'I make the fires when I go ice-fishing with my dad,' she explained. 'I can help you if you want?'

'Well . . .' I hesitated before realizing that not only were my damp bras in the grass not making a political statement but the numbness creeping up my legs was probably the start of frostbite. Because I wasn't speaking to Mary Kate, I couldn't ask to borrow her long johns, so I'd worn my fox-print tights under my jeans instead, but they weren't helping. I looked up under the flaps of my hat at the ever-darkening sky. Temperatures were supposed to drop below freezing tonight.

I handed her the lighter.

Katie Casey may not have been a rebel, but she turned out to be pretty useful. In no time at all, she had a good-sized fire going. Sure, her fire didn't have that whole roaring, destructive vibe I was going for – it was happy and crackling, sending up cheerful sparks, a better fit for a Girl Scout sleepover or a cozy Christmas Eve than a violent protest. But the quad was colder than Princess Elsa's asshole, so Katie Casey's friendly fire was probably saving my life.

This time, when she sat down in the grass again, I sat down next to her.

'You know, Alex, I've always wanted to get to know you better,' she confided. 'I always thought you seemed super cool and original. I know a lot of times we were, like, coming from different places for the event, but I also feel like we're so similar.'

'Similar?' I raised an eyebrow, holding my hands in their fingerless gloves out to the fire.

'Kinda like . . . I'm here on campus trying to save people's hearts,' she said sweetly. 'And you're here, like, saving the vaginas.'

That wasn't the same at all to me. But Katie Casey had just said the word *vaginas* in the shadow of the Virgin Mary statue, and she'd also kept me from freezing my tits off tonight. Plus, I kinda liked the idea of myself as some kind of vagina superhero. The Wondervulva. Clitwoman. So I took a deep breath of cold, smoky air and said something I never, ever thought I'd say to Katie Casey.

'I guess you might be kinda . . . partly . . . right.'

Then I changed the subject. I asked her why she didn't like recruit parties, and she told me.

'Freshman year, this guy in my Latin class invited me to a recruit party in his dorm,' she began. 'It was for that basketball player from Wisconsin – remember, the really tall guy with the thyroid problem everyone was so excited about? Before they got him good medical treatment and he stopped growing, of course,' she added.

'Yeah,' I recalled. 'What a bummer. I heard he shrank back to six foot four.'

'So I show up to the party,' Katie continued. 'And I'm super excited because it's my first real party at St Mary's, and I love basketball because I always watch the college tournaments, so I'm looking forward to meeting everyone. And right away this senior basketball player starts talking to me, and telling me how only the prettiest girls are invited to recruit parties, to make a good impression on the recruit.'

'What a pig!' I exclaimed, and threw a handful of grass on the fire for emphasis.

'The senior says the party is too loud, and he wants to go somewhere quiet so we can talk. So we go back to his room . . .' Katie looked at the fire, her eyes shining. 'We were on the futon, and he kept trying to kiss me and get me to lie down. It made me super uncomfortable, and finally I *said* I was super uncomfortable, so he walked me out.

Nothing actually really *happened*, so I guess I'm lucky, but . . .'

'Lucky?' I spluttered, my infuriated breath freezing in the cold air. 'What a creep! How pathetic is a guy who has to, like, corner a freshman girl and lure her back to his room? *He's* the lucky one! He should, like, light a fucking gratitude candle that you were even willing to set *foot* in his gross sweatsock-smelling room. Seriously!'

Wait, was I defending Katie Casey? Was I saying someone was lucky to have her in their room, when a few weeks ago I would have refused to let her into mine even if she brought amazing and super-fattening baked goods? What was happening here?

'So I left,' Katie continued, huddling into herself. 'But, as I was going down the hallway, I overheard the senior talking to another guy. They were talking about me. And he said, "Three words: *waste of time*."'

I shook my head in silent, indignant sympathy.

'And that's when I decided,' she said, her clear, strong breath cutting through the smoke, 'that my body was *mine*.'

'Hell, yeah!' I stood up.

'And that *I* got to decide what I did with it!' She stood up.

'Right on, sister!' The fire was climbing higher and higher, crackling and hissing now, and my face was hot.

'And that I was going to save myself for marriage!'

Hold up. That just took a turn I wasn't cool with.

'Um,' I interjected. Pricks of pain were bringing the feeling back to my legs, and I was stomping my feet. 'You do realize it's possible to have a totally consensual hook-up where you're in control and there's lots of sexy fun and laughter and possibly dulce de leche sauce involved, right?' Then I waved that little life lesson away. 'You know what? Forget that for now.'

Katie Casey was staring greedily at the fire, and I could see the flames leaping in her wet eyes. Turning to me, she confessed in a low, excited voice: 'I kinda want to burn something.'

'Oh *hell*, yeah!' I said again.

The bras I'd brought were still lying in the frosty grass because Katie had built the fire out of my physics quizzes. I picked up two and held them out to her.

'Balconette or racerback?'

'Actually . . .' Katie pursed her lips mischievously. She unzipped her ski parka, reached inside and pulled out . . .

A bra. A baby-blue, lace-trimmed bra.

'You brought your own bra to burn?' I squawked in disbelief. 'Yes! Let's do this!'

I went first. I stepped up, yelled 'FUCK THE PATRIARCHY!' into the cold, smoky wind, then hurled the mystery balconette bra from the laundry room on the fire, and thrust my arm above my head in triumph as the flames devoured it.

Next it was Katie Casey's turn. And she hesitated at first, dangling her bra by the strap, coughing a little at the smoke in her face, her voice wavering in the wind: 'F . . . F . . . F . . .'

I don't think the chick had ever dropped the F-bomb before. But all of a sudden it burst out of her: 'F-F-FUCK THE PATRIARCHY!'

And she flung the cute bra into the flames. Shoulder to shoulder, we watched the fabric of our bras burn away, exposing the underwire, which lit and twisted, glowing orange. It was pretty fucking awesome. Katie started giggling for some reason and couldn't stop, and then I started giggling, and someone walking by probably would've thought we were drunk. Obviously, Katie Casey dropping her first F-bomb and being actually drunk at the same time was way too 'Never Have I Ever' for one night, but I have to admit it was a crazy natural high – the flashing flames, the swirling smoke, the adrenaline-pumping ecstasy of annihilation and anarchy which I know so well and she was tasting for the first time.

The fire blazed on, even in the howling wind, and Katie and I raced around the quad, giggling like psychopath arsonists, grabbing sticks and leaves and throwing them on the fire, emptying our pockets of crumpled graph paper and cough-drop wrappers (her) and old clove cigarettes (me). The flames climbed higher.

'Bring on the destruction!' I growled enthusiastically, punching the air and hopping from foot to foot like a boxer. 'BURN, BABY, BURN!'

'Someone's definitely gonna come yell at us soon,' Katie said, and she sounded excited about it.

'Hell, yeah!' I affirmed. 'They can't ignore us!' I flung my arms out wide and yelled to the frozen sky: 'YOU

CAN'T IGNORE US! WE'RE SETTING ST MARY'S ON FIRE!'

Inhaling a deep, frosty breath, I was filled with savage satisfaction.

And then, at that exact moment, because the universe likes to give me a metaphorical purple nurple at every possible turn, one thing happened – the one thing that would one hundred percent definitely, indisputably, irrevocably ruin my last act of violent disobedience at St Mary's.

It began to snow.

The first flake fell on my nose. The second on my eyelashes. *Oh great*, I thought. *Snowflakes on my nose and eyelashes. Now I'm Maria from the friggin' Sound of Music. I'm supposed to be a raging Amazon death-goddess of destruction here!*

The snow was swirling and swirling, covering the bare tree branches and the stone buildings. In just a few minutes, the Mary statue was cloaked in white, and Katie and I, too. And our fire . . .

'It's going out!' I shouted. 'Defend the fire! Defend the fire!'

'The wind is blowing this way,' Katie calculated quickly. 'If we both stand here, we can block it.'

But the fire was already flickering lower, and, as we hurried to stand shoulder to shoulder in defense of our flaming protest, we saw through the whirling white snowflakes another enemy approaching: people. Lots of people.

Here's the thing about St Mary's . . . you would THINK, being in Minnesota and right on a lake where we get ridiculous dumps of lake-effect snow every day in the winter, we would hate snow. And we DO hate snow – when it's January and we're trekking to class in Ugg boots that smell like wet dog. But something miraculous happens every spring and summer: we lose our memories. And, when it snows for the first time that year, it's like it's snowing for the first time ever: we fall in love with it all over again.

So now, mere minutes after the first flakes, joyful, shouting, whooping parades of people were streaming towards us from Boys' Quad, Girls' Quad, all directions.

'It's magical!' girls in woolly hats cried, jumping up, grasping each other's mittened hands and twirling in the white downfall. 'It's a winter wonderland!'

Not only does every St Mary's kid love snow, but we've got students from all over the country – California, Florida, the Deep South – which means some freshmen are literally seeing snow for the first time. A skinny, bright-eyed freshman in an earflap hat with the price sticker still on it wandered around in a daze of enchantment, lay down on the white-blanketed ground and began a slow-motion snow angel. In rapture, in wonder, his blue eyes fixed on the whirling shower of soft white flakes from the heavens above, he said in a deep Alabama drawl: 'I'll never, ever forget this moment.'

'Hey!' I barked, kicking snow into his open mouth. 'We're burning our bras here!'

Then a herd of sophomores thundered by me and I whirled around. 'WATCH OUT FOR OUR FIRE!'

One turned to me and frowned. 'What fire?'

'What FIRE?' I raged. 'What FIRE?'

Then I turned and saw that our fire was dead. Katie was scrambling around in a mess of garbage caked in white.

'Light it again, Katie!' I called out, tossing her my cigarette lighter. 'I'll stand guard!'

But people were everywhere – running, jumping, twirling in the snow – and playing defense wasn't easy. The Cupcakes had reappeared, and they were building a snowman – giddily rolling a giant snowball right up to us. 'I've got a carrot in my room!' one called out gaily.

Another chirped, 'He can have my scarf!'

'Hey!' I shouted. 'Back off! This is still a protest!' Spotting a blackened bra cup left in the snow, I snatched it up to use as a slingshot, loading the cup with a snowball and releasing the strap with a snap and a loud yell: 'Get out of here!'

It backfired immediately.

'SNOWBALL FIGHT!' a freshman cried, and a boisterous cheer rang out across the blizzarding quad.

Before you could say *frostbitten nipples*, snowballs were whizzing every which way, hitting the backs of people's coats and beanies and exploding into soft confetti. Great fluffy flakes were swirling around, people were running and leaping through the fresh white drifts, skipping carelessly over my charred physics quizzes and almost somersaulting over Katie Casey, who was crouched intently in the snow with my lighter. She managed to get a small circle of flame going again in the wet, whirling wind.

'Defend the fire, Katie!' I called back to her, and I was defending it myself, racing around, fending people off, blocking them with my body, loading snowball after snowball into my slingshot and launching them through the smoky air. My heart was pounding, I was hot and sweaty inside my coat and a strange exhilaration was pumping through me. Even though I took my protest seriously, I couldn't fight off a stray thought that made me smile: *This is kinda fun.*

But then I saw something that wiped the smile off my face. My fury roared with flaming power that put our reborn baby bonfire to shame.

Pat.

Pure Minnesota through and through, he wasn't even wearing a coat. No hat, either – no gloves, no scarf. His green fleece was open over his sweater, his tousled hair damp with snowflakes, and he strolled through the snow flanked by his douchelord hockey cocks (including Lundqvist the Ginger Viking), infuriatingly casual as ever.

Flinging my slingshot aside, I snatched up a handful of snow and hurled it as hard as I could. It hit Pat right in the face. Surprised, he turned his head. There was a bright red mark on his right cheek where the snowball had hit him. Sure, I'm no Hulked-out Mary Kate with a football, but I'm not bad.

'Hey!' He frowned.

But I was already launching another snowball. *Pow!* It hit him in the stomach and all the white snow clung to his sweater. He took off running, and I took off after him. Crushing snow castles, stomping through snow angels and shoving aside cheerful snow bunnies, I pursued him, scooping up snow and packing and throwing snowballs as I ran.

Pat was bobbing and weaving between people in puffy coats and pompon hats; at one point he ducked behind a snowman and I hurled a snowball straight at it and its head exploded. But he just kept running, laughing as he ran, and, as I raced after him through the gale of snowflakes, he began to scoop snow and toss snowballs back at me. It didn't even look like he was aiming, but the first hit my left cheek with a wet, cold *splat*. Then another – *whoosh!* – in the side of my head. And *boom!* A third snowball hit me right in the boob.

'You sexist bastard!' I shouted at him, panting. 'This is supposed to be a bra-burning!' Then – punctuating each word with a hurled snowball: 'This. Isn't. A. Snowball. Fight!'

Pat shrugged in his annoyingly carefree way. 'Now it is!' he called out cheerfully, taking a few running steps and launching a snowball high into the air. It plopped down exactly on top of my head and I stood there with ice particles slowly dripping down the leather earflaps of my hat, looking like I'd dressed up as a snow cone for Halloween. Which made me really mad. I growled, tossed aside my handful of snow and made a beeline for Pat, plowing straight into him.

We collided. Pat was knocked back to the ground and I tumbled on top of him, straddling him in the soft, fluffy blanket of snow, panting heavily in his face. His hair was wet and messy and starting to curl, his face bright red, white specks on his long eyelashes.

'How dare you show up here!' I panted. 'This is a protest against misogyny and douchebag jocks and . . . and whatever wearing a bra symbolizes! This is a protest AGAINST YOU!'

'Hey, I would never tell you to put on a bra,' Pat said. 'In fact, I came to join your protest. Mary Kate was at the recruit party and she told me what you were up to. I came here to help.'

'Oh yeah?' I was still panting. Damn, this snowball-fight thing could be the next cardio exercise craze. 'How could *you* possibly help? Unless you want to be our symbolic, overprivileged male sacrifice voodoo doll and let us light your hair on fire.'

He ignored that offer. 'I brought you something. And, if you would get off me a second, I'll show you.'

Curiosity got the better of me. I sat back in the snow and let him sit up. Shaking white flakes from his hair, he reached inside his pea coat and pulled out . . .

'Is that a BLOWTORCH?'

The metal glinted irresistibly through the falling snow. I grabbed it.

'Hell, yeah!' Pat grinned. 'I mean, obviously it's a *mini* blowtorch. Lundqvist uses it to make crème brûlée. He got hooked on *The Great British Bake Off*,' he explained.

I turned the blowtorch over in my gloved hands.

'So if you want our help . . .' Pat trailed off.

I couldn't help it – I flung myself on top of him again, almost smacking him in the face with the blowtorch, and kissed him.

Soon we were standing in front of another roaring fire. This fire was way bigger than the one Katie and I had made. AND I'd gotten to use the blowtorch.

It turned out Pat's bros actually had come for the protest, although they weren't the most legit supporters in the world.

'I'm a feminist!' one insisted. 'I place bets on women's basketball games.'

'I brought something to burn,' another offered. 'A pair of boxer briefs that really ride up.'

'That does not count as gender-based oppression,' I snapped.

'I brought ManSpanx,' Lundqvist said. We all frowned at him and he mumbled, 'My mom said I inherited my dad's pear-shaped figure.'

'Well, that's some kind of oppression,' I allowed. 'Throw 'em on the fire!'

Sparks rose up in the navy, snow-flecked sky, and a big cheer rose up, too. A whole crowd was gathered around the fire, and growing. So it was no surprise that, as soon as the ManSpanx caught fire, a red snowplow appeared, speeding from the east side of campus, flashing and wailing like a fire engine, with a school maintenance man shouting through a bullhorn:

'PLEASE CLEAR THE QUAD! STUDENTS, EVACUATE THE QUAD!'

I rubbed my fingerless gloves together with glee and turned to Katie Casey. 'Ready to get in trouble?' I asked her.

Her freckled face looked anxious – a deer-in-the-snowplow-lights look. And she was about to get more anxious because the snowplow dude wasn't the only authority figure rolling our way. A second later, a senior came running up to the crowd and shouted: 'Father Hughes is coming! The banquet for Mama and Papa Beast just ended, and he's coming back this way!'

The crowd scattered, all the little snow bunnies scampering away, dropping random mittens in the snow in their haste to escape. At the same time, a new group of tall dudes came jogging towards us.

'What's up?' Pat greeted one of them, clasping his hand and pulling him in for a chest bump. 'What happened to the recruit party?'

'Busted,' the tall dude replied. 'Someone fell off the pool table and the dorm priest broke it up.'

'What happened to the Beast?' Pat asked. 'Where is he?'

'He left with a girl. Took her back to a room. Actually, it was that girl *you* were talking to before. Little brunette, real cute?'

Pat looked at me. I looked at Pat.

'Mary Kate!' I gasped.

We both looked up at the sky.

'Oh my God!' My shocked breath froze in the air between us. 'The first snow! Mary Kate! She went back to a dorm room with the Toothless Beast? Oh my God, it's the first snow, she's desperate, she's not thinking clearly!'

'Alex!' Katie Casey was tugging on my coat sleeve. 'Look!'

A golf cart was speeding towards us. It was charging up the main avenue, clearly coming from the Mendoza Banquet Hall where St Mary's had hosted the welcome dinner for the Toothless Beast's parents. A young priest was driving the golf cart with one hand, holding a bull-horn in the other, shouting, 'STUDENTS! BACK AWAY FROM THE FIRE!'

And in the passenger seat was Father Hughes.

I looked west to Boys' Quad, from where the hockey players had come with the gossip, where Mary Kate was imprisoned in a strange room with a potentially murderous Canadian. Little Mary Kate, who still bought three-pack training bras from GapKids.

I looked south. Father Hughes had stepped down from the golf cart and was striding towards us through the wintry storm, his long dark coat blowing behind him.

Heat was blazing at my back. This was my chance. This was the moment I'd been building towards for two and a half years. I had literally set fire to the campus, and now I got to stand in front of a righteous flame and face down Father Hughes – got to look into the stern grey face of the patriarchy and declare: *You can't make me wear a bra. Or a green-plaid skort that gives me wedgies. And you can't make me feel like I'm any less important than some 'roid-rage human jockstrap with no nerve feeling left in his shoulders. Fuck the patriarchy, and fuck you, Father Hughes!*

Fuck you, Father Hughes – and goodbye.

But I couldn't stop imagining Mary Kate's face, remembering her big, scared brown eyes during that first dodgeball game.

I turned to Katie Casey. 'I've gotta go,' I told her.

'WHAT?' All her freckles stood out in her pale, shocked face. 'Where are you going?'

'You know in *Beauty and the Beast* when the brunette dweeb who likes to read gets chained up by this, like, big hairy monster and a bunch of French furniture, and her dad goes into the village and has to get that muscle-bound prick to go break her free?' I explained hurriedly. 'It's kinda like that.'

'I think I'm the muscle-bound prick,' Pat contributed over my shoulder.

Father Hughes was waving away the smoke from the fire as he walked towards us.

'Look.' I grabbed Katie's arm. 'You don't have to get in trouble if you don't want to. You can tell him I started it, and you tried to stop me. He'll believe you, trust me. If you saw my disciplinary file, you'd know why. Tell him I started the fire – tell him I made you start the fire – tell him I tried to set *you* on fire. I don't care.'

And, before she had a chance to respond, I grabbed Pat and sprinted off through the snow.

I had a best friend to find.

18

Snow was swirling. It was impossible to see. We slipped and slid and struggled against tundra winds that almost blew us over. Even Pat was panting heavily, clutching his fleece closed, shaking his wet hair out of his eyes. It seemed like a thousand miles to St Ambrose Hall. How would we ever get to Mary Kate?

'Here!' Pat grabbed my hand suddenly and yanked me to the side. He knelt down and began digging through the snow like a dog. It took me a minute to wipe the snow from my watering eyes and see what he was doing, and another minute to understand.

The tunnels.

This time, I trusted him. I followed him immediately down into the pitch-darkness, racing down the wooden ladder so rapidly I stepped on his head.

Down in the tunnels, it was dry and dark and a little warmer. We hit the ground, both breathing heavily, and hurried forward. When we reached a turn, I asked, 'Which way is Boys' Quad?'

'No, we should go to Girls' Quad.'

'Why?'

'Because look . . .' Pat held out the phone he'd been using as our flashlight.

'You have service?' I asked excitedly.

I had been trying and trying to call Mary Kate, and Pat had been trying and trying to call the guys at the party. The cell coverage on our campus is always shitty, which has me convinced the administration made a pact with either the devil or T-Mobile to keep us from sending sexy Snapchats. But tonight, in the howling wind and whirling blizzard, it was downright non-existent.

'No service, but look at the time,' Pat said. 'It's eleven already. It's after curfew! She's gotta be back in your room. Has Mary Kate ever missed curfew?'

'SHE'S NOT HERE!' I wailed. 'I TOLD YOU, SHE'S DEAD!'

I was tearing around our little dorm room, yanking the duvets off our beds, flinging the wardrobe doors open, searching for Mary Kate in all these tiny, weird places even she couldn't possibly fit.

Pat was shutting the window. We'd raced through the underground tunnel towards Girls' Quad, climbed out, dashed through the snow to my dorm and climbed in through the window so Sister Hellda wouldn't see Pat.

'She probably just forgot because she was having too much fun at the recruit party,' he said. 'Hey! It's the first snow! Maybe she fell in love!'

'You said it yourself – Mary Kate NEVER misses curfew,' I panted. 'And there's no way she fell in love. That party was full of jock misogynist CREEPS. They probably spiked her drink. She's probably being used in some weird satanic hockey sex ritual right now with blood smeared on her forehead and guys in helmets all around her, chanting.'

'We don't usually do that ritual on Fridays,' Pat reassured me. 'That's more a Wednesday kinda thing. Besides –' he pulled me in for a hug – 'not every guy on the hockey team is a sex-crazed psychopath, you know.'

For a moment, I let myself lean against him, resting my head against his wet fleece, inhaling the bonfire smell of his sweater. Then a horrible parallel occurred to me and I was hit by a fresh wave of panic.

'THE ICEMAN!' I cried. 'This is EXACTLY what happened to the Iceman! He was out after curfew, it was snowing and he DIED! Mary Kate is gonna be a ghost! She's gonna be the Icewoman! Which would actually be kind of badass and feminist if we had a female ghost, too, but . . .'

'You don't believe in the Iceman,' Pat reminded me.

But I didn't care. I was going back into the blizzard to find Mary Kate. I was going to save my best friend.

Just as I was climbing onto my desk, there was a crisp rap at the frost-covered window. I reached for the sash and yanked it open, letting in a gust of icy wind and a flurry of snow. Then, blinking, I saw . . . an enormous monster carrying Mary Kate!

Okay, so it wasn't a monster – but the dude WAS enormous, and his red varsity jacket set off stranger-danger alarm bells in my head. That wasn't a St Mary's jacket! Where was his green plaid? Who the hell was this guy?

Although actually his face did look a little familiar . . . *Did* I know him?

No time to find out. In the wild swirl of the snowstorm, in the stranger's arms, Mary Kate was whimpering and holding her left snow boot. 'It's her ankle – I think it's broken,' the stranger cautioned me as I reached through the window to grab her, pulling her inside so fast I almost smashed her head on the window.

I was shouting in her face, 'Mary Kate! Are you okay?' then staggering to climb down from the desk and carry her over to the bunk bed, apologizing profusely the whole time.

'I'm sorry! I don't care if we fought about feminism and unicorn buttholes, I didn't mean for you to end up frozen in the snow after curfew. I thought you were gonna die like the Iceman and come back and haunt me by hiding the gummy bears –'

But suddenly I was interrupted when Pat strolled to the window, shaking his still-soaked hair, and crowed, 'DOMINIC!'

Dominic?

'Oh my God!' I cried out in sudden recognition, turning around. 'You're the Toothless Beast!'

There he stood, in the snow, his famous face floating outside our window like he was the BFG – the most talked-about celebrity on this campus for months, the notorious enemy-turned-hero, the royal baby himself: Dominic LeClair.

I whipped my head back to Mary Kate, who was sitting on my bed, struggling to get her soaked pea coat off, and hit her with a barrage of questions.

'What the hell happened to you tonight? Why are you with the Toothless Beast? What happened at the recruit party? How did you miss curfew?'

At the same time, Pat was urging Dominic to get inside.

'Come on, dude, it's freezing out there, and there's a bunch of priests and ghosts and stuff. We gotta get you inside. If you catch pneumonia before you even play hockey for us, everyone will be really pissed.'

The Toothless Beast said, 'I don't think I can fit.'

'C'mon, just climb up.'

'I don't know.' The Toothless Beast had a soft voice, and he sounded nervous. 'I've seen *Winnie the Pooh*. I don't know if climbing through a window is such a good idea.'

Meanwhile, Mary Kate was trying to gently remove the boot from her injured ankle. 'Do we have any ice?' she asked me, wincing.

As Pat was suggesting, 'What if you dive? Just grab the windowsill!' I hurried over to our minifridge. *Ice? Ice?* No ice. Nothing but half-empty cans of iced coffee and a bag of Milky Way minis ... wait! A distorted, crusted-in-ice Pepsi can on the brink of explosion! Triumph! I thought, *Everything is going to be A-okay ...*

And I looked up just in time to see the Toothless Beast launch himself head first through our window. He careened across my desk, scattering shards of ice, pencils and bobby pins everywhere, and crash-landed in the center of our floor with an enormous, 200-pound man-thud that rattled the bunk beds and dressers, that at its worst would alert Sister Hellda and at its best knock out the last of his badass baby teeth.

'SHHH!' I hissed furiously. 'Be quiet!'

'Sorry,' the Toothless Beast mumbled, standing up and brushing off his snowy jeans. In a corner of my hyped-up mind, I noticed that he was actually pretty cute. I mean, he was so enormous he took up sixty percent of the space in our tiny dorm room and his curly brown head practically touched our ceiling, but he had a baby face, and – if you weren't too distracted by the two-inch gap in his mouth to notice – cute dimples when he smiled apologetically.

But there was no time to ogle him right now.

'It's fine, it's fine,' I said hurriedly, standing in the center of the room, gripping the frozen Pepsi. 'We just need to be quiet so our dorm nun doesn't catch you guys in here!'

Mary Kate looked up from propping her bare foot on a pillow to frown at me, and then I frowned, too – what was wrong with me? My heart was pounding, I was all jittery, and I couldn't stop shooting anxious glances at the wall we shared with Sister Hellda. Why did I feel so weird? What was it about boys in the dorm that was making me so uneasy? Was this two and a half years of ignored Catholic guilt finally catching up with me?

'It's fine,' I repeated, trying to calm myself mostly, going over to shut the window before handing the Pepsi to Mary Kate for her swollen ankle.

'We all just have to be super quiet,' I continued in a whisper. 'It doesn't sound like Sister Hellda's in her room; she must still be guarding the front door. So, as soon as we hear her coming for bedchecks, Mary Kate and I will intercept her and show her Mary Kate's ankle. Then she'll take us to the infirmary, and you guys can leave. But, for now, we can all just stay here.'

As I sank down on my bunk beside Mary Kate, my pulse began to slow a little. My hands stopped shaking. I took a few deep breaths and told myself, *It's gonna be okay.*

Then a shrill, horrible sound rang out through the dorm.

'Shit!' I cried, jumping up.

'Shit!' Pat cried.

'Oh no!' Mary Kate cried, hopping up from my bed in panic. She accidentally put weight on her bad ankle, shrieked in pain and promptly dropped the can of frozen Pepsi, which exploded all over the floor in a foamy, sugary flood.

'What is that?' the Toothless Beast asked helplessly, covering his ears with his hands and looking like a giant little boy caught in Willy Wonka's supersized gumball machine. 'Is that the fire alarm?'

Right on cue, we heard Sister Hellda's footsteps of doom down the hallway. Her piercing voice carried even over the wailing alarm: 'THIS IS AN EMERGENCY. I REPEAT, THIS IS AN EMERGENCY. DO NOT

RUN BUT WALK SWIFTLY. EVACUATE THE DORM AT ONCE. I NEED ALL DORM ROOMS CLEARED OUT IMMEDIATELY.'

'Is there actually a fire?' The Toothless Beast looked in rapid panic from me to Mary Kate.

'Yes!' I said.

'How do you know?'

'BECAUSE I STARTED A FIRE!' I shouted at the top of my lungs. There was no point in being quiet anymore; the alarm was blasting, Sister Hellda was yelling and Mary Kate was whimpering. Pat was racing to button up his pea coat, which made me suddenly aware that the fox-print tights under my jeans were twisted and bunched up, giving me a worse wedgie than my skort. But even worse than the shooting pain in my butthole was a strange, unprecedented shooting pain in my heart.

'I started a fire on Academic Quad – it must have spread!' I burst out. 'And Sister Hellda probably found out I started it and now she's coming to get me and she's gonna catch us with boys in our dorm room – which at St Mary's is, like, basically as bad as arson!'

'Really?' The Toothless Beast sounded pretty nervous for a guy who looked like he had eaten five lesser lumberjacks. 'Mary Kate, are you gonna get in trouble? I'll tell them it was my fault. It *was* my fault . . .'

'No, not Mary Kate!' I said. 'Everyone loves her! They hate me! If Sister Hellda comes in here and catches me with Pepsi all over the floor and two hockey players in my dorm room, one with condoms in his pocket and one with no molars, she's gonna think I'm hosting some kind of kinky diabetic Canadian Tooth Fairy pyromaniac orgy in here while St Mary's burns to the ground, and I am gonna be in deep shit!'

Slowly, I raised my head and looked at each of them in turn: at Mary Kate, her Bambi eyes big and her wet, tangled hair streaming down her snow-dusted sweater; at the bewildered Toothless Beast, looking from side to side as if he expected someone to burst through the bookcase and check him into the bunk beds; at Pat, frozen and alert like a freeze-tag player. The fire alarm was wailing, Sister Hellda was pounding on doors and, what's more, I thought I could smell smoke . . .

It was then – that exact moment – that the realization hit me. And, when it hit me, it broke over me again and again like waves of foaming Pepsi, shouting inside my head like an anal-retentive nun, deafening as a fire alarm, impossible to ignore.

'I don't want to get kicked out!' I wailed, shocked by my own words. 'I don't want to leave St Mary's!'

These past two days had been my weirdest days yet at boarding school – and that included the misogynist Labradoodle. But they had changed the way I saw everything. Maybe it had been the unexpected thrill of racing around the quad with Katie Casey, throwing things in the fire and watching sparks fly; maybe it had been kissing Pat, breathless, in the freshly fallen snow; maybe it had been seeing Mary Kate's face at the window after my heart-racing panic, after two days of not speaking to her. The fear of losing something, then the deep, warm hug feeling of finding it again. And now I was going to lose it all . . .

'Okay, stop. Wait,' Mary Kate said. Taking a deep breath, she took hold of the bunk-bed ladder and pulled herself up. Even balancing on her one good leg in the Pepsi flood, she looked stronger somehow, taller, and when she spoke her clear, strong voice projected over the screeching fire alarm.

'It's going to be fine,' she told us. 'Pat and Dom will just go out the way they came in. They came in the window – they'll go out the window. Simple!'

'It wasn't so simple for Winnie the Pooh,' the Toothless Beast said doubtfully.

But I was reassured. 'Right!' I agreed, nodding rapidly. I was too relieved and tense to notice that Mary Kate had called the Toothless Beast 'Dom'. Doing my best to self-soothe, I kept repeating, 'Simple! In the window, out the window, simple!' The guys would be gone in no time, and no one would ever know they'd been in here.

The plan was in motion. Toothless Beast was climbing onto my desk. Pat was lined up behind him, ready to shove him forcefully into the snow should a *Winnie* situation occur. The Toothless Beast was yanking open the frozen window. Wide open. Escape. Freedom. He was about to climb out when . . .

Sister Hellda appeared on the quad in her winter coat, leading a long parade of girls with parkas thrown on over their pajamas through the snow. The line came to a halt right smack in front of our window.

'Everyone, line up right here! Young ladies, form a line in front of this window!'

They formed a line. A human wall of snowy coats blocking our escape.

The Toothless Beast slammed down the window immediately.

Mary Kate said, clearly and distinctly, 'Shit.'

I groaned, squatting (which made my wedgie a billion times worse) in the Pepsi spill. 'Seriously? As soon as I decide I don't want to get in trouble, I end up in THIS friggin' situation? Irony, I hate you *and* Alanis Morissette. We're doomed!'

'We're not doomed!' Mary Kate snapped. 'We just need to *think*. We're four smart people – I mean, sure, Dom's had a few concussions, but I'm sure we can come up with an idea. How do we get Pat and Dom outside without anyone noticing them?'

Fuck Harry Potter, because my first thought was, *Invisibility cloak*. I'm telling you, I'm not great in a crisis.

'We need them to blend in.' My room-mate was talking rapidly and gesturing with her hands, like she was playing charades and there were five seconds left. 'We need them undercover. In disguise. Ooh, I've got it! We'll dress them up!'

'Yeah, why not?' I said sarcastically. 'Pat will get on Dominic's shoulders and we'll throw on my trench coat and that straw fedora you thought you could pull off.'

'*No*,' Mary Kate said impatiently. 'We'll dress them up like GIRLS! We're not supposed to have boys in the dorm, so we'll dress them up like GIRLS! We'll dress them up in our clothes!'

Thrilled by her own creativity, she hopped over to her dresser and started yanking clothes from the hangers.

'Mary Kate!' I called over the fire alarm, which was ringing in my brain now and driving me crazy. 'They won't FIT in our clothes! And, even if they did, don't you think someone is gonna notice that Dominic is an enormous hairy beast in a plaid skort? I mean, the kid is six-four. How is he POSSIBLY going to blend in? It's not like there's a bunch of GIRLS walking around our hallway who are six foot . . .'

It dawned on me and Mary Kate at the exact same moment. When our eyes met, this insane smile stretched across her face, like we were Marie and Pierre Curie and we'd just decided to blow up radium for the first time. Pat and the Toothless Beast – Dom – kept looking back and forth, wide-eyed, from Mary Kate's insane smile to me. I was terrified.

'We can't!' I told Mary Kate.

But already she was hopping determinedly across the sticky floor, snatching something off her desk on the way. She opened the door (the alarm blared even louder) and scuttled one-legged out into the hallway – and I had to follow.

A confused mass of yoga-pant and pajama-clad girls were shuffling towards the door, covering their ears against the alarm and blinking in the flashing emergency lights. They were obediently evacuating. But Mary Kate limped her way forcefully through the crowd, pushing people aside, and walked straight up to the door of the room we had always dreaded: room 102.

It belonged to the Rowers.

'We can't!' I was still protesting over the wailing siren. 'They'll kill us! They will literally kill us. They almost killed you already, and you hadn't even stolen their shit!'

'They're not here,' she said rapidly, trying the handle. The door was locked. 'Read the whiteboard.'

Out of town for Springfield varsity regatta read the message board on their door. *Back Sunday after bedchecks. Go, SM Crew!*

'How did you know that?' I asked Mary Kate.

'I keep the crew schedule in my planner so I know which weekends are safe to go down to the laundry room.'

She had stuck an eyebrow brush (that's what she'd grabbed off her desk) in the door handle and, with an impressively expert series of turns, jiggles and clicks, she picked the lock. The door swung open.

I stood gaping in the doorway. But Mary Kate was already inside, recklessly yanking open drawers and wardrobe doors. When she found what she was looking for, she held them aloft above her head in triumph: two grey varsity sweatsuits, size XXL.

'Mary Kate! That's stealing!' I said in astonishment and admiration, my ears ringing now from shouting over the alarm. 'You just broke into their room and *stole* their shit!'

'Good!' Mary Kate cried, whirling around with savage joy flashing in her eyes. 'They broke my friggin' nose – it's about time I got my revenge!'

The whole time, I was holding my breath. Between that, the wedgie and Mary Kate digging her little claws into my shoulder to keep her balance with her bad ankle, it was a really friggin' uncomfortable seven minutes. And it felt like an eternity because it was as tense as hell.

There we were, proceeding down the hallway in an orderly fashion as instructed – outwardly calm, obediently evacuating the dorm. There we were, just Mary Kate and I . . . and two six-foot-plus figures in grey XXL sweatsuits looming over us with their hoods drawn down low over their shadowy faces. Nothing out of the ordinary. Nothing you wouldn't see on an average night in St Theresa Hall. Nothing remotely sketchy, shady or suspicious – right?

There we were, at the open front door. The cold wind and snow were on our faces. There we were on the front steps. No Long Huggers in our way (*phew*). There we were, walking down the steps. Four steps to go – three steps to go – two, one. Our boots touched down in the snow, and the boys bolted across the quad, disappearing into the anonymity of the whirling blizzard.

Safe, I thought, finally exhaling.

We tramped through the snow to join the rest of the dorm girls, and I managed to pick my wedgie through my winter layers. But, just as I got rid of that pain in my ass, there came another one – Tambourine Spanker, who was wearing her L.L.Bean ski parka and kitten-print pajamas, and acting as Sister Hellda's little helper by counting all of us, suddenly called out:

'Wait! Sister Hilda, there's a problem! The girls from one oh two!'

Fire trucks were flashing, honking, driving right onto the quad. The sirens were screaming accusations at us, the blinding red and white lights flashing in our eyes like interrogation lamps. Mary Kate and I stood shoulder to shoulder, frozen with guilt. Tambourine Spanker must have spotted Pat and Dom! All that stress and worry, all that effort and secrecy and Mary Kate's genius and holding my breath and my wedgie and the exploding Pepsi can and risking concussions to break into the Rowers' room and steal their enormous clothes for invisibility cloaks, all for nothing.

I was gonna get kicked out. And, for the second time that night, I thought how much I really, really didn't want to.

But then, as Sister Hellda hurried down the dorm steps towards us, Tambourine Spanker finished her thought: 'I haven't seen them at all!'

Mary Kate and I exhaled heavily.

Sister Hellda stormed over, her dark eyes wide in panic above her hawk nose, but right then Mary Kate piped up in a sweet voice: 'They're at the regatta, Sister Hilda, remember?'

'Yeah, the varsity regatta at Springfield,' I chimed in. 'Remember? They'll be back Sunday night.'

'Oh.' Sister Hellda looked flustered. 'Right. Of course. Right.'

Then she studied us more closely, suspiciously. Disheveled? Yes, but deceptively sweet, smiling, so helpful and innocent in the virgin snow, looking extra adorable because of the way Mary Kate was leaning against me, like red panda cubs sharing a branch.

'Thank you, girls,' she said rather stiffly.

Sister Hellda hurried off, Tambourine Spanker scurried after her in her kitten pajamas, and we stood there in a strange new world. The snow was falling, the fire trucks were flashing, and the realization dawned on both of us in the bizarre light.

'We got away with it,' I whispered in astonishment, exhaling.

'We got away with it!' Mary Kate echoed, more excitedly.

We had gotten away with it! We had successfully broken curfew and gotten away with it! Ecstatic, we did a little dance in the snow, Mary Kate hopping around in a peg-leg parody of her usual *Charlie Brown Christmas* bop, me breakin' it down in my boots and accidentally giving myself another wedgie.

Then Mary Kate stopped bopping. 'Except . . . you did set the campus on fire, like, less than two hours ago.'

'Fuck,' I said loudly.

19

The best view at St Mary's Catholic School is from the top floor of the main building, right under the famous golden statue of the Virgin Mary. From there, you can see the whole campus, covered in a fresh blanket of white snow, with one long stone walkway cutting a path through the white-draped trees down to the frozen lake.

Take a good look, I told myself. *This could be the last time you ever see it.*

Here I was in the principal's office again, but this time everything was different.

First off, I was friggin' terrified.

My sweaty palms kept slipping as I tried to grip the green leather chair, my legs were trembling violently in my black tights and, as my glance flitted anxiously from mosaic to mosaic on the wall of torture, I felt every arrow in St Sebastian's body piercing my own arms and legs. There was a new mosaic, too: Joan of Arc screaming as she was burned alive. I was pretty sure Father Hughes had just put it up this morning as some kind of subliminal message about me and the fire. Or to scare the shit out of me. It was working. I was scared shitless.

The second big difference was the one Father Hughes pointed out himself.

'Well, Ms Heck, I wish I could say it was unexpected to find you here for a disciplinary meeting,' he began, serious as always behind his desk. Then he turned his head and his tone changed. 'But it *is* rather unexpected to have you here with her, Ms Casey.'

Katie Casey was sitting in the green leather chair next to mine. For once, she was not smiling.

'I believe the last time we met in this office,' he told her, 'we were awarding you a mentoring prize, yes? And today we are here for something very different.'

Katie Casey held her breath as Father Hughes opened a folder and removed the dreaded yellow sheet – the incident report. Her first. My last. The almighty mahogany stamp sat like a loaded weapon on the desk.

'At approximately ten forty-five p.m. last night, the school maintenance team discovered a fire on Academic Quad. A group of students, which included Ms Casey and Ms Heck, was repeatedly told to leave the quad, but did not comply. By the time I arrived, once again asking the students to evacuate for their own safety, Ms Heck had left, but Ms Casey, who was still present, indicated that she and Ms Heck had started the fire as a form of protest.

'Shortly after curfew, fire alarms went off in St Theresa Hall. All dorm residents were evacuated. The fire department reported to the scene and investigated, discovering that a piece of ... *debris* ... from the earlier fire on Academic Quad had been carried by the strong winds eastward, settling in the shrubbery behind the dorm and generating enough smoke to activate the fire alarms before ultimately being extinguished by the heavy snowfall.'

I frowned. 'Debris?'

Father Hughes reached under his chair, brought up a Ziploc bag, withdrew an object and set it carefully on the desk in front of us. It was a long, skinny, charred piece of purple fabric, with a metal clasp in the center.

'Oh my God,' I breathed. 'My BRA STRAP set the dorm on fire?'

My brave little bra strap! It had sailed across campus on the wind and kept the fire of rebellion burning. Well, kind of.

'Ms Casey,' he said, 'you have a long-standing record of responsibility and concern for the spiritual and physical well-being of your fellow students. Can you illuminate for me what happened last night?'

Katie Casey swallowed, and prepared herself to speak.

I prepared myself, too, because I knew exactly what she was going to say. The speech was ready. I'd coached her. I could practically mouth the words along with her.

Early this morning, Katie Casey and I had met up at the statue of an old singing nun on Girls' Quad, halfway between our two dorms. I got there early and, as soon as I saw her coming towards me in her adorable ski-bunny gear, I lunged at her across the knee-high snowdrifts and

288

immediately offered to take the blame. I'd offered last night, of course, when I left her alone with our raging fire, the cigarette lighter and all the incriminating evidence, but maybe she'd been all high on the excitement, or peer-pressured by my West Coast badassery, or dizzy from smoke inhalation. Say what you want about my morals, I knew I had to give her another chance to back out. I was probably done at St Mary's for good, but that was no reason for her to get screwed over.

She said no. She would come with me to our disciplinary hearing with Father Hughes.

'Well, in that case,' I said, 'there are magic words that will get you through your first disciplinary hearing at St Mary's. Kinda like Dorothy and the ruby slippers and "There's no place like home" – except you're not trying to get sent back to bland-ass Kansas. You say this, exactly this: "I'm so sorry. I made a mistake. I've never done anything like that before, and I'll never do it again."'

She looked doubtful. 'That works?'

'Well, not for me,' I clarified. 'Once you keep getting called into the principal's office, like, forty times for different alcoholic and sexual escapades, plus vandalism involving an obscene spray-paint mural, the magic wears off. But for YOU, a first-time offender, it will work. Trust me.'

So now, in Father Hughes's office, I waited for the magic words. There wasn't a chance in hell for me, but it was possible Katie could save herself.

'I . . .' she began.

I'm so sorry, I thought intensely, trying to telegraph the words over mindwaves to her, and almost began to whisper it: *I made a mistake. I've never done anything like that before . . .*

Instead, she said, 'I do have something to say.' And she took a breath and started.

'I *am* sorry about the fire. It was dangerous, and it wasn't fair to the fire department or the school maintenance staff who had to come out in the snow because of it.'

Okay, I thought, watching her with interest. *She did the apology. A little more detail than I suggested, but ya know, to each her own . . .*

'But I'm sure you'll understand that we were super disappointed. Alex and I have been working this whole semester on the festival. It was important to us. But St Mary's decided that sports were more important.'

Wait . . . where was she going with this?

'I know that hockey is really exciting,' she continued, sitting up straighter in the chair, 'and the school spirit is really great – all the pep rallies and the marching band and everything. But, just because one group of people may be louder than another, it doesn't mean their voices are more important.'

'HELL, YEAH!' I burst out, jumping out of my chair, all my tension exploding in sudden surprise and excitement. Father Hughes gave me a look and I sat back down, mumbling to Katie Casey, 'No – you keep going.'

'Alex and I were super frustrated,' said Katie Casey, 'because an event which was important to us – and which we thought should also be important to the St Mary's administration – was canceled suddenly, with barely any notice, and no apology. We thought it was right to protest. And I get that our protest was dangerous – but maybe it was extra dangerous because so many staff were at the banquet. I mean, the first fire on Academic Quad went out and we started a whole other bigger one before anyone noticed! We basically had no supervision.'

'Well, let's not complain about that right now,' I cautioned her. 'Personally, I think a little less supervision could be healthy for us. Give us some space, inspire some independence, we can make our own mistakes . . . anyway, you guys can talk about that later . . .'

Katie Casey concluded: 'I don't think what Alex and I did was right. But I don't think what the school did was right, either.'

Wow.

Did Katie Casey seriously just tell off Father Hughes? Had she actually helped me set the quad on fire and then told Father Hughes *he* was wrong?

I looked up at screaming Joan of Arc. Even she looked impressed.

Father Hughes lifted the mahogany stamp over the incident report. I braced myself for the resounding thud, the authority of it, the finality. But he hesitated and, when he did, Katie Casey picked up something else from his desk: my burnt bra strap.

'I can't help thinking,' she said, 'about the burning bush.'

I frowned at her in total confusion, and not just because of all the 'smoldering loins' jokes running through my head.

'In the Book of Exodus,' Katie Casey explained to me, 'God talked to Moses through a bush. The bush was on fire, but it didn't actually burn, and no one got hurt.' She turned to Father Hughes. 'Because the burning bush wasn't an act of destruction; it was an act of communication.'

Father Hughes considered this. He looked at Katie Casey; he looked at me; he looked back at Katie Casey.

And then – miraculously – he set the stamp down.

'I do hope,' he cautioned sternly, 'that all future acts of communication on this campus take a less . . . *incendiary* . . . approach.'

But that was it. He put my bra strap back in the Ziploc bag, gave it to me and stood up to shake our hands.

'Have a nice Saturday, Ms Casey, Ms Heck,' he said. 'I suggest you take some time for rest and schoolwork.'

Wait – what?

'Me too?' I asked dumbly.

'Yes, Ms Heck.'

'Me? I should have a nice Saturday? And get some rest? And do my homework?'

'Yes, Ms Heck. As I have told you before, your junior year at St Mary's is an exceptionally important one. It prepares you for your future – most immediately, for your *senior* year at St Mary's.'

'My senior year at St Mary's?' I repeated.

And, with that, he waved us out of the door.

Out on the stairwell, Katie and I looked at each other.

Who *was* this chick? What kind of witch was she? The fact that she hadn't gotten in trouble wasn't too surprising, given it was her first time in the principal's office and she'd been a favorite of teachers and nuns for years now. But this time she hadn't been sucking up. She'd told Father Hughes the truth; she'd told him he was wrong. And, instead of punishing her, he'd listened.

He'd listened – and he'd let me stay.

It occurred to me in some part of my dazed, dumb brain that it was actually possible I could learn something from Katie Casey. I mean, not about politics, or sexuality, or the morality of masturbating to the sweaty Judas from that Bible video we watched in freshman theology – because she was totally clueless and wrong on all that stuff – but about getting people to listen. Getting your way. Maybe she was kind of like Machiavelli, or Sun Tzu if he wrote *The Art of War* in pink, sparkly gel pen.

I took a deep breath and said – 'Katie?'

'Uh-huh?'

'So . . . we have one last meeting of the Feminist Club after finals. I was thinking . . . you could come, if you want? In case we wanna talk about the *Monologues*, or the festival, or . . .'

Katie's smile returned. 'Yeah! Definitely! Let me know when – I'll be there!'

I was staying at St Mary's.

At first, I felt this massive relief. Then I felt a little bit of regret when I realized I would actually have to catch up on all my homework, and study for my finals, too. But overall, by Sunday, the weekend felt kind of anticlimactic. I hadn't gotten in trouble; Sister Hellda never found out about the guys in the dorm. The snowplow had cleared away any evidence of our fire on the quad, the mini bra-strap fire in the smoldering bush had been put out, and no one had gotten hurt.

Oh – well, except Mary Kate. Her ankle was broken. After a trip to the hospital with her new best friend, the school nurse, her parents picked her up and took her home early for Thanksgiving.

I spent Thanksgiving break catching up on physics labs, watching trashy reality TV and eating dining-hall turkey with exchange students from Chile, and by the time Mary Kate got back we were in the last weeks of the semester. Seniors were running around, freaking out about college applications, and that whole strange, snowy night *The Non-Vagina Monologues* never happened might have been forgotten – except there was one very interesting result, one very important consequence whose revelation would rock the whole campus: the Toothless Beast announced he was coming to St Mary's.

The news broke Monday when I was waiting in line for the new candy-cane mocha at the coffee shop. Suddenly a sophomore in glasses streaked through the student center, holding a school newspaper above his head and shouting, 'Breaking news! Breaking news! THE TOOTHLESS BEAST IS COMING TO ST MARY'S!'

The whole place erupted in cheers. Preeti from the dorm happened to be behind me and she grabbed my arm.

'Oh my God!' she said. 'Mary Kate! I bet he's coming because of Mary Kate!'

'What?' I said. 'You know about that?'

Preeti rolled her eyes. '*Everyone* knows about that, Alex. A bazillion people at the recruit party saw them leave together. And a bunch of people saw them sneak out after curfew, too.'

'So?'

'So . . . he comes to St Mary's, goes to a party full of pretty girls, leaves with Mary Kate and *boom!* He's on our team.'

I bolted. I pushed my way through the cheering crowd to the exit. I ran straight back to our dorm and burst in the door.

'Did you hear?' I blurted out, breathless. 'He's coming to St Mary's! The Toothless Beast! DOM!'

Mary Kate was at her desk studying. Her crutches were leaning against the dresser and there was a bottle of ibuprofen next to her textbook. She glanced up briefly but avoided my eyes. Her lips tightened into a perfectly straight line.

'Oh,' she said. 'That's nice.'

It had been three days since she'd returned to school, and Mary Kate still hadn't told me what had happened between her and the Toothless Beast. To be fair, she'd been dealing with a painful injury and the subsequent realization while using crutches in the snow that disabled access at St Mary's sucks as much as everything else at this school. That's why I hadn't pushed her. I hadn't even said the guy's name. But it had taken a lot of willpower because three days is like an entire friggin' Neptune year when you're waiting for hook-up gossip.

And there was no avoiding the issue now. I mean, the Toothless Beast was coming to campus! Were they going to be friends? Were they going to DATE? Were they going to awkwardly avoid each other because they'd hooked up? *Had* they hooked up? Well, whatever the truth was, now that he was coming to campus, she would have to tell me, right?

She didn't.

December

20

Study days are tense. The whole week had basically been one metaphorical clenched butthole.

But that Saturday the entire school got a big stress reliever. It was a special occasion guaranteed to relieve the tension that had been building all week: it was the first varsity hockey play-off game, and the Toothless Beast was playing.

The whole campus was lively and buzzing, with cheering and laughter on the quads and everyone bustling around in hockey sweatshirts, painting their faces green. Dominic LeClair had arrived at St Francis Hall that morning, and would be putting on his St Mary's jersey for the first time that afternoon.

Everyone was getting into the spirit. Even Mary Kate had put away her textbooks and shelved her flashcards. I dug out the green pompon hat I'd bought in the bookstore freshman year to cover my illegal cartilage piercings; Mary Kate pulled her hair back into a ponytail with a big green bow. We took turns drawing the St Mary's logo on each other's cheeks with my Wicked Bitch of the West green eyeliner.

As I traced the logo on Mary Kate's cheek, I asked casually, 'So, has Dominic told you anything about the game? Is he nervous?'

(I had decided that maybe Mary Kate was insulted when I called him 'the Toothless Beast', and a personal approach would be better.)

But Mary Kate turned her head away instantly, which really messed up my face-painting. 'Nope. Hasn't said anything.' And her lips tightened into that straight line again.

I pushed a little. 'But have you talked to him at all? Do you have his number?'

'I have his number,' she said pertly. 'We text sometimes.'

They TEXTED sometimes? What the hell! In the past, when Mary Kate got a *Candy Crush* invite from a guy on Facebook, we'd spend hours bent over her phone like two greedy British archeologists decoding an ancient tablet they'd stolen. Now she was texting a guy! Without me! This was too much!

'Mary Kate,' I said sternly, 'what happened between you and the Toothless Beast?'

Nothing. That's what I expected her to say. That's what she was going to say. Of course nothing had happened. This was Mary Kate!

Instead, she pursed her lips, avoided my eyes and said very primly: 'I don't kiss and tell.'

'Kiss?' I squawked. 'So you KISSED him?'

My room-mate just tilted her chin up and looked away, which drove me even crazier.

'So you DID kiss him! Oh my God, you kissed him! Did you . . . oh my God . . . Mary Kate! DID YOU SLEEP WITH THE TOOTHLESS BEAST?'

Hundreds of contradictory thoughts raced through my head. She must have slept with the Toothless Beast! Why else was she out after curfew? Why else was she acting so weird? But she *couldn't* have slept with the Toothless Beast! Mary Kate didn't sleep with guys! And she definitely wouldn't sleep with someone she'd just met! I knew Mary Kate!

But *did* I really? She had been so weird lately. So calm. So collected. So discreet. So mature. She wasn't even braiding her hair anymore. Maybe this newfound maturity meant she had lost her virginity!

No way. That whole idea that 'losing your virginity' is some kind of milestone that makes you an adult is bullshit, left over from the days of Queen Victoria when you sold your daughter for a stable of racehorses. You don't get any kind of mysterious wisdom from having sex. The only thing most teenagers get out of first-time sex is a urinary tract infection and that sad-faced kid from sixth-period Spanish following you around like a puppy and henna-tattooing your name on his pasty ass. Oops, just me then? Anyway . . .

But the Toothless Beast was pretty cute. And seemed nice.

Mary Kate looked me straight in the eye. 'Actually . . .' she began.

Right at that moment, a deafening blare sounded across the quad: the fucking St Mary's Marching Band, with their impeccable pain-in-my-crotch timing, was crossing in front of our dorm, blasting the school fight song at full volume. A massive, cheering crowd streamed behind them.

'Oh look!' Mary Kate chirped with obvious relief, pointing out of the window. 'The band! Let's go – we don't want to miss the march-out!'

And, throwing her green scarf over her shoulder and snatching up her crutches, she hobbled rapidly out of the room and disappeared down the hallway. I'm telling you, for a chick with a broken ankle, girlfriend can MOVE when she wants to.

21

Out on the quad, seventy-seven trombones and that one lone dude piccolo player were all blowing and banging and trilling their little hearts out. Blinding early-winter sunlight was reflecting off the brass instruments, a dizzying array of flags was waving and a crowd of green-clad sports maniacs was pouring out of every dorm.

The crowd swept us across campus to the sports center, into the frosty arena and up into the hot crush of the bleachers. We teetered trying to balance standing up on the four-inch wooden benches, a group of screaming girls with spray-dyed green hair behind us and, in front, a line of shirtless dudes body-painted with big letters: G-O-S-T-M-A-R-Y-S-! The exclamation point was the worst part. This super-hairy senior had actually *shaved* an exclamation point into his chest hair AND his back hair. How does a high-school guy even get that hairy? Clearly, this dude does not need ancestry.com to know his great-grandma was getting down and dirty with a grizzly bear.

So there Mary Kate and I were, swallowed up by this mass of freaks, and every time the feral fangirls went wild cheering – which was every five seconds – we were shoved face first into the Exclamation Point's back hair.

How the hell am I gonna get it out of her HERE? I thought.

No, this was not the place to have a sensitive and nuanced discussion about Mary Kate's nascent sexuality. I would just have to creepily stare at her and use the skills I'd picked up from three seasons of *Sherlock* to figure out what had happened by her reactions.

So, while everyone else was cheering and chanting, I was watching my best friend, who was balanced on her crutches on the narrow bleachers. Other than glancing down when Pat was introduced, to see him race out onto the ice and stop short with a showy flourish sending up a spray of ice that would have made a killer snow cone, I was intensely studying Mary Kate.

'AND NOW,' the announcer thundered, 'MAKING HIS ST MARY'S VARSITY ICE HOCKEY DEBUT, NUMBER SIXTY-SIX, RIGHT WING . . . DOMINIC LECLAIR!'

It was pandemonium. The whole arena was on its feet. The band was going berserk. The entire student section was shouting, cheering, roaring, stamping, whistling. The guys in front of us were pounding their bare chests like Tarzan, the girls behind us screaming. Any second now, they would pull their bras out from under fifteen layers of thermal long johns and throw them onto the ice.

And beside me, right in the middle of it all, Mary Kate, balanced calmly on her crutches, was clapping a polite little clap like she was Princess Friggin' Kate watching a polo match with her shiny-ass hair. Her lips were once again glued together in that neutral, inscrutable, infuriating line.

But she wouldn't be able to stay neutral much longer. It started with a whisper here, a knowing look there. Then, slowly and surely, gossip began to spread through the crowd. Rumors. Rumors about the Toothless Beast . . . and Mary Kate.

Preeti had been right: everyone knew. Maybe it had begun with the guys at the recruit party who saw them leave together, maybe later. But everyone had found out that our new star hockey player had spent his first night at St Mary's breaking curfew with my best friend.

And they wanted to know more.

People were poking each other, swiveling their beanie-clad heads around to stare at Mary Kate and wriggle their eyebrows suggestively. Then we heard the first audible whispers: 'That's her!'

Between bursts of cheering or booing, we could hear:

'That's the girl who got him to come to St Mary's!'

'I heard it was love at first sight!'

'I heard he gave her his championship ring – is she wearing his championship ring?'

'I can't see – she's wearing mittens!'

At first, Mary Kate bravely ignored it – just as she had been bravely ignoring me for days. She kept her eyes straight ahead, pretending to be deeply absorbed in checks and hat tricks and other hockey-ish things. But soon it got harder to ignore.

It was a close game. The other team were killers: seven-foot-tall, fully bearded dudes with rage problems from a school in the northern Minnesota woods. The action on the ice was aggressive and violent, and the energy in the arena was tense.

When the refs made a questionable call, the whole crowd booed and hissed and threw stuff. And, when the Toothless Beast made a good play, the whole student section turned to Mary Kate and burst into ecstatic cheering, like she was the queen reigning over a gladiator battle and Russell Crowe had just stabbed another man homoerotically through the thigh.

The rumor mill was still churning, and by the second half it was turning out some pretty juicy stuff.

'How do you think she *really* convinced him to come to St Mary's?'

'I heard she did that frozen-grape trick from *Cosmo*.'

'I never really understood that one . . .'

'I heard another hockey player walked in on them.'

'I heard Father *Callahan* walked in on them – and, when he saw what they were doing, he started performing an exorcism. That's how dirty it was.'

'No *wonder* the Toothless Beast wanted to come to St Mary's!'

It was too much. Mary Kate's right eye started to twitch. Then her left eye, too. Her cheeks were burning. And, after one particularly filthy comment about what she and the Toothless Beast had supposedly done on a St Ambrose Hall bathroom sink, she refused to take it anymore.

She sat down.

Now that sentence might sound pretty simple to you. *She sat down.* Subject, verb . . . okay, whatever, I'm not a grammar dweeb, but it's simple: the chick sat down. At a normal school, that would be a normal thing to happen. At a normal school, she could have sat for the next forty-five minutes, staring at people's butts, unable to see a friggin' minute of the game action, but perfectly content and left alone.

But here's the problem: St Mary's hockey, like everything else at this school, has rules. At a St Mary's hockey game, you don't sit down. And this is a long-established, widely believed, sacred superstition, like walking around the lake. You cannot sit down at a hockey game or the team will lose. So our whole student body *stands* on the bleachers for the whole length of the game. It can be negative twenty degrees in the arena, you can be numb in every extremity going into triple overtime and so weak from exhaustion that your legs are like string cheese, but no matter what happens: *You. Do. Not. Sit. Down.*

So when one of the guys in front of us – the Shirtless M, to be exact – turned around and saw Mary Kate sitting down on the bleachers, he did not take it well.

'We stand with the team!' he reminded her. 'If you sit down, you let the team down!'

'Oh, c'mon,' I said. 'Leave her alone.'

He ignored me and hit the guy next to him – the Shirtless T – on the shoulder. The Shirtless T was even more outraged.

'How DARE you sit down at a hockey game!' he

roared. 'I don't pay fifty thousand dollars a year in tuition so you can sit DOWN at a hockey game!'

My room-mate stared straight ahead and refused to reply.

'Hey!' I snapped. 'She has a broken ankle! If she needs to sit down, she gets to sit down!'

'I've failed three scoliosis tests, but you don't see *me* complaining!' the Shirtless T said self-righteously, puffing out his scrawny painted chest.

'Yeah, and besides . . .' The Shirtless M narrowed his eyes and pointed his finger at Mary Kate. 'We all know exactly HOW she broke her ankle.'

'Do you?' I asked eagerly, without thinking. 'Because I'd really like the details . . .'

But then my loyal indignation came rushing back and I pushed the Shirtless M, who was getting all up in our personal space. 'It doesn't matter HOW she broke her ankle. The point is, the girl needs a second to sit down!'

Unfortunately, just then the other team scored a goal, putting them ahead by two. A huge *boooo* went up from the crowd.

'See?' the Shirtless M exploded, his man-nipples pointy with rage. 'THAT's what happens when you sit down!'

Cupping his hands around his mouth, he made an announcement: 'Fellow students! I call your attention to something SHAMEFUL going on here. The Toothless Beast's girlfriend is sitting down – I repeat – SITTING DOWN – during the game!'

The crowd erupted in righteous fury. They were shouting,

hissing, spitting. Everywhere I turned was body heat, angry breath and the crush of impending doom. My chest was tight with panic. I was a trapped animal. The booing and hissing swelled into a single angry, manic chant:

'STAND UP, STAND UP, STAND UP, STAND UP!'

This is how it ends, I thought in terror, my heart racing under my puffy coat. *Iceman, get ready – you're about to have two rival ghosts on campus.* Any second now, the two of us would be ground to dust beneath a thousand pairs of snow boots.

I looked down at my room-mate for one last glimpse of her before the angry mob swallowed us whole, expecting to see her quivering like a tiny white rabbit in a meme that said, 'PWEASE HELP ME.'

But she wasn't. She was small, yes, but her narrow shoulders were drawn proudly back, and her jaw was set: everything in her body language showed steely determination.

And then something happened, something heroic and shocking and incredible: Mary Kate stood up.

She stood up, planted her crutches on the bleachers and, in a clear, angry, self-confident voice that carried over that entire thousand-person crowd, yelled, 'SHUT UP!'

Everyone was staring at her.

'All your little whispers and rumors and lies. It's all BS!'

My jaw dropped. This wasn't the kind of language my room-mate used in her *Downton Abbey* fan fiction!

'In fact, this whole *school* is BS!' Mary Kate plowed on, a savage relish in her voice. 'I've tried to fit in here. I've tried to be a perfect St Mary's girl. But I walk around the lake and what happens? I get BARFED on! I try to play football – because sports are *soooo* friggin' important around here – and what happens? I get my nose broken!'

Whatever was happening on the ice, none of us cared anymore. What was the score? No one knew. Everyone was riveted by Mary Kate's rant. And I could tell from the light in her eyes, from her chest heaving with excited breaths, that she was enjoying holding court. I don't think she'd ever raised her voice that loud in her life.

'So now guess what?' she announced. Her eyes were flashing; she was building to a vicious crescendo, ready to deal her final death blow to the trembling crowd. 'I'm not standing up for you. I'm not even STAYING for you! I don't give a frozen poop about hockey, so I'm leaving. And you can stay, and you can whisper about me, and you can judge me all you want. But none of you knows, and none of you will EVER know, what I did – or didn't do – with my VAGINA!!!'

Shock struck the crowd dumb. Even the marching band was quiet. We could hear the sticks scratching and the puck sliding and the skates scraping on the ice, the shouts of the players through their spitty mouthguards, but it was all distant background noise as Mary Kate's almighty word echoed in the frosty air: *VAGINA VAGINA VAGINA VAGINA* . . . No one dared speak after it.

My best friend had just won the vagina game.

And she followed it up with a really righteous storm-out. Slamming her crutches down, she stalked with single-minded, reckless determination towards the exit. The shocked crowd parted for her like a body-painted Red Sea.

I should have followed her right away, but I was too surprised to move. I just stood there on the bleachers. The whole student section was stunned. Which I guess is why it took us all several minutes to realize that the action on the ice had stopped – the game was on a time-out, and a single player had skated over to us and removed his helmet.

It was the Toothless Beast. His curls were damp with sweat and he held his helmet with the mouthguard dangling.

'Hey!' he called up into the bleachers. 'What's going on? Is Mary Kate okay?'

The Shirtless T called back, 'She wasn't standing up, Beast!'

Man, his scoliosis had really made him bitter.

'She has a broken ankle!' Dom called back. 'She should sit down.'

'If you sit down, you let the team down!'

The other dudes around him cheered in agreement, but went silent when the Toothless Beast opened his mouth to speak.

'Ya know,' he said, 'I know you guys have a lot of traditions here, but I don't think we need to sweat all that standing-up and sitting-down stuff. I mean, now that I'm here . . . and you don't suck at hockey anymore.'

'Oh shit!' the shirtless dudes called out. But they loved it. They were laughing and cheering, and down on the ice Dom was grinning a little shyly, flashing his gums. He started to put his helmet back on, but then paused.

'Oh, and by the way, nothing happened between me and Mary Kate. I'm gay. So . . . I hope that's cool with everyone.'

Tugging the cage of his helmet down, he skated back to the game.

The scoreboard said we were down by one goal, but no one cared. Finally, after several long and uncomfortable moments, the Shirtless M broke the silence.

'What did he mean by that?' he said, watching the Toothless Beast body-slam a rival player into the boards. 'He hopes that's cool with everyone? We're cool with that.'

All the shirtless letters nodded in agreement, and the Hairy Exclamation Mark spoke up in indignation. 'I mean, what does he think we are?' he said. 'A bunch of homophobes?'

And, rubbing his big, underage beer belly, he let out a loud, wet belch.

That revolting burp was the most cheerful thing I'd heard in a long time. As I made my way down the bleachers, a great big cheer went up through the crowd. Dominic LeClair had scored a goal, tying the game. '*TOOTH-LESS BEAST!*' everyone chanted. '*TOOTH-LESS BEAST!*'

I felt warm all over in that chilly arena. Maybe, despite everything Mary Kate had said, and everything I had always believed, this school wasn't one hundred percent closed-minded and terrible after all. I think my heart grew three sizes that day.

I hurried to catch up to Mary Kate at the open doorway of the hockey arena, where bright daylight was streaming inside, and where two loving figures were embracing, green pea coat to green pea coat, framed in the blinding-white winter sunshine. It was the Long Huggers.

Seeing them, Mary Kate did not slow down. She did not step aside. Powering ahead, she went straight up to them and cleared her throat loudly. Then, when they didn't move, she said loudly, 'Ex-CUSE me!'

The Long Huggers looked up, startled, then pulled apart – each of them stumbling backwards a step, dazed at their sudden separation. Mary Kate plowed forward between them and left the hockey arena without looking back.

Okay. So maybe my heart grew *four* sizes that day.

22

It was the last St Mary's Feminist Club meeting of the semester.

Finals were over. We had survived. I had even survived my last and worst exam, physics, and when it was done I burst out of the doors, tore up my lab notes, flung them into the frosty air and shouted, 'I'M DONE, MOTHERFUCKERS!' Then I jogged across Academic Quad, where overjoyed seniors in brand-new college sweatshirts were waving acceptance letters in the air, where the big Christmas tree sparkled with tinsel. Mary Kate was waiting for me on the south hill with two trays from the dining hall, and, using them as sleds, we raced down the snowy hill towards the frozen lake, shrieking and laughing.

Now this club meeting was my last responsibility of the semester. But meetings are never that productive right before a break. It's usually some kind of party and the club president brings snacks. Luckily, Katie Casey had taken care of that for me – showing up with her ever-present smile and a tray of brownies.

And, for once at a Feminist Club meeting, I had nothing to say. I had nothing to rage about. I was – for the moment – chill.

A festive mood cheered that moldy basement room. Sarah and Sophia were wearing matching Santa hats; Claudia's Mistletoe Mistress lipgloss left merry stains on her candy-cane mocha cup, and even Robbie Schmidt looked happy as everyone chattered about winter break. I only interrupted to introduce Katie and say, 'Honestly, I don't really have any plans or any ideas right now, so . . . let's get freaky with these brownies!'

But, as I reached across the table, Sarah/Sophia stopped me.

'Wait!' she said, looking around. 'What happened to Father Hughes? Father Hughes is supposed to be here, right?'

All of us looked at the empty seat at the end of the table.

Katie Casey said politely, 'Father Hughes?'

'He was our club advisor,' Claudia informed her. 'After Alex killed the first one.'

'I didn't kill Sister Georgina!' I said. 'She's just, like, living a peaceful life in a warmer place.'

'That's what my dad said about my hedgehog,' Robbie Schmidt said sadly.

'Maybe –' I looked pointedly at Claudia – 'Father Hughes just decided he could trust me to run the club by myself.'

'And what do you think made him trust you?' she asked. 'The fact that you set the campus on fire?'

I looked across the table at Katie Casey and a brief flash of camaraderie passed between us. 'Father Hughes and I have come to ... an *understanding* ... about the fire,' I said.

And maybe, I thought, he had actually listened to my suggestion about giving us more freedom. Did I have total control over the Feminist Club now?

Just then, there was a knock at the door. The woman who came in was a stranger to me. She was wearing the green blazer St Mary's teachers wear when they're not priests or nuns. But she also looked young and cool: she had an asymmetrical bob.

'Ms Chan!' Claudia crowed. Then she turned to us and said, 'Does everyone know Ms Chan? She's the new art teacher. And she was my personal advisor on my AMAZING black-and-white self-portrait series.'

'Hi, everybody,' the young teacher said. 'Father Hughes sent me over to check on you guys. I heard you might be looking for a new faculty advisor?'

'You're a teacher here?' I said in surprise. 'How long have you been at St Mary's?'

'This is my first year teaching,' Ms Chan said. 'But I was actually in the first co-ed class to graduate from St Mary's – one of the pioneers! The school was *not* ready for girls ... but we did get to live in the science building and play ping-pong on the lab tables at night.'

I invited Ms Chan to sit down. She did, and when she tucked the shorter side of her bob behind her ear, I saw that she had at least four ear piercings. She definitely

LOOKED cool. Of course, it was possible Father Hughes had gotten extra devious in his spying on us. But all we were doing today was eating brownies anyway, so . . .

Looking around the table, Ms Chan asked in surprise, 'Is this everyone?'

I was about to say yes when there was another knock on the door and Maggie, my Planned Parenthood road-trip buddy, appeared. She had another Save Your Heart girl with her.

'Are we in the right place?' Maggie asked. 'Is this the Feminist Club? We want to join.'

And then Preeti arrived with a friend.

Then two more freshman girls turned up – one tall and one short. The tall one looked familiar, but I couldn't place her. The short one pointed at Mary Kate and whispered, 'That's the vagina girl!'

Her friend corrected her. 'No, *that's* the vagina girl' – and, when she pointed to me, I saw her black nail polish and the faded shadow of a henna tattoo on the inside of her wrist. It was my potential rebel from the September Club Fair – ready to be rebellious at last.

We were making room for everyone, shifting our puffy coats and backpacks off the last free chairs, when two tall figures appeared in the doorway, casting long shadows across our table. It was the Rowers. Mary Kate and I looked at each other in panic.

'Is this the Feminist Club?' asked the Rower with a long braid over her shoulder. 'We need your help. The Toothless Beast just got to St Mary's, and he's getting all this attention.

He got a whole welcome banquet just because he's a guy and he plays hockey. *We* won the National Varsity Crew Championship last year and barely anyone even showed up. It's not fair, and we want to do something about it.'

I was flustered. 'Well . . . yeah. Definitely. That is unfair. We'll . . . we'll see what we can do.' I looked around the table. 'Does anyone else have something they want to change?'

Preeti spoke up. 'I'm in sex ed right now and it's ridiculous. Ms Hyde is totally clueless. I don't think she's ever even had sex. I'm pretty sure she wears a tankini in the shower.'

Maggie chimed in. 'Well, *I* was gonna say we should have peer counsellors for sex ed. Older students you can go to and ask anything, and it's confidential.' She gave me a small, grateful smile before adding quickly, 'Not that *I* have questions, but . . . hypothetically.'

'These are actually good ideas,' I said. 'I should –'

Before I'd even finished the sentence, Mary Kate was sliding a crisp, blank notebook and uncapped blue pen in front of me.

'What about the dorms? I mean, single-sex dorms, boys or girls. It's so, like . . . *gender-binary*. Can we talk to the school about that?'

That suggestion came from Sarah – or was it Sophia? I made a hurried note in the margins: *Sarah = baby bangs. Sophia = good eyebrows.*

Mary Kate reached over and, with her red pen, corrected it with a double-sided arrow.

'What about an LGBTQI-plus Alliance?' asked Black Nail Polish. 'Do we seriously not have one?'

Ms Chan answered, 'St Mary's always said they couldn't have an official club for gay students because it's a Catholic school.'

'Yeah,' Sophia – it *was* Sophia – replied, 'but isn't everything different now? The Toothless Beast is here and he's gay. And I know St Mary's is really into being Catholic . . . but they're really, *really* into hockey.'

Everyone nodded in agreement and one of the Rowers rolled her eyes and muttered, 'No kidding.'

I jotted a quick note: *Learn the Rowers' names, too.*

Katie Casey's sweet voice rang out. 'What about you, Alex? Have you thought of anything?'

'Actually . . .'

I looked around the room – at Maggie, who gave me another shy smile; at Preeti, my freshman buddy; at Ms Chan and her funky ear piercings; at the Rowers. One of them was twirling the end of her braid nervously; the other had a cute spray of freckles across her nose that I'd never noticed. They didn't look so scary now.

'This semester, we tried – and failed – to put on *The Vagina Monologues*,' I said. 'Most people were totally against it. But *some* people supported it. And what I learned from that is that you can't judge a book by its cover. Or a virgin by their crucifix. Or a feminist by their purple fauxhawk. Or a hockey player by their . . . bloody gums. Even in a place like this, people have stuff going on underneath that you have no idea about, ya know?

'We've all got stories. We've all got voices. So let's tell *our* stories in *our* voices. We'll write our own play. Like . . . *The St Mary's Monologues: Sex, Love and the Lack Thereof.* Ooh, that's good! I just came up with that.'

'I think that's an awesome idea, Alex!' Katie Casey said. 'And I know a whole bunch of Save Your Heart girls who will totally do it, too.'

'Can I still wear a black turtleneck and hide backstage?' Robbie Schmidt asked.

I said yes, and everyone around the table seemed to be nodding in agreement. Then one clear, decisive voice said, 'No.'

Mary Kate was sitting up straight, with her hair in a big bun right on top of her head. The bun she'd started doing during finals, claiming she didn't have time for braids, but I think in reality she liked the three inches it added to her height. Now that she'd told off the entire student body, everyone on campus was a little bit scared of her, and I think she liked that, too. She was walking around all sassy these days, with her shoulders thrown back and that big bun bobbing on her head, like a Russian gymnast who'd just done an illegal triple-flip dismount off the balance beam and was daring anyone to accuse her of using steroids.

I knew she had changed, but even I was surprised when she declared: 'I don't want to put on some watered-down version of this play. We need to put on *The Vagina Monologues*.'

'WHAT?' I couldn't believe my ears.

'This is the Feminist Club, and *The Vagina Monologues* is a feminist play. We've been working on it for months now, and next semester it's time to actually do it.'

I was staring at her in disbelief, shaking my head. Clearly, an alien had possessed her body, right? That would explain the bun – to hide the space antennae.

'At the beginning of the semester,' she continued, 'Alex made a vow. She vowed to stage the first-ever St Mary's Catholic School production of *The Vagina Monologues*. Semester vows are very important,' she added, wincing a little.

I sighed. 'Look, I obviously think it's a good idea. It was *my* idea. But we already tried it, and it didn't work.' I paused and looked across the table. 'What do you think, Ms Chan?'

She considered. 'I do love the show. I did the *Monologues* when I was in grad school in Seattle. It *is* usually for older students . . .' She leaned back in her chair and crossed her legs. 'But we could try some kind of compromise. What if we performed off-campus? Or for juniors and seniors only? Or got permission slips from parents? I think, if we all put our heads together, we can make it happen.'

Everyone in the packed room nodded.

'All right then!' I said. 'So, next semester, we're gonna . . .' Looking down at the list, I summarized: 'Rectify the gender-binary bias in campus housing, enforce equal treatment in varsity sports, revamp the St Mary's sex-ed curriculum and student-health resources, and – finally, at long last, for real this time – produce "St Mary's

Catholic School presents *The Vagina Monologues*." What do we think?'

Everyone nodded. Preeti gave a little cheer. The Rowers clapped.

Ms Chan interrupted. 'Before any of that,' she said sternly, 'there's something important I need to address.'

Shit. I knew she was a spy!

But Ms Chan's face softened into a smile as she looked around. 'I think,' she said, 'we're gonna need a bigger room.'

23

In two hours, we would be gone.

Our dorm room was unnaturally clean – the beds made (both by Mary Kate), the floor swept (also by Mary Kate). We were ready to go home for Christmas break. I had stuffed all my crap into my old army duffel, which was now covered in Pussy Riot pins, and tossed it in the corner of the room. My room-mate, on the other hand, had meticulously rolled and tissue-papered her clothes, studiously following the commandments of that North Korean Closet Dictator who swears the universe doles out good karma based on how you color-code your underwear. Her floral-print suitcase stood neatly to attention beside the door, with Sir Shackleton, wearing his Christmas sweater, perched on top.

Now we were working together on the checklist Sister Hellda had slid under our door that morning.

'Okay,' Mary Kate said, sitting on my desk, swinging her legs as she read off the list. 'Have we . . . turned off the radiator?'

I checked. 'Check.'

'Unplugged all our electronics? Swept the floor? Thrown out or tightly packaged all food?'

'Check. Check. Check.'

She looked up from the list and her face darkened suspiciously. 'What about those joints you were keeping in your laptop case?'

'Don't worry.' I yawned casually. 'I dumped them in the rhododendrons. They're looking super-duper chill this morning.'

That was a lie. Actually, I'd split the last one on the roof of the science building with the Hairy Exclamation Mark. We had run into each other buying candy at the student center and kinda bonded. Funnily enough, his actual name was Mark.

There was a knock at the window and I went over to answer it. Pat, in ski parka and jeans, was standing in his Chucks in two feet of snow.

'Hey! I wanted to say goodbye. When are you guys heading out?' he asked.

'My dad's flight just landed and he rented a car,' I said. 'He's gonna drive us to Minneapolis to meet Mary Kate's family and go ice skating. It's gonna be disgustingly sweet and adorable.'

'Disgustingly sweet sounds pretty good to me,' Pat said. 'Hey, Mary Kate! I've got a Christmas present for you!'

He pulled out of his jacket . . . a bright neon box of tampons, with a red bow on it.

'They're very useful,' he explained. 'And you can decorate your tree with them, too. Or they look great in your hair – Alex taught me that the night I met you guys.'

Mary Kate snatched the box, shaking her head and trying to hide a smile. 'I'm taking them so they don't go to waste,' she told him loftily, and went back to her dusting.

Next Pat pulled out a present in reindeer wrapping paper. 'And this one's for you.'

I grabbed it and shook it. 'What is it?'

'Nope.' He shook his head. 'Can't tell. Santa would sue me.'

I leaned further out of the window. 'Come on! I always snoop on my gifts beforehand.'

'Not this time. Pinkie swear or I'll take it back.'

He threatened to grab it, so I sighed and hooked my pinkie in his. Then I pulled him close and kissed him.

Something light hit me in the back of the head and dropped to the floor. A purple tampon. I looked up and saw Mary Kate armed with another one, grinning.

'*Oooooooh*,' she said in a teasing sing-song. 'Alex has a *boyfriend*.'

I picked up the tampon and threw it behind her. When she turned around, I grabbed Pat again, kissed him even harder and pushed him away.

'Get outta here,' I said. 'Mary Kate and I have to go on a walk.'

'We do?' Mary Kate asked.

'See you in January. Merry Christmas!'

'Merry Christmas!' Pat called, and jogged off across the quad.

A light snow was falling on white-blanketed Girls' Quad as we crossed through the soft drifts, bundled up. The dorms were hushed and dark. Most people had already gone home. Academic Quad was frozen as still as a postcard, the Mary statue wore a white hat of snow, and the golden doors of the main building were locked. The late-afternoon sky turned pink and orange as we walked down the long avenue of pine trees, and, when we came to a little flight of stone steps, I stopped.

Mary Kate, who was wearing furry earmuffs with her power bun, looked around. 'Where are we going?'

I held out my hand.

She narrowed her eyes suspiciously. 'What are you doing?'

'We're walking around the lake,' I told her proudly.

She looked out at the lake, which was pink with reflected sunset under branches bowed by sparkling snow. She groaned and shook her head.

'You're in love with me, aren't you?' she said. 'Well, I guess in the back of my mind I've always known. This explains why you kept trying to spoon me the night the radiator broke.'

'What? No! This is a SYMBOL, Mary Kate. This is me helping you fulfill your semester goal. This is a gesture! Not a romantic gesture, but a friendship gesture.'

She sighed heavily, pulled off her mitten and held out her bare hand. I took it, and we walked down the steps and set off on the tree-lined trail around the lake.

'This doesn't count as achieving my semester goal, you know,' she warned me.

'*Actually*,' I said, 'you might be wrong about that.'

A few nights ago, I'd called my dad to ask him about this whole lake thing. Since he'd been right about the tunnels, I figured he might know some other St Mary's stuff, too. And, according to him, the true meaning of the tradition wasn't being 'boyfriend-girlfriend'; walking around the lake with someone meant you'd be together forever.

'This actually means we'll always be in each other's lives,' I explained. 'We'll be friends forever.'

'No way!' Mary Kate shook her head. 'In a few years, we'll be leading totally different lives. You'll be staging a topless sit-in at Berkeley to protest the government, and I'll be with Rupert in the Bodleian Library at Oxford, wearing adorable matching hand-knitted scarves and studying Shakespeare's sonnets.'

'First of all,' I began, 'you're never going to learn to knit. You've tried three times and it's still a Pinterest pipe dream. And, second of all, we're still going to be friends. Who else is going to bail me out of prison when my sit-in gets busted?'

'I'm not coming to bail you out of prison.'

'One call, Mary Kate! I get one call!'

'Nope. You made your bed, you lie in it.' Then, rolling her eyes, she added, 'Not that you've ever made your bed in your life, but maybe prison will teach you.'

'Will Rupert come bail me out?'

My room-mate gave me a saucy look from under her big bun and wiggled her eyebrows suggestively. 'I think Rupert will be pretty busy.'

We both cracked up laughing.

'Uh-oh, watch out! So you're wearing that hand-knitted scarf and nothing else, huh?' I clucked my tongue in mock disapproval. 'You've gotten really naughty this semester. I don't know who or what corrupted you.'

We continued along the snowy path and came to the bend where you could see the seminary. Mary Kate pointed out where Caleb had told her he was going to be a priest. I kept insisting we were going to stay friends.

'I mean, sure, we might drift apart in college, but we'll reconnect when we're adults. You know, after your English professor husband is caught having an affair and you're a single mother of five freckle-faced kids . . . oh my God! Maybe our kids will get married!'

Mary Kate shook her head, laughing. 'No way. My kids are *not* marrying your kids. My kids are going to the Sorbonne and playing the oboe in the New York Philharmonic; they're not getting derailed because your kids gave them some new-millennium strain of HPV.'

'Fine. We'll reconnect when we're older. It can be like *Golden Girls*! But it will be, like, 2064, so it'll be *Golden Girls* on the moon! You can be Rose and I can be Blanche!'

She wasn't into that, either. 'I'm going to be a wealthy matriarch managing my literary legacy, donating all my letters to universities and things like that. I'm gonna be way too busy to move to the moon with you.'

'C'mon, let me be your moon Blanche!'

The sun was in its final fiery orange blaze above the fringe of pine trees, and we were more than halfway around the lake, still holding hands.

'You know,' I said, 'you never told me what you ACTUALLY said to the Toothless Beast to get him to come to St Mary's.'

'Well,' Mary Kate began, 'first of all, you were right. The recruit party was horrible.'

My room-mate had found herself in a sweaty, crowded common room, surrounded by drunk dudes slapping each other, burping, and – in one case – doing a graphic re-enactment of the time he tore his kneecap off playing street hockey. Mary Kate went to hide in a corner and fill a red Solo Cup with ginger ale to pretend she was drinking beer, when she found the Toothless Beast – Dom – hiding in a corner and doing the same thing.

'So we decided to leave together,' Mary Kate said. 'Of course, all the hockey guys noticed, and they started cheering and making dirty jokes.'

'They're fucking medieval,' I said. 'I'm surprised they didn't come banging on the door afterwards asking to see the bloody sheet.'

'Well, they wouldn't have gotten one,' Mary Kate said. 'This school may think the only possible reason you could be in a room with a guy after eleven p.m. is if you're *boning* each other, but we were just drinking tea and talking. We ended up having this whole heart-to-heart. I asked him if he didn't like any of the girls at the party, and he ended up telling me he didn't like girls, and was having all these problems at St Luke's. And I told him the problems I was having dating at St Mary's. Speaking of which . . .'

She looked around at the bench by the lake, and the trees and bushes covered in snow.

'I think this is where I got puked on.'

'Ew!' I said, looking down at my feet like there'd still be puke there. But everything was covered in a clean, fresh white layer of snow.

'I don't get it,' I said. 'You told him some doofus puked on you in the woods, and that made him want to come to school here?'

'No. I told him St Mary's was different from St Luke's. I told him all the stuff I thought freshman year – that we were all like a family, and the dorms were like the houses from Hogwarts. And I told him about the *Monologues*, too, and Feminist Club, and how the school was changing.' She sighed. 'So now I have to go to confession for getting him here on false pretenses.'

'I don't think so,' I said. 'St Mary's might suck a snowman's balls, but it's definitely better than St Luke's. That place is like a gulag with prom. Here we have a few good things at least . . .'

'Yeah?'

'Yeah! Like when we convince Father Brian to let us have philo class outside in the spring. Those shirtless southern guys with the glow-in-the-dark Frisbee. The big Christmas tree on Academic Quad. Oh, and Fajita Friday.'

'I do really love the big Christmas tree,' Mary Kate had to admit, resting her head on my shoulder. 'And Fajita Friday obviously.'

Looking across the lake, I took a deep breath and inhaled the crisp winter wind blowing off the water. I felt suddenly sentimental, with the golden Mary statue atop the main building looking down on us.

'Of course,' Mary Kate continued, 'a half-hour after I told Dom how progressive and welcoming St Mary's was, I was being catcalled by a bunch of shirtless guys leaning out into a snowstorm to watch me sneak out of a second-story window. And, five minutes after that, I was falling to certain death in the whirling blizzard after losing my grip on the windowsill.'

'Hey, that's how I fell in August! Second-story window, St Ambrose Hall! Same thing! Those windows are crazy slippery.'

'Yes! It's a total health hazard! They need to fix that.'

'If they're gonna set such a strict curfew, they really need to make sure we have a safe means of sneaking out when we break it. It's only fair. Let's get Health and Safety Standards on it.'

'We should sue.'

'Seriously.'

'This place –' Mary Kate narrowed her eyes critically, surveying the lake, snowy woods, the bare branches – 'needs a lot of improvement.'

'Oh, definitely,' I agreed, musing.

But, in the distance, a faint silver moon and stars were shimmering now in the lavender twilight sky. They looked like the sequins on the puffy eighties prom dress my mom tried to make me wear to a middle-school dance, which at first I thought was totally tacky before I realized it was SO tacky it actually came around to being vintage cool again. It was pretty.

We were still holding hands.

'But right now, with no priests around, no nuns spying on us with binoculars in the bushes, no homework, douchey jocks or hairy backs, and the prospect of three peaceful weeks of free and unfettered sin ahead of me . . . it actually looks kinda badass,' I said.

And, together, we took the last few steps.

Acknowledgments

First and foremost, thank you to my agent Gemma, who was the warm and humorous light at the end of a long tunnel of work and worry. She not only guided me through the submission process with confidence and positivity, but also suggested key editorial changes that made the plot work. Most importantly, she liked my vibrator joke.

Thank you also to the whole team at the Bent Agency.

Another person whose incredibly insightful suggestions shaped *Bad Habits* for the better is my talented, collaborative, and respectful editor Natalie. She made the dreaded revision process a breeze! Thank you also to Wendy and Jane for their eagle-eyed copy-editing and creative problem-solving, and to the whole team at Penguin Random House. As a bigger Anglophile than even Mary Kate, I am thrilled to have my book published in the UK!

Thank you to my first agent, Dan, and my first editor, Elizabeth, for giving me my start in YA publishing ten years ago.

On a personal note, I am grateful to my family, friends, and teachers for their support. Most specifically, thank you to my fellow artsy folks from the Arteles Creative Center in Hämeenkyrö, Finland, where I wrote a key draft of this manuscript. As I plugged away at my 2,000 words a day, they alternately cheered me on and distracted me with naked saunas and frosty beers. Both approaches were extremely conducive to productivity. *Kiitos!*

An Interview with Flynn Meaney

Where did the inspiration for St Mary's as a setting come from?

Definitely my time at the University of Notre Dame in the early 2000s: we had the wild sports fanatics, the apocalyptic snowy winters, way too many priests, and even a pair of long huggers – who always seemed to be blocking my path when I was in a bad mood. To this day I don't know who they were, because I never saw their faces! I wonder if they've let go of each other by now . . .

Why did you choose to write a YA novel about feminism?

Students at my college actually did try to put on *The Vagina Monologues*, and in the end they had to perform it off-campus. I wasn't involved, but I remember sitting in the dining hall – me, a New York fish out of water in the conservative Midwest – reading outraged letters in the college newspaper from alumni who were offended by the word *vagina* and thinking to myself, *How ridiculous are these grumpy old dudes?*

But the truth is a lot of us are uncomfortable with the word *vagina*, or uncomfortable buying tampons, or uncomfortable talking about gender and sex. So I didn't set out to write a book about feminism, but it was interesting to explore our complicated feelings about those issues. And because I was exploring those feelings in a very enclosed, specific environment through small (and strange!) incidents – fighting the president of the purity club to put gynecological stirrups in the school play, using terrible homemade birth control because you can't get condoms, nip-slipping at the school swim test – I could explore the humour in them, too.

Who do you most closely identify with? Alex, Mary Kate, or another character in the book altogether?
When I was sixteen, I was definitely Mary Kate! It was easy to write her because I took so many things from my own life, like my love for British mini-series and school supplies (I really had – and loved – the tiny purple stapler with tiny purple staples). Now, in my thirties, I think I've got a bit of Alex in me, too. I'm more comfortable speaking my mind – and buying tampons!

What were your own favourite books growing up?
My absolute favourites were the Betsy-Tacy books by Maud Hart Lovelace. The first books in the series are children's books and the later ones are YA, so I grew up with them

and they influenced my life so much! I am also a big Beverly Cleary fan, and both those authors were so great at showing human dynamics in small everyday interactions.

At the same time, I loved reading about experiences that girls had in other time periods or countries in memoirs like *Red Scarf Girl* or *Warriors Don't Cry*.

In my teenage years, I was into reading diaries – Anaïs Nin, Anne Morrow Lindbergh. While studying French in college, I discovered Colette and Marguerite Duras, who both mixed fiction and memory in a way I found fascinating. Then in graduate school I read *The Sisters – the Saga of the Mitford Family* by Mary S. Lovell, and wrote my poetry thesis about the Mitford sisters. All these are narratives of women leading unconventional lives in restrictive societies – a story genre I think both Alex and Mary Kate would enjoy!

About the Author

Flynn Meaney is the author of *The Boy Recession* and *Bloodthirsty*. She studied marketing and French at the University of Notre Dame, where she barely survived the terrifying array of priests and nuns, campus ghosts and bone-crushing athletes who inspired *Bad Habits*. Since completing a very practical MFA in poetry, she works for a French company and travels often between New York (when she's in the mood for bagels) and Paris (when she's in the mood for croissants).

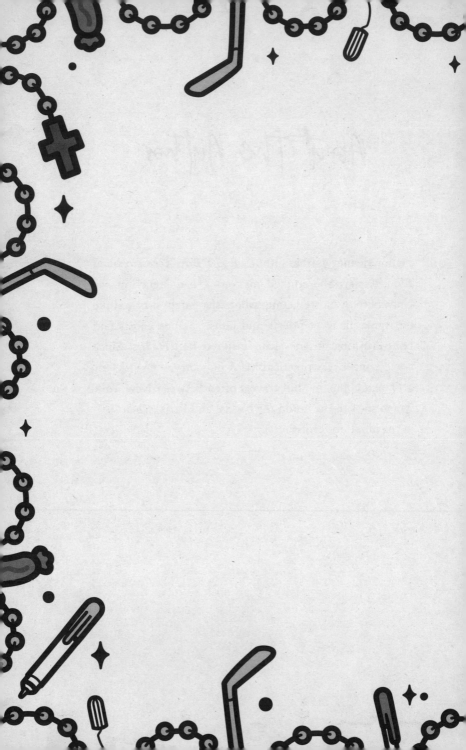

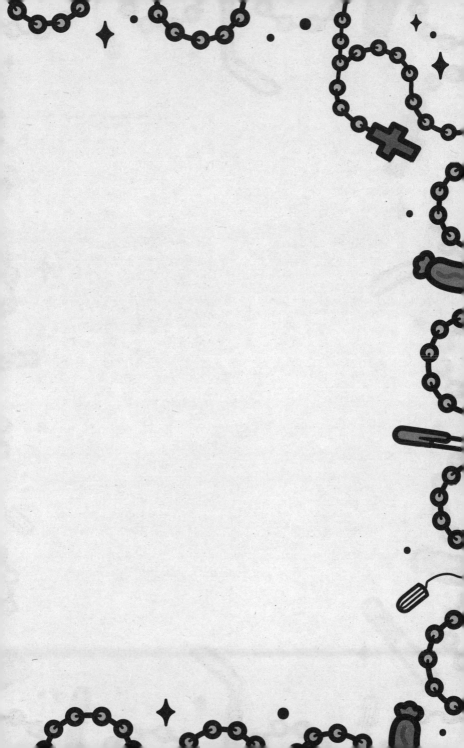

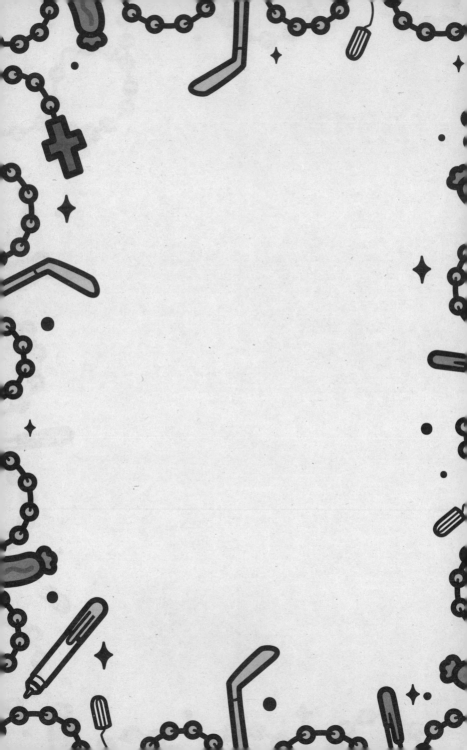